THE SCORPION STONE

The "Stone Collection" Book 10

NICK HAWKES

Hawkesflight Media

Titles in The Stone Collection:

The Scorpion Stone

First edition published in 2022 *(v.1.1)*
by Hawkesflight Media

ISBN: 978-0-6451202-3-3

www.author-nick.com

Cover Design by Karri Klawiter

To my grandchildren.

The Scorpion Stone

a novel

by
Nick Hawkes

Malaya, 1963

Chapter 1

The old Chinese mansion had its shutters closed against the tropical heat. Some of them hung askew on broken hinges. Dark stains of mold streaked the face of the building.

Sam reached out and held the arm of his older brother. Isaac was fourteen years old, and Sam needed to feel his extra two years of bravery. "I... I don't want to go into the house," he whispered.

Isaac looked at him scornfully. "I thought you wanted to explore the place."

"I don't like it."

Isaac shrugged himself free of his grip. "We'll just have a look in that old outhouse then. The door has partly fallen away. We can get in easily."

Sam looked back to the arched gate in the sea wall that led out to the beach. They'd crept through it a few minutes earlier. Now Sam wanted to be back on the beach. 'Beach' was a generous term. There was nothing pretty about it. It was mostly mud, and the water was brown – doubtless from pollution from the river that ran along the western edge of the ancient Portuguese trading town of Malacca. A bamboo gantry over the edge of the river served as the public latrine… before the water flowed past the fish market and out into the sea.

Sam wanted to be back on the beach, where he could search for the prehistoric-looking horseshoe crabs with their fearsome tail spine – or maybe splatter some of the hundreds of mudskippers with his catapult.

The walled garden, such as it was, was overgrown. No one had even bothered to collect the coconuts that had fallen from the trees. Climbing a coconut tree, like the Malay children could, remained Sam's burning ambition. It was, as yet, unfulfilled.

Sam followed behind Isaac as they made for the outhouse.

"Here, help me shove the door open," said Isaac.

The two boys heaved at the edge of the wooden door, pushing it against the vegetation that had grown against it.

Emboldened by a shaft of light they'd let into the gloom, they stepped inside.

An instant later, they stared in disbelief at two boat-shaped Chinese coffins that were laid out on trestles. Dust covered them like a shroud. A third coffin had broken open and lay on the floor, its rotted wood split and broken. Fortunately, it was empty.

Sam wanted to turn and run, but something caught his eye. A shaft of sunlight caused something to glow with luminescent gold. Whatever it was, it was beautiful. Sam reached out tentatively to tug it out from under the ruined coffin. As he did, he discovered that he was holding a dagger. Its blade was rusted, but the hilt of twisted metal was still intact. At the end of the pommel, a golden stone lay imprisoned by metal clasps.

"What have you got there?" demanded Isaac.

"It's mine. I found it," retorted Sam, hiding the dagger behind his back.

An instant later, the two boys were wrestling for control of the dagger.

It was a fearsome fight, although with no real malice. It was like so many others that had characterized them growing up together. Isaac was always going to win. Sam let go of the knife as Isaac wrenched it from his hands.

As he did, the tip of the dagger jerked into Isaac's stomach. He howled in agony.

Sam stood transfixed to the spot.

Isaac pulled the dagger out of his side and screamed again.

Sam knew that something deadly serious had occurred. He pulled off his t-shirt and pushed it onto the belly wound to staunch the bleeding. Then he pushed him toward the gate in the sea wall.

Isaac stumbled before him, staggering left and right. Sam pushed him along with one hand and kept pressure on the wound with the other.

They came out onto the muddy sand.

Almost immediately, he heard the voice he least wanted to hear.

"Ay you. Where you go with that knife? Give it to me."

It took a moment for Sam to realize that his brother, Isaac, was still holding the knife he had stabbed himself with.

A group of older adolescent Malay youths, dressed only in shorts and showing off their lean, muscular bodies, stood in front of them. They were angling for a fight. Sam was never sure why animosity sometimes flared up between this group of local youths and Isaac and himself. It could have been due to one of the army officers telling them to 'clear off.' The youths would sometimes loiter along the half-mile of cul-de-sac that ran inland from the beach at Batang Tiga to join the main highway. The cause of the problem was the brothel that was on the highway just opposite the laneway. It was called 'The Suzi' and was one of a number of 'massage parlors' that existed between Malacca and the British army camp at Terendak, six miles away. The women who worked there were Chinese. Some of the men took their girls down to the beach, much to the fascination of the local Malay youth. They watched everything.

Isaac was bent over, staggering to keep himself upright and moaning in pain.

"Give me the knife," said the largest of the five youths.

Sam pleaded. "My brother is hurt. I need to get help."

"The youth lifted his chin. "The knife," he repeated.

In irritation, Sam snatched the knife from Isaac's hand.

Glancing briefly at the golden stone in its hilt, he was filled with anger. He grabbed the stone and twisted it in anguish. Surprisingly, the stone broke off in his hand. The rusted clasps that held it in place snapped. In one movement, he slipped the golden stone into the pocket of his shorts, then swung his arm back and hurled the knife into the turbid waters of the sea.

There was a cry of angry protest, some of the youths splashed into the water seeking to retrieve it, whilst two others stayed on the beach and circled around them.

Sam had wasted no time and was now manhandling Isaac through the gate at the top of the beach. Their house, the house of the Hastings family, was one-hundred-and-fifty yards away along the cul-de-sac. He was never going to get home without being beaten up. Sam doubted whether Isaac could survive the ordeal.

The youths who had waded into the water to try and find the knife, splashed back out empty handed and were now heading toward the gate.

Isaac sank to his knees on the asphalt, whimpering as Sam eased him down. Reaching into his back pocket, Sam removed his 'ding.' It was what he called his catapult. Both he and Isaac had perfected its use over the months they had lived in Malaya.

Sam picked up three stones from the edge of the roadway and waited for the first youth to come through the gate. When he came through, he let fly.

The stone hit the youth in the shoulder causing him to spin in the air and crawl for cover behind the bushes to one side.

He loaded up the slingshot with another stone and sent it zinging through the foliage beside the gate.

A head that had appeared ducked for cover.

No one else attempted to get through the gate.

He put the catapult back into his pocket and pulled his brother to his feet.

This is NBC News. Here is Peter Hackes in Washington. President Kennedy has been shot. As of now, there is no final official report on his condition. Here now pieced together, the news items we have, that have reached us from Dallas, Texas...

The shocking news came from a transistor radio owned by the soldier in the hospital bed next to Isaac. The whole ward, containing eight beds, was silent – overawed by the news.

Outside the hospital, the growling of thunder from a tropical downpour added to the sense of unease.

Isaac wasn't really sure about the significance of what he was hearing, but he had the sense that something historically momentous had happened.

The ward remained silent after the broadcast. No one seemed to have words. The soldier in the next bed was, like Isaac, a long-term patient. He had used the tedious days of recuperation to assemble a large plastic model of the German ship, *The Bismarck*. Even the gun turrets swiveled. Isaac was captivated by it.

There had been little else to captivate him in the last two months. His knife wound had become infected, and a large section of his gut had been removed. At one point, it was thought that he might not live. Fortunately, he had little memory of the days of delirium and raging hot temperatures. He just knew that he was now very weak... and that he'd missed all the activities of Christmas.

The hospital in Terendak Camp was near the beach. There was only a thin strip of jungle in between. Isaac was grateful for the jungle, because it meant that there were always monkeys outside ready to entertain him with their antics. There was a notice under the ward window saying that feeding the monkeys was strictly prohibited. None of the patients heeded it, least of all Isaac – and much of the fruit given to him at meal times ended up being thrown out to his greedy friends.

Isaac and Sam had developed a long-standing relationship with monkeys during their time in Malaya. When they saw one in the jungle strip at the back of their house, the two of them would whoop and holler at it. The monkey would respond by hollering back... an action that would attract other monkeys to the scene.

The boys would then run away, causing the monkeys to swing down from the trees and chase them. Isaac and Sam would stop, turn round, and charge toward the monkeys, who scampered away and swung themselves back up the trees. The seesaw game continued until the monkeys became progressively bolder as their numbers grew. The boys would end the game by running onto the beach and diving into the water. The monkeys would hoot in outrage as the boys swam a few hundred yards down the coast where they would emerge back on the beach well pleased with themselves. It was a delicate game of brinkmanship. But it was a dangerous game. A bite could be serious. Some of the monkeys had rabies.

Isaac drifted off into an uneasy sleep.

He woke to find Sam beside his bed, shaking his arm to wake him.

"Shh," said Sam. "Dad told me not to wake you." He paused. "You frightened me. I thought you were dead."

"Where's dad?"

"Talking to the doctor." Sam scowled and looked across to his father standing by the doorway talking to a man in a white coat.

"What's the matter?" demanded Isaac.

"Huh?" Sam screwed up his face and shrugged with irritation. "Dad discovered my collection of scorpions, and he squashed the lot of them."

Isaac nodded his sympathy.

Their parents rarely intruded on the life he shared with Sam. Their relationship with their sons seemed to be different from those he'd seen in other families. The Hastings family was more disconnected. Isaac didn't mind, although he did admit to himself that if it weren't for Sam, life would be unbearably lonely. Their father was an army chaplain to the British forces. He was fretful, emotionally distant, and completely unaware of what his two sons were up to most of the time. Their mother, in contrast, had once trained for the theater. She was vivacious, funny, and totally unearthed in reality. She spent most of her time smoking cigarettes and reading. She hated conflict, abhorred injustice, and was suspicious of reality. For most of the time, she retreated to the safety of magazines and novels. She was greatly encouraged in this by the fact that she had a cook, a wizened Chinese man called Ah Soi, a gardener whom she could never remember the name of, and Rosna. Rosna was the wash amah and cleaning lady. She was a lovely Malayan woman with a wide smile and a ready laugh. She was the only adult who had at least some idea of what the boys got up to. This was due, in part, to the fact that the boys conspired to spend as much time in Rosna's tiny *kampong* as possible. Her house was squeezed between the jungle and the wide expanses of flooded rice paddies.

"Are you going to die?" asked Sam.

"Nup."

Sam lowered his head. "That's good, then."

Silence hung between them.

Isaac thought it time he exerted his status as the old brother. "The hospital has a library with an almost complete set of Encyclopedia Britannica. I've been swatting up on the history of Malacca and the spice trade with Portugal."

He was rewarded for this comment by an expression of exaggerated boredom. "Why, for goodness sake?"

"Because the knife we found was not a Malay knife. The classic Malay knife is a kris. It has a wiggly blade and an angled handle."

Sam shrugged, but Isaac could tell that his interest had been roused. He pushed on. "I think it's an old Portuguese knife."

"Wow! D'ya reckon?"

"Yeah. I've studied pictures of their weapons."

Sam furrowed his brow. "But what would a Portuguese knife be doing in a Chinese coffin?"

"Dunno."

At that point, their father interrupted them. He walked over to Isaac and laid a string bag of rambutans on the locker beside his bed. "These are from Rosna," he said without preamble. "And the doctor has asked me to tell you that it is not the role of nurses to fetch and carry books for you from the hospital library all day."

As a form of greeting, Isaac felt it left a bit to be desired. But he was grateful at least for the rambutans. They were his favorite fruit, and he wouldn't be feeding them to the monkeys. The fruit's red leathery skin was covered in soft spines, and once you'd peeled the skin off, the translucent flesh was delicious eating. Its flavor reminded him of grapes. But if you ate the raw seed inside it, you died. At least, that's what he'd been told.

He ventured to ask, "When can I come home?" He'd asked the same question every day for the last two weeks.

"In three or four days if everything stays normal." His father managed a smile. "That's just one week before your school exams."

Sam helped himself to one of the rambutans. "I wouldn't worry Dad. I betcha Isaac will still top the class."

His father grunted. "Just see that you behave yourself." He ruffled Isaac's hair. The act was the nearest thing to intimacy he allowed. Then he turned and made for the door.

Sam, however, held back. He looked as if he wanted to say something. In the end, he put his hand in his pocket, withdrew it and thrust a closed fist at Isaac.

Isaac looked at him with a puzzled frown and held out his hand.

Sam brushed his nose with his sleeve. "This is for you – now I know you're not going to die."

Isaac gave his brother a grim smile. "Only presidents are dying at the moment."

His brother frowned his incomprehension. He'd obviously not yet heard the news. Neither, he suspected, had his father.

Sam dropped the golden stone into Isaac's hand. "This stone came from the end of the dagger. Sam shrugged. "It broke off." He paused. "Keep it… at least for a while. It's as much yours as mine."

He looked as if he wanted to say more, but his father called out, "Get a move on, Sam."

Chapter 2

It was the school sports day, and Sam wasn't enjoying it. It had nothing to do with his sporting prowess. He was a good athlete. Years of wrestling and competing with an older brother had ensured that he had strength and fitness well beyond his years. He won the 400 meters, came second in the 200, and ran the second leg of the winning team in the 4 by 100 relay.

The object that cast a pall over the occasion was the sight of his brother, standing disconsolately on the sidelines watching. The sports day would normally have been an occasion for Isaac to shine. He'd been a superb sportsman. Rather annoyingly, Isaac had been one of those boys who was good at everything. He read voraciously and found academic study easy. He'd been particularly good at athletics. But not anymore.

Sam didn't really understand himself. He couldn't enjoy the fact that sports day was a day for him to excel, whilst his brother stood watching – a shadow of his former physical self. This was the first sports day Sam had experienced in his new school. The Slim School in Terendak Camp catered for secondary students, so Sam had joined his brother at the school earlier in the year. He'd not found it an easy transition. Everything was different. The school required him to change clothes to play sport, and had prefects who handed out punishments. It also required him to wear shoes – always. As a result, his feet had become soft and now felt the prickles from the mimosa plants that grew amongst the grass.

The mimosa plant had intrigued him when he first encountered it. Its leaves closed up and drooped down when touched. After a while, they opened up again. Sam was sure that the plant must have eyes. Isaac had told him that it didn't, but he wasn't convinced.

Sam's old school had been located in the converted wooden barracks of a Malay army camp on the beach at Tanjung Kling. A tired Bedford bus had driven him two miles to the school, which was not far beyond the local mosque. The mosque's multi-galleried minaret leaned at an alarming angle, and Sam wondered how long it would be before it fell over. It was also the site of the local grave-yard. The gravestones looked like elaborate stone lanterns, and they leaned at odd angles under the trees. Nothing seemed to be straight. There was a sour lime smell about the place that Sam didn't like. It was the smell of death.

There were only two classes in the school, both with a dozen senior primary students. The novelty of European children attracted a good deal of attention from the local Malay boys. Perhaps it was the presence of the girls. This suspicion was in no way dispelled by the disturbing habit of some of the older local boys, who, when the teacher was well out of sight, put their penises through the cyclone mesh of the security fence and called out unintelligible things to the girls in Malay. One or two of the girls were intrigued, but they pretended not to be. They giggled, but were prim enough not to go too near the fence.

One side of the security fence ran, rather frustratingly, along the sea front, which meant they couldn't get to the beach. They had to be content to watch local fishermen walk along the shallows with a net over their shoulders. Every now and then, they would cast the net so that its weighted edge would fall over a school of tiny fish. The fish were usually fried and used to garnish curries.

Sam rubbed his forehead.

"Cheer up, Sam. We won."

Sam jerked himself out of his reverie and conjured up a tired smile for his friend Rohit. His friendship with Rohit Tapit was almost the only good thing to come from his move to the senior school. Rohit had run the last leg of the relay and had been responsible for them winning the race.

Rohit was an enigma. He was a Ghurkha, and as far as Sam could tell, the only Ghurkha in the school. He was also quite unlike his fellow countrymen in that he was tall. The Ghurkhas were tough, nuggety men recruited to the British army from Nepal. They had a fearsome reputation as fighters.

Both he and Rohit were in the A stream at school, but unlike Isaac, neither were natural academics. Sam's main skills were in English and woodwork. He was particularly good with his hands and had impressed his brother by making a serviceable crossbow. Whilst Sam was not at all careful with his schoolwork, Rohit was meticulous. He underlined all the headings in his textbook three times with red ink.

Sam looked at his friend with a sense of guilt, or was it embarrassment? There was a reason he lingered on the far side of the playing field. The reason was hard to admit, and even harder to verbalize. The reason was a girl: Doseena Wonaeamirri.

For over a term, Sam had watched her covertly from afar. Today, however, he'd had more courage and stayed on the far side of the running track to watch her start in the final of the girl's 200 meters. He'd even managed to say gruffly, "I hope you win," before he felt himself coloring and walked away to hide his embarrassment.

Doseena won – as she usually did. She had fantastically long legs. But that was not what had originally captured his attention. Doseena wrote the most beautiful stories about her homeland; the Tiwi Islands off the north coast of Australia. She wrote of her people telling stories of the last ice age, even though it had happened 9,000 years ago. Doseena painted pictures with words – of how the cicada songs increased in volume with the build-up to the wet season. She spoke of paperbarks, woollybutts, and mangroves, and the small patches of rainforest where spring water occurred. All her writings betrayed a deep sense of connectedness to her ancestors, whose lives were celebrated with *tutini* – painted grave posts decorated with clay, charcoal, and ocher.

She'd once shown the class a cowrie shell she said she kept in her bag to remind her of her people. Her father was part of the Australian regiment that was garrisoned at the camp. When Doseena had first been invited to read her essay to the class, Sam was in shock. Sam's untidy essays were full of action and information. Doseena, however, used words that painted emotions and feelings, and these made her stories come alive. Sam was not the only one to appreciate this. The whole class loved to hear her read. She was spellbinding, and there was almost a sigh of disappointment when she stopped. The irony was, that Doseena never sought to show off. She was serene, gentle, and had a self-effacing shyness.

Sam was both captivated and bewildered… and had signaled the fact by putting a green tree frog in her desk. She had found it, kept it secret, and handed it back to him at the end of the day.

How had she known it was him?

Sam stood with his friend Rohit and kicked disconsolately at the turf.

Not far away, a *kebun* (a gardener) was cutting down the tall grass at the edge of the field with a scythe. His dirty vest, conical palm-leaf hat, and dark glasses forestalled any sense of him being the 'grim reaper.' *Kebuns* were a common sight around the camp.

Rohit pointed over to where the army were setting up a small display marquee. They had parked a Saladin and a Ferret beside it. The Ferret scout car had tires that could keep running even when punctured… and the big six-wheeled Saladin had a 76 millimeter gun. This was the sort of information that was important for Sam to know.

"Are you going to have a look?" asked Rohit. "We're allowed to after the prize-giving."

"Suppose so," said Sam, without any real conviction.

The explosion, when it came was shocking.

A shock wave punched Sam in the chest and sent him spinning into Rohit. He had a vague impression of the Ferret being upended and crashing down. A soldier had been on the top, helping a little girl down through the hatchway.

Sam felt searing pain, and then he lost consciousness.

The first visitor Sam actually remembered was not either of his parents, although he'd been told they'd come earlier. It was Hamish O'Brien. He was the senior chaplain at Terendak. The man's eyes, usually crinkled by a smile, were not smiling at the moment. Sam felt him lay a hand gently on his right shoulder. "And how are you feeling, young man?" His words came out with his characteristic soft Scottish brogue.

Sam tried to sit up in his hospital bed, but the chaplain forestalled him. "Sit back and rest easy. The last thing I want is to tire you out." He paused. "I just wanted to see how you were going."

There had been a question lurking half in and half out of Sam's consciousness. It was a terrible question, one that had given him nightmares. He swallowed, and stammered: "There was a soldier and a little girl on the Ferret…" he trailed off.

The chaplain's expression changed to one of infinite sadness. For a long time he said nothing, as if weighing up what he should say. Eventually, he said, "Both the soldier and the girl were killed." The chaplain drew in a deep breath. "He was called George, and she was called Annie."

Sam nodded; his worst fears confirmed. "Was anyone else…?"

"No. The Saladin sheltered those in the marquee from the blast. You were the only other casualty."

"My friend, Rohit…"

"He's fine. He had a head wound and was in hospital for two days, mainly for observation."

"What happened?"

"The investigators think it was a bomb, the work of saboteurs."

Sam wanted to know more, but Hamish O'Brien wouldn't be drawn further.

"Your job, young Sam, is to get better. There are so many things out there waiting for you to explore and wonder at."

Sam couldn't help but smile at the man's irrepressible positivity and kindness. Rather guiltily, he compared him to his own father. The two were so different. His father was stern and fretful, and the services he conducted were formal and dull. When Mr. O'Brian took a service, it was full of life, passion, and conviction. His talks were sometimes punctuated by stories from his rugby-playing days. He'd played fullback for Scotland. The two men were so different that he wondered if they actually believed in the same God.

Would God smile at children, Sam wondered? Mr. O'Brien was always smiling. To be fair, his father sometimes tried to smile when speaking to other people's children. In fact, he thought he was good at it. He'd pull silly faces to try to get them to laugh. The younger children did so, but the older ones smiled nervously and shifted uneasily on their feet… and Sam would die with embarrassment.

Dying with embarrassment. Stupid. Two people had died, a man called George and a girl called Annie. It was all too much. Sam closed his eyes.

When he opened them again, Hamish O'Brien had gone.

Sam's next visitor was equally a surprise. His old friend, Rohit, came into the ward, accompanied by a Ghurkha soldier whom Sam assumed had driven him to the hospital. The soldier stayed by the door as Rohit approached his bed. Rohit looked terrific. He had a dramatic white bandage around his head. The bandages Sam had were not as obvious. He'd sustained a nasty gash on his upper left arm, and the left side of his torso had multiple wounds. The doctor told him that none were very serious and that he should be out of hospital soon. The weirdness of being in hospital so soon after his brother was not lost on him. Up to that point, neither of them had needed medical attention.

For a long while, his friend said nothing. He just looked at Sam, as if storing up data in his mind.

Sam broke the spell. "Hi. How are you going?"

Rohit ignored the question and said, "You protected me from most of the blast."

Sam didn't know what to say. He had little recollection of what had happened.

His friend continued. "I have something for you." Rohit reached out and placed something in Sam's hand.

When Sam looked at what he was holding, he saw that it was a brooch of a miniature kukri in a decorated sheath. A real kukri was a large curved knife that was carried by Ghurkha soldiers. Rohit had told Sam that a Ghurkha soldier would never unsheathe his kukri without shedding blood, so they would nick a finger with it whenever they took the knife out to sharpen it. Sam thought that was fabulous.

He pulled the tiny kukri from its sheath, pretended to cut his finger with it, and put it back.

Rohit smiled. But moments later, his stern expression returned. "My people… my battalion… are very angry. They want to fight."

Sam was not the least bit surprised. The Ghurkhas loved to fight. They, more than anyone else, embodied the warrior spirit. Sam held up the small brooch and smiled. "Thanks for this, Rohit. It will always be special to me."

Rohit nodded, then turned to rejoin his driver. Sam watched him go. His friend was looking considerably older than his twelve years.

"*Terima kasih* (thank you) Rosna." Isaac leaned back in his chair at the card table and accepted the plate of *bubur cha-cha* she proffered. His mother had bought the table so that the family could reclaim the dining table. Isaac routinely frustrated the cook by covering it with his books when he was researching something.

"You eat," demanded Rosna.

Isaac looked at her distractedly. "Um, yes. I will."

Rosna was not to be so easily fobbed off. She reached forward and flicked his ear.

"Ow!" complained Isaac. He gave her a rueful grin and reached for a piece of the colorful, multi-layered, dessert.

Isaac had been told that he needed to eat little and often, as so much of his gut was missing. Rosna had taken it on herself to ensure he did. She bullied him like a big sister. Technically, this should have been the job of the cook, but Rosna held the cook, the taciturn Ah Soi, in some contempt and didn't trust him to look after Isaac at all.

She stood over him until he'd eaten two pieces. Rosna then flashed him a wide smile, and left.

Her smile was a tonic. The atmosphere amongst the army personnel in Terendak and amongst the tiny community in the "hirings" of the Batang Tiga cul-de-sac had changed. The carefree life they had once enjoyed was gone. Soldiers had been posted to watch the coast at Terendak, and security at the guardhouse into the camp had been beefed up. However, those living in the outpost community of Batang Tiga had no guardhouse and almost no soldiers. Non-combatants such as the headmaster of the primary school, and the boys' father, a chaplain, occupied the sixteen houses on either side of the road.

There was only one proper army officer, Major Shelbourne, and he lived next door. He was considered to be the local 'officer commanding.' The major was a loud, florid man, whilst his wife was a tiny timorous woman who was always wringing her hands. She was, however, kindly disposed toward Isaac and Sam and occasionally gave them a piece of cake. They had won her favor when she'd come round in high distress one night because a rat was running rampant in her kitchen storeroom. Her husband was away on a temporary deployment to Sarawak at the time, and she was on her own.

Sam and Isaac ran round to her house, with some glee, and dispatched the rat with their catapults. They still argued over which of them actually killed it.

"Hello, dear." Isaac's mother paused at the doorway of his bedroom. She was dangling an empty coffee mug in one hand. It was about the time of day that her coffee drinking gave way to sherry. Her voice was low and husky – a smoker's voice. Isaac thought it was lovely. "Your father is driving into Terendak this evening to see Hamish O'Brien."

Isaac raised a questioning eyebrow. His mother continued. "It's something to do with last minute changes to the little girl's funeral tomorrow."

"Her name was Annie, mum."

His mother waved a hand in irritation.

"Will you be going?" asked Isaac.

His mother shuddered. "Certainly not. It will be ghastly." She stepped into the room and looked over his shoulder. "What are you reading about?"

"The Egyptian pharaoh, Tutankhamen."

"Ah, the magnificent mummy that's been found."

"Yes." Isaac wondered briefly, how much he should say. He decided it was safe to tell her a bit. "Did you know that he had a pair of daggers wrapped up with him?"

"Really. I wonder why?"

"No one knows." He pointed to a picture in the National Geographic magazine. "The daggers were beautifully made. Here, look. They had a decorated gold handle and a gold sheath."

"But the knife blade doesn't seem to be rusted at all," said his mother. "I wonder why that is."

"Well that's the thing, mum. There wasn't much iron around 3,300 years ago. What there was came from meteorites. The ancient Egyptians saw meteorites as gifts from the gods, and iron was prized more highly than gold. Evidently, iron from meteorites hardly rusts at all."

"Extraordinary." She patted his shoulder. "I sometimes wonder what's going to become of you."

"I'm going to be an archaeologist."

"Archaeology takes a lot of painstaking physical work."

"I'm not an invalid, Mum."

"But you have more physical limitations than most."

Isaac hated to be reminded of it, and he sought to change the subject. "Did you know that smithies who worked with iron in ancient Turkey were considered to be the same as shamans?"

His mother raised an eyebrow.

Isaac rushed on. "Yes. Iron was thought to be sacred, and both the fire that melted it and the smith that worked it were, *ipso facto*, also sacred. Because the smith could manipulate the iron, he was considered to be a priest."

His mother laughed. "What on earth made you research that?"

Isaac swallowed. "Because the ancient Turks also put a knife in the coffin of the dead."

"I would have thought that you have had quite enough of knives – more than enough to last a lifetime."

Isaac thought it propitious to again change the subject. "Yeah. Er, can you tell dad that I'll come in with him so I can see Sam?"

After his mother left, Isaac sat at his table absent-mindedly tapping his fountain pen on a book. The talk of knifes, coffins, and Sam, confirmed in him a conviction he would share with his brother.

Chapter 3

Isaac's relief at finally being home was tempered by his frustration at not being fit enough to accompany his mother to Malacca. It was mid morning, and he was feeling more than a little desolate. The cook, Ah Soi, had not yet arrived, and Rosna had gone to visit a friend who was the wash amah for a family across the road.

He was lounging in a cane chair behind the hibiscus bush with his catapult in his lap. He had peppered most stationary objects in the garden during the morning. But there was an agreement between him and Sam that the most prestigious target was the giant black carpenter bee. They were huge and loved to visit the red hibiscus flowers.

As he waited, keeping as still as possible, he was conscious of a movement in the corner of his eye. Through a gap in the foliage of the hibiscus, he saw a Chinese girl. Her long black hair fell away from a face that was stunningly beautiful.

Isaac was transfixed. He was conscious of holding his breath as he watched.

The girl's eyes searched the back of the house, presumably for any signs of human presence. Then, seemingly satisfied, she ran to the back of the garden where the papaya tree was growing and tried to reach for one of the fruit. However, she was not very tall, and the fruit was frustratingly beyond her reach.

She was now so preoccupied that she didn't hear Isaac creep up behind her over the buffalo grass. When she finally noticed him, she gave a yelp of surprise and cowered away from him.

The girl was wearing black slacks and a white blouse. Her figure was slight and showing the first flush of womanhood. But it was her face that captured Isaac's attention. It had been exquisitely carved by the gods and was quite extraordinary.

She edged sideways so she could run past Isaac to safety. Isaac forestalled her by moving to block her path. "What is your name?" he asked.

The girl looked at him, fear evident in her eyes. Isaac's question caused her to frown, as if surprised. She didn't answer him.

He tried a different tack. "Why do you want to take our papayas?" Isaac pointed to the tree, unsure if she could understand him.

He was shocked to hear her reply in surprisingly good English, "I am hungry."

The girl's expression had changed to one of defiance... even disdain. It was disturbing.

"Did you not have any breakfast?" It was an inane thing to ask, but he wanted to keep their conversation going for as long as possible.

"No. No breakfast."

It was now Isaac's turn to be surprised. He thought quickly. "Then I'll help you get a papaya, and you can have breakfast."

The girl's expression turned to fright.

Isaac held up a placating hand. "Then you can go and eat breakfast wherever you like."

He was relieved to see the girl's fearful expression begin to dissipate. "I'll get the pole from the washing line to pull the branch down." Months earlier, Sam had driven a nail into the forked end of the pole for that very purpose.

Isaac continued to speak to her as he got the pole. "I'll pull the branch down, and you pick the fruit."

Isaac didn't want his conversation with this extraordinary girl to stop, so he took his time in hooking the branch down. "You speak English very well. Where did you learn it?"

The girl was now concentrating on the papaya that was coming within reach. "My mother said I must learn. It good for business."

"You've been a good student." He paused. "What is your name?"

"Anything you want."

Isaac could detect a touch of venom in her voice. He let the papaya he was pulling down bend back so that it was further out of reach.

She recognized the game he was playing and answered crossly. "Yet Mee. My name is Yet Mee."

"Well Yet Mee, it is nice to meet you. My name is Isaac."

He pulled the branch down so she could pick the papaya easily. Once she'd done so, she put it into her shoulder bag. As she did, she pointed to the ugly scar on Isaac's stomach. Although the stitches had all been taken out, the edges of the wound were still pink and puckered. Isaac had not chosen to wear a tee-shirt as he still found it uncomfortable on the wound. "What happen to you?" she asked.

Isaac didn't want to revisit the drama of the last two months. "An accident."

The girl nodded and made to move away.

"Where do you live?" he blurted out.

Yet Mee stopped and didn't answer.

Isaac had to get more information about this remarkable girl. "Where do you work?"

Yet Mee lowered her head and remained silent.

Isaac blundered on. "You can take a papaya whenever you are hungry."

She turned and looked at him, her lips compressed together as if in defiance. "I work in The Suzi."

Isaac's mouth dropped open as the awful realization of what he'd heard hit him. But he couldn't say a thing. This gorgeous girl was one of the prostitutes who worked at the massage parlor. For an instant, he was overcome by revulsion that such a beautiful person could be so defiled. He wanted to scream in protest and rage at the injustice of life. Above all, he wanted to protect her – but he could do nothing.

Yet Mee nodded, bitterness now making her face pinched and ugly. She turned and began to walk away.

Isaac called after her, "Yet Mee."

She stopped in her tracks.

"That changes nothing. Take a papaya any time you are hungry."

This was Isaac's second visit to his brother, so the sense of *déjà vu* and dread he had first experienced at being back in hospital was now fairly muted. He even wondered if he should first visit his friend who was building the model *Bismarck*, but decided that was a step too far.

He pushed through the swing doors leading into Sam's ward and waited for an orderly to finish removing the remains of Sam's evening meal. The smell of it caused his stomach to turn. It held too many memories.

Isaac sat down on the edge of Sam's bed, affecting a normalcy he did not feel. "Have you been feeding the monkeys?"

Sam grinned and nodded. "And have you been feeding Sir-lettuce-a-lot?" Sir-lettuce-a-lot was a tortoise that Sam had rescued from being eaten alive by ants. He'd found it beside the jungle track that led to Rosna's *kampong*.

"Yes," Isaac lied. He made a mental note to feed the animal before he went to bed.

"I'm coming home in two days."

"That's good." Isaac wasn't sure what to say next. He wasn't yet ready to put his proposal to Sam. The one subject everyone was talking about was the bombing, so he decided to begin there.

"Do you know what's going on with the bombing?"

Sam chewed on his lip, as if being made to face a monster he didn't want to see. "A bit," he said eventually. "I asked the nurses, and they said I should ask Dad. So, I asked Dad, and he said I wasn't to worry about such things." His brother shrugged. "So I asked Rohit, and he told me." Rohit was the usual line of communication about things the adults didn't want the boys to know.

Isaac was eager to learn the details, and was slightly mortified that his younger brother should know more than him. "What did he say?"

"Well… you know that Malaya became Malaysia a few months ago?"

Isaac nodded.

"Evidently, the move cheesed off Indonesia's President Sukarno. He thought the joining together of Malaya, Sarawak, and Singapore was a plot by the British to keep being the boss-man around here."

Isaac shook his head. "Gee, you'd think he could have solved the problem by having a chat to a few people."

"Yeah. Rohit tells me he's been a right pain in the arse for a decade or so. He supported the communist terrorists during the war here a few years ago."

"What's that got to do with the bombing?"

"The word is: Sukarno is now sending terrorists across to Malaya to blow things up and cause trouble."

Isaac nodded slowly. "Wow! So he's responsible."

Sam shrugged. "Dunno for sure. Probably."

For a while, nothing was said.

The evening sounds of the jungle could be heard coming through the fly-screen on the window – the chirruping of insects and frogs. Someone in the distance had the radio on. He could hear the Beatles singing "She loves you, yeah, yeah, yeah." When heard against the background of their conversation, it sounded crass. Paranoid politicians were killing little girls.

Isaac rubbed his temples. Would they ever get their old care-free life back? Would he ever again be able to do the things he once did with his brother? The two of them had loved going with their parents to the 'officers beach club' at Terendak. It was a swimming pool and café by the beach. With their parents safely out of sight enjoying their gin and tonics, the two of them would sneak down to the beach, straddle a coconut log and paddle out to Bat Island. It was a granite island just offshore. They'd called it 'Bat Island' because it had a cave in it that gradually dipped down vertically to disappear into the bowels of the earth. It was a mark of bravery to get as close to the vertical as possible without slipping. The exercise was made even more interesting by the bats that flittered round their ears as they edged toward the point of no return.

Would he have the strength to paddle out there again, and then pull himself up onto the rounded granite rock? It wasn't easy even when he was fit.

He sighed. In the last few weeks, both he and his brother had been brought face to face with death, and it wasn't a comfortable experience.

Isaac reached into his pocket and took out the golden stone that had once been fixed at the end of the dagger's pommel. He held it between finger and thumb, and lifted it up to the neon ceiling light. It glowed with gold, like honey. There were tiny flecks of black in the stone. Isaac had examined them with a magnifying glass and identified what he thought must be a tiny midge imprisoned within the stone. He handed it to Sam.

His brother looked at him questioningly.

Isaac pointed to it. "I'm pretty sure this stone is a piece of amber."

"What's that?"

"It's fossilized tree sap that has turned into rock. Sometimes it includes insects that have been trapped in the resin."

"Wow."

"Sam, I don't know how long you or I are going to live." He shrugged. "Life is pretty uncertain right now." Isaac fished around, trying to find the right words. "You and I are probably going to need help now and then." He smiled. "I'm going to need your help when I'm in trouble…"

His brother continued the sentence, "And I'm going to need your help when I'm in trouble."

"Exactly."

"So together, we're kinda like a scorpion."

Isaac raised his eyebrow. "What?"

"If a scorpion can't defeat its enemy with its claws, it uses its lethal back up – the sting in its tail." Sam grinned. "I've got you; you've got me. We're each other's back up."

Isaac nodded. "Yeah. I like that." He paused, "So, here's the deal: Neither of us owns this stone. It gets given to whichever one of us needs the most help. At the moment, that's you. It's a reminder that the one of us without the stone has a duty to help the other."

"A duty?"

"Yeah. As you would if we were blood brothers."

"Blood brothers?"

"Yeah. Like Huckleberry Finn and Tom Sawyer, when they swore an oath to each other on the Mississippi."

Sam weighed the stone in his hand. "So this is… the Scorpion Stone."

"Yes."

"I reckon we need some blood to make it real."

Isaac rolled his eyes. "And just how are we going to do that?"

"Easy." Sam opened the drawer of the cabinet beside his bed, took something out, and held it up for Isaac to see. "Rohit gave me this. It's a small kukri brooch. The knife comes out, and it's sharp. We can prick a finger with it and join our drops of blood together."

―――――――――

Isaac was lounging on top of what remained of a wall, in which there had once been an elaborate arched gate. Only the archway and a small section of wall now remained – a lingering reminder of a bygone era. It stood amongst the undergrowth beside the entrance to their cul-de-sac. Isaac and Sam sometimes sat on top of the ruin to watch the traffic on the highway. There was always something interesting to see: a slow-moving bullock cart with its giant wooden wheels and iconic curved roof, tricycle rickshaws, racing taxis or trucks carrying bales of rubber.

And every now and then, a taxi drove into the front car park of the brothel. It never seemed to close, although it was much busier at night.

He recognized her when she was still a hundred yards away. The hair, the sway of the hips – how could he forget? He felt his mouth go dry. Mustering all his self-control, he waited until she was twenty yards away and was about to cross the road. Then he yelled out, "Hey, Yet Mee." He gave a friendly wave.

She looked at him and hesitated.

"Have you had breakfast?" he added.

His comment seemed to unlock her reserve, as she smiled and came over to him.

Isaac clambered down from the wall. Moments later the two of them were standing together behind the broken masonry. Yet Mee looked round briefly and was apparently satisfied that the two of them were almost invisible to anyone who might be passing.

"Have you had breakfast?" he repeated.

She nodded. "Your tummy, is it better?"

"It's fine." His reply completely exhausted his vocabulary, and he couldn't think of what to say next. And yet, there were so many questions he wanted to ask. Eventually, he settled for the standard safe inquiry between two young people. "How old are you?"

Yet Mee looked at him sharply. After studying his face – during which time, Isaac felt he must look like a blundering buffoon, she relaxed her shoulders. "I am eighteen," she said. "How old are you?"

Isaac thought about lying, just as he was fairly sure he'd been lied to, but in the end, he told the truth. "I'm fourteen."

Silence hung between them for an eternity. In the end, Isaac could hold the question that was burning in his soul in for no longer. He kicked at a tussock of grass and said without looking at her, "You are much too beautiful to work at The Suzi. Why do you work there?"

She bristled immediately. "You imperialist bullies know nothing," she spat.

It took a moment for Isaac to recalibrate his thinking to match where her mercurial mind had gone.

"Are you a Communist?" he asked aghast. "You can't be a Communist. You are beautiful."

Yet Mee laughed harshly. After a while, she said in a softer tone, "Sometimes, being beautiful is no good. I wish I were ugly."

Before he realized what he'd done, he'd taken one of her hands in his own and said, "Oh no. Never say that. You are lovely."

She smiled a sad smile and took her hand away from his.

Isaac looked forlornly at his feet, not trusting himself to look at her. "How did you come to work in…" he couldn't bring himself to say the name, "over there?"

Yet Mee lifted her chin, as if daring Isaac to challenge her. "My mother was a slave… and had me as a result of her master. He was old man." She shrugged. "Laws changed, and he had to marry my mother. She became 'Number two' wife. But 'Number one' wife beat her all the time. When I was twelve, my father's 'Number one' son raped me."

Isaac's mouth dropped open. "He raped you?"

"Yes." The matter-of-fact way she spoke of it was unnerving. She continued. "And then my father got money trouble with some bad men, and I was sold to The Suzi." Yet Mee dropped her head. "I am the youngest. Very popular. I make my boss much money."

Isaac thought of her not having breakfast and very much doubted much of the money filtered down to her.

He could hear the sound of a bus snarling down the highway. Somewhere in the distance, a food-cart was being pushed. Every now and then, the driver would stop and bang his two clap-sticks together and shout, *"Makanan. Makanan"* (Food. Food). He'd probably be selling *apom balik* (stuffed pancake) or *nasi lemak* (Rice Cooked in Coconut Milk). Sometimes, he'd sell iced lollipops in decorated plastic tubes that you had to bite the end off.

Isaac was desperate to continue the conversation. "What did you really want to do when you grew up?"

She looked away from him and began to absent-mindedly strip the head off a stalk of grass.

"What?" he insisted.

She smiled sadly. Isaac thought he saw her eyes begin to well with tears, but she turned her head away.

He rushed on. "I think you could do anything." Isaac was trying to be valiant, but somehow it didn't come out right.

Eventually, she said in a voice that was barely audible. "I want to be teacher." She sniffed. "I want to teach children."

"I think that is wonderful," he said.

She laughed. The harshness was back in her voice.

Isaac was devastated. Nothing he had said had been the least help to her. Then he had an idea. He turned to her. "I want to give you something to help you become a teacher."

She laughed again. "What you give me?"

Isaac held up a hand. "Wait here. I'll only be a minute."

She favored him with a sardonic expression that eloquently expressed her disbelief.

He ran across the cul-de-sac and sprinted down to his house.

Within a few minutes, he was back clutching one of his prized books. It was volume 4 of *Junior World Encyclopedia*. "Here," he said, thrusting the book out to her. "Teachers need to know stuff."

She took the book with a puzzled frown.

"I've only got two volumes in this set. I'd like you to have one of them." He hurried on, "You can borrow the other one if you like… if you give it back."

Yet Mee looked at the book, nodded and put it into her shoulder bag.

Then she turned and walked away – toward the massage parlor.

England, 1963

Chapter 4

"**B**last that pig! He's escaped again. Can you fetch it in, lass?"

Sophie Hunter pulled her smock straight against her overlength dress. Both were second hand. The smock was now well smudged with the toils of the day: collecting the eggs, digging up potatoes, and helping her mother churn the butter. At twelve years of age, Sophie was expected to pull her weight on the farm.

"Sure, Dad."

The pig would undoubtedly be Ethelred, so called because of the red tinge to his hair. He was always pushing his way through the woven wooden palisade in order to seek some free-range morsels, or sex.

"Did you see where it was going?"

Her father, Walter, climbed down from the tractor, removed his cap, and scratched wearily at his tangle of hair. "I saw summat trotting down the path to the spinney. Can't be sure." Walter, Sophie's father, had poor eyesight and never seemed to find time to get new prescription glasses. He said he didn't really need them during the day, and at night, he was too tired to read. Walter was the stockman in charge of the calves on the farm where he had worked all his life.

He lived with his wife and their only child, Sophie, in one of the farm's tied cottages.

The farm formed part of the Chessington Estates, and once boasted a magnificent manor house. Sadly, the manor was now a ruin, having been bombed during World War II by a German bomber that had been trying to target the US air base next door. The airfield had long since been returned to agriculture. Golden stubble was now all that was left of the winter wheat that had been grown there this year. The thatchers had gone home, having done their job thatching the top of the haystacks.

Sophie loved this time of year. It was as if the Suffolk country-side, deep in the heart of England, sighed and paused for breath before the winter cereals and sugar beet were planted. They needed to be sown before the frosts set in, a sure sign that Christmas was on its way.

Sophie enjoyed going down to the spinney. She often saw hedge-hogs there. It was a long, thin paddock dotted with trees. Her father used to put the cows that were in calf there, so he could keep a closer eye on them.

The pigs were kept beside the track that led down to the spinney and to the woods that lay beyond it. One of the estate cottages was tucked in against the trees, as if seeking shelter. It was one of the larger cottages, and had a pretty front garden that featured red and white roses.

Sophie set off down the track. Cows could still be seen in the spinney. Their udders were full of milk, as they had now been sepa-rated from their calves. It was Sophie's job to teach the calves to drink from a pail of milk rather than their mother's teats. She did it by putting her hand into a pail of milk and letting the calves suck greedily on her fingers as if on a teat, slurping up the milk as they did. It always surprised her how rough their little tongues were. Fortunately, it didn't take long for her fingers to be redundant.

She scanned the hedges, fields, and tracks for signs of the errant pig. And then she saw it. To her dismay, Ethelred had pushed through the coppiced fence at the end of the spinney into the garden of the cottage. The wretched animal was munching on the roses with every appearance of contentment. Sophie didn't dare think of the damage it was doing… and her father would be none too pleased that Ethelred had managed to push through his coppiced fence. He prided himself on the quality of his coppicing. He'd spent many hours instructing Sophie on the art of cutting young saplings two-thirds of the way through, a foot or so from their bases, and then leaning the broken sapling sideways, weaving them in and out of the neighboring saplings. It was hard work, and she'd come home covered in scratches and cuts from the billhook. The net result, however, was pleasing. The plaited timber continued to grow and helped form a stock-proof fence.

But not today. Ethelred was now snorting about at the base of the roses looking for goodness-knows-what. Sophie grabbed a length of broken branch and let herself into the garden through the front gate. "Oh Ethelred; look at the damage you've done. Come away." She gave the pig a sharp smack across the haunches with her twitch. "Come on. Move, yer blighter. Back home with you afore I turn you into bacon."

Above her, Sophie heard an imperious voice ring out. "Get that wretched animal out of my garden. It's ruining my roses."

It took a moment for her to locate the source of the indignation. It came from a woman. She had opened the dormer window above her. Sophie couldn't make out what she was wearing but was instantly struck by the woman's strong facial features and long, iron-gray hair.

Sophie stood with her mouth open, rooted to the spot.

The woman continued to speak. "Girls who have their mouth open for reasons other than speaking or eating, look particularly unintelligent."

Sophie stammered, "Er, sorry ma'am. Ethelred is forever escaping into mischief. I'll quickly get him home."

The woman sniffed. "It's a pity you have to do so with a split infinitive."

Sophie had no idea what she was speaking about, but she wasn't given time to dwell on it.

"What is your name, girl?"

"Sophie Hunter, ma'am. I'm Walter Hunter's daughter." She added, "He looks after the calves."

"And the pigs, it would seem."

"No ma'am. Jimmy Stanground looks after them. But we help each other when there's need."

The woman looked at her appraisingly. Sophie squirmed and wished she was wearing her better dress. No longer able to bear her inspection, she dropped her head and looked at her work boots.

Ethelred took advantage of the inaction and began chewing on some more roses.

The woman appeared not to notice.

Sophie risked a question. "I thought old Mrs. Lutkin lived here."

"She died three months ago. It is now 'old' Georgina Chessington – Miss, who lives here."

"Oh no, Miss. You aren't old like her. You're beautiful." Sophie had blurted the words out before she realized it. She hung her head again to cover her embarrassment and hurried on. "You must be related to…" her voice trailed off.

"Yes. I am Sir Robert Chessington's aunt. He has graciously let me hide on his estate."

Sophie couldn't think what Miss Chessington would need to hide from, but didn't say anything.

Miss Chessington interrupted her thinking. "So you do odd jobs around the farm?"

"Yes, Ma'am – when I'm back from school. But I'm not paid or anything."

"How would you like to do a small job for me and get paid?"

"Oh, ma'am. You wouldn't have to pay me. I'd be happy to help."

"I will pay you," insisted the woman. She said it with a conviction that brooked no argument. "I need someone to fetch shopping from the grocer's in Thurston village. I phone him my order on Tuesday and Friday mornings. Would you be able to bring it to me on those days?"

"Yes, ma'am. That's easy. The school bus drops me off at Thurston."

"Where do you go to school?"

"In the town, Miss. In Bury-St.-Edmunds."

Miss Chessington nodded. "You will receive half a crown each week."

Sophie blinked. To her, it was a fortune.

Sophie spooned the last of the shepherd's pie into her mouth but still managed to say, "Dad, I didn't know old Mrs. Lutkin had died." Quite why Mrs. Lutkin had always been referred to as 'old' was a mystery. Presumably, there must have been a young Mrs. Lutkin once.

"Aye, lass. She gorn six months ago."

Her mother pointed a fork at her. "Don't speak with your mouth full."

Sophie swallowed obediently. "There's another person living there now. She looks like a real lady."

Her father grunted. "Aye. She's a strange one, that. Keeps to herself. I've dropped firewood off for her a few times. She never comes out or says anything. The word is, she suffers from the melancholy."

Sophie's mother shook her head. "Such a pity. I hear she used to be the headmistress of a fancy girl's school somewhere in Kent. But she packed it in."

Her father grunted. "I don't hold with girls being educated. What do they need it for? You just need a bit of readin' and writin'. I were workin' on the farm at your age. You don't need schooling to cook like your mother."

Sophie's mother got to her feet and fetched the rhubarb crumble to the table. "It's no good you sweet-talking me, Walter Hunter. Sophie needs a good education. Things aren't like they were. Women are getting good jobs and getting ahead. And our Sophie is top of her class. There's no end of things she could do with education." She patted Sophie on the back of the hand. "You continue with it for as long as you can, dear."

Her father picked up his spoon and growled, "Things hain't been the same since they put women in trousers."

Sophie lifted the brass knocker on the door and banged it as hard as she dared. Her school satchel was slung over one shoulder and she held a wicker basket under one arm. It contained Miss Chessington's groceries. They didn't amount to much: mainly fruit and vegetables. She felt a pang of guilt at being paid for doing so little – the more so because she knew that most of the fruit and vegetables could be obtained at no cost from somewhere on the farm.

The door opened just a crack, and Sophie had the impression of an eye inspecting her. After a moment, the door was taken off the chain and opened fully. Miss Chessington stood before her in all her majesty. Her graying hair hung in rich profusion almost to her waist. It was the longest hair Sophie had ever seen. The woman wore a silk kaftan. It was dark red, and it shimmered in the light. To Sophie, it looked like a royal gown. Miss Chessington's face was, however, white and pinched, but she still managed a smile. "Little Miss Ridinghood, I presume."

"No ma'am. It's Sophie Hunter with your groceries."

Miss Chessington stepped to one side. "Bring them through to the kitchen."

Sophie entered the hallway leading to the kitchen. As she did, she was able to see into the front parlor. She had a brief impression of antique furniture and, wonder of wonders, two large bookcases filled with books. The hallway had a narrow sideboard along one wall. A photograph of a dark-haired man was displayed prominently on it. Sophie paused to look at it.

Miss Chessington noticed. "That young man was my lover. He was killed in the war."

Sophie wasn't sure she was meant to know that Miss Chessington once had a lover. It sounded scandalous. She gulped and managed to say, "I'm very sorry. That must have been horrible."

"What? No censure? No outrage?" Miss Chessington laughed a brief but bitter laugh. "How old are you?"

"I'm twelve, ma'am."

Sophie placed the basket on the scrubbed kitchen table. "I've got to take the basket back to the grocer when I wait for the bus tomorrow morning."

Miss Chessington nodded and began unpacking the basket. "And what's this?" she said, holding up the book Sophie had been reading on the bus. It was a copy of Louisa Alcott's 'Little Women' and she'd nearly finished it.

"Sorry, Miss. I've been reading it."

Miss Chessington frowned and handed the book to Sophie. "Read it to me." She sat herself down at the kitchen table.

Sophie took it obediently and started to read from where she'd put the bookmark. She got so caught up in the pathos of the story that she discovered she'd read four full pages, and had done so with the passion she felt the story deserved.

Miss Chessington held up a hand to stop her.

Sophie stood mute, embarrassed at having become so carried away.

"Well, well. What an interesting girl you are. Do you harbor any ambitions for your life in adulthood?"

Sophie hung her head.

"Speak up, girl."

"Please Miss; I do have dreams, but they are only dreams."

"Only dreams?"

"Yes, Miss."

"Tell me your dreams."

For a long while, Sophie said nothing. Then she jutted out her chin, almost in defiance at the foolishness of what she was about to say. "I want to study history and write… and maybe…"

"Maybe?"

"Be a politician – so I can help change history." She shrugged. "Right decisions do so much good. My dad says that a moment's pause for thinking saves weeks of regret."

"Your father is very wise."

"But he doesn't want me to continue long at school. He says it doesn't do women any good."

Miss Chessington frowned. "Does he now."

Silence hung in the room. Miss Chessington seemed lost in thought. In the distance, Sophie could hear some of the cows bellowing for their calves. For them at least, life was simple, if a little sad.

Sophie broke the silence. "My dad said you used to be a head-mistress of a school. Is that right?"

Miss Chessington started into consciousness, looked at Sophie, and coughed a bitter laugh. "What I did was to over-educate breeding stock for over-privileged and unimaginative businessmen who worked in the city."

Sophie was not sure she understood her reply but nodded anyway. "They must have been very lucky."

"Lucky?"

"Yes. Lucky to have been taught by you." Sophie began leafing through the pages of 'Little Women,' half imagining what it would be like to be an author like Jo March in the story. "I would give a lot to be taught by someone like you."

Miss Chessington managed a smile. "And what would you give?"

Sophie hadn't expected to be taken seriously and had no time to prepare an answer. Before she had time to think, she blurted out, "Half a crown."

Miss Chessington raised an eyebrow. "A week?"

"Yes."

The headmistress nodded and smiled. "A princely sum indeed."

Sophie felt herself coloring. "I'm sorry, Miss."

Miss Chessington raised a hand. "No. Don't apologize." For a while, she looked at Sophie saying nothing. Then she said, "All right then. I will accept your terms, exacting as they are. I am prepared to tutor you for an hour or so when you bring my groceries. But you must get your father's permission first. I daresay that I'll be taking you from some of your responsibilities on the farm – chasing pigs and the like."

Sophie's mouth dropped open. She couldn't believe what she was hearing.

"Wow! Would you? Wow, wow, wow." Then she furrowed her brow. "What things will you teach me?"

"Manners. Then English and history. And when you are a little older, we'll explore the classical philosophers."

Sophie found herself hopping from one foot to the other. "I can hardly wait." She rushed on. "And I'll pick you some St. John's wort from the hedgerows. Mum makes tea with it and gives it to dad whenever he has one of his bouts of depression."

"St. John's wort?"

"Yes."

Miss Chessington smiled. "I look forward to testing its magic."

Malaya, 1963

Chapter 5

"You're out," shouted Sam.

Sam was now home, and the two boys were in Sam's bedroom playing cricket. It wasn't a game anyone from Lords would recognize. The boys were taking it in turn to toss a matchbox into the ceiling fan. If the fan knocked the matchbox to the floor, it was one run. If it hit the wall, it was six runs. If someone caught the matchbox, or it went through and hit the ceiling, you were out.

"Boys, come here." Their mother's voice called them from the living room.

Sam turned off the fan, and the two of them went to join her.

They found her talking with Mrs. Shelbourne from next door. Their neighbor was a bit of a mystery, as she seemed to spend as much time away as with her husband.

Their mother wasted no time getting to the point.

"Mrs. Shelbourne has quite a lot of shopping to do in Malacca and was hoping I might come and assist her. However, I'm busy, so I've volunteered the two of you to help. You are both driving me crazy kicking around the house doing nothing."

Sam repressed a smile. He knew his mother wasn't busy at all but found the incessant chatter of Mrs. Shelbourne hard to bear.

Her face, however, was full of sincerity and bonhomie. She was a magnificent actor. Nor was he surprised that his mother had forgotten that neither of her sons was currently in a great physical state.

"Sure mum. Happy to help," he said. It was half true. He loved going into Malacca.

Ten minutes later the two boys were being bounced up and down in the back of an army Land Rover. Mrs. Shelbourne was in the front seat, and an army driver, Private Saunders, was driving them.

It was when they were approaching the outskirts of Malacca and about to cross the bridge into town, that Sam voiced a growing concern to his brother.

"Isaac, don't make it obvious that you're watching, but do you see that taxi that's three cars back. It pulled out behind us when we turned onto the main road and its followed us, never getting too far from us, or too close to us, ever since."

Isaac leaned forward and took a brief casual look over the tail-gate of the Land Rover.

"Yeah, I see it. You don't think it's a coincidence?"

"No."

His older brother looked at him. "Why is it you see things other people don't?"

"Do I?"

Isaac laughed. "You're kidding me, right? The whole house is filled with critters you've seen and collected."

Sam took another covert look at the taxi. It was, as most Malayan taxis were, a diesel-driven Mercedes painted in the livery of the local taxi company: green with a white roof. Quite how Mercedes had lowered themselves to provide taxis for Malaya was beyond his comprehension. Mind you, the taxis had been stripped of all things luxurious, and all of them seemed to need a tune-up. They belched acrid exhaust smoke behind them wherever they went. They were a common sight along the highway and in the car parks of the brothels. He turned back to his brother. "Could you ask if Saunders is going to stay with the Land Rover?"

Isaac nodded. "Yeah."

In the end, they needn't have worried. Saunders himself told them he would stay with the vehicle. He said he was obliged to, but Sam rather suspected that he was seeking peace from Mrs. Shelbourne's incessant chatter.

The town of Malacca was a strange 'other world' to Sam. It had once been the Portuguese trading port at the heart of the spice trade. Many of its old civic buildings had been built by the Portuguese and, for some reason, were painted red. The Chinese, however, dominated the town's commerce. Shuttered, dark, oriental shops held secrets, treasures, and smells. The upper level of the shops was built over a covered walkway that collectively formed a colonnade to keep shoppers in the shade. The air was thick with the smell of joss sticks, excrement, and a thousand different spices. Monsoon drains beside the road were ready to trap the unwary. They doubled as the communal toilet.

The town was a melting pot of cultures: Chinese; Malay, and Indian – overlaid with a Portuguese heritage, and there was always something going on. Although Indians comprised only five percent of the population, they more than made up for this with the extravagance of their religious festivals. Some were deeply disturbing. Their priests would put people into a trance and then stick metal skewers through their neck and cheeks. Sam wondered what sort of god would require such a thing.

The Chinese occasionally set up a theater in the streets. They featured richly attired figures with faces masked by huge amounts of makeup that gyrated and gesticulated dramatically to discordant music. It seemed to Sam that the music made up with bangs and crashes what it lacked in meter or tune. The Chinese, however, loved it.

The Malays were altogether more demure. They loved watching their shadow puppets – grotesque, intricately carved characters that were worked by sticks.

The air was hot and sultry and Sam was glad to be back in the Land Rover an hour later. Mrs. Shelbourne had, in the event, bought very little, but both Isaac and Sam dutifully carried the raffia bags that contained her shopping. Sam suspected that Mrs. Shelbourne was just seeking company, or perhaps respite from her overbearing husband.

Sam was in no doubt that he would soon be speaking to Major Shelbourne. The taxi they had first seen following them into Malacca, was now back behind them. It was currently trying to hide behind a bus.

Major Shelbourne's personal Land Rover was in the driveway when they returned, indicating that he was back home. Private Saunders dropped them off, and then returned to the highway and on toward Terendak.

Mrs. Shelbourne took the three bags of shopping from the boys, nodded her thanks, and began to head toward the door. Sam squared his shoulders and said, "Mrs. Shelbourne, may I speak with your husband please."

She paused and looked over her shoulder. "No. I don't think so. He'll be very tired." She forced a smile. "He's not at his best after a long day."

"Please, Mrs. Shelbourne. It's important."

Isaac spoke up in support. "It concerns an important security issue."

Sam could see that the poor woman was conflicted. "Oh, oh, I suppose so. If you must." She led the way inside and called out loudly to her husband. "Arnold. The boys from next door want to tell you something important."

When Sam stepped inside the cool of the living room, he saw the Major sprawled in an armchair. He had a bottle of Tiger Beer in his hand. Three empty bottles were beside him. His khaki shirt was undone, and his feet were bare. The Major had left his boots in the middle of the room.

He looked at the two boys and sniffed. "Ah, the rat catchers have come. Have you come to scrounge some more cake?"

Sam blinked, but managed to stammer. "N, No sir. It's a security issue."

The Major laughed. "And what would you know about security?"

"It concerns your security, sir."

The Major looked at him incredulously. "Mine?" He laughed again. "You cheeky blighter. I can look after my own security."

His wife fluttered in the background. "Perhaps you should listen to him, Arnold. The boys have been a great help today."

Sam wasn't quite sure he followed the logic of Mrs. Shelbourne's reasoning, but he was nonetheless grateful for her support.

The man waved his hand dismissively. "Humph. They're just toadying for more of your cooking, Esme. You spoil them."

Sam's fear was now giving way to anger. He held his arms stiffly by his side and clenched his fists. "All I've come to tell you, is that our Land Rover was followed into Malacca this afternoon by a taxi – a green and white one, and that the same taxi followed us back."

The Major tilted his head back and laughed. "A taxi followed you. Now who would have thought it?" he shouted out theatrically, "Let's call out the guards. No… the air force. Let's run to our nuclear shelters."

The outburst was enough to stun Sam into silence. He felt his face redden.

Mrs. Shelbourne walked from behind the settee with her arms out, seeking to shepherd the boys out of the house. "I think you should go home, boys."

Sam glanced at his brother.

Isaac did not move. A moment later Sam was amazed to hear his brother say, "Major, Sam has come here in good faith to report something which any reasonable person would consider suspicious. He needn't have done so, and he only has your well being at heart. You have no right to demean him."

"Why, you cheeky whippersnapper. I'll show you. Who do you think you are?"

His wife screamed. "I can't bear it. I can't bear it," and ran from the room with her hands over her ears.

Isaac still didn't move. "You ask who I am, Sir. I'll tell you. My name is Isaac Hastings, and I am Sam's brother."

By this stage the Major had slipped off the webbing belt from around his generous girth and was lurching forward from his chair.

Without any pretense at dignity, Sam grabbed his brother and pushed him toward the door. The end of the Major's belt clipped his calf as he ran from the house. Sam was quite sure that if he hadn't grabbed Isaac, his brother would have stood his ground and received a sound thrashing.

Sam was never more proud of his brother than he was at that moment.

Isaac was tired of reading, so he made his way through the house and walked outside to the end of the driveway, driven by a morbid curiosity about how many squashed frogs there would be on the roadway outside. It was almost impossible for a car not to squash one when going down the road after dusk.

What he did see was infinitely more unpleasant than squashed frogs. Yet Mee was walking with a young Chinese man who had draped his arm around her shoulder. He could see them speaking together and laughing.

A momentary start of surprise was the only clue Yet Mee gave of her discomfort at seeing Isaac.

When they drew level with Isaac, the Chinese man called out to him. "Hey, Johnny. You got papaya."

Isaac shot Yet Mee an interrogating look.

She gave just the tiniest shake of the head. Isaac chose to interpret it as an apology and remained silent.

The Chinese man pulled Yet Mee closer to him and gave an arrogant grin. "You get me a papaya, and my girl will show you things – sexy things."

Isaac was appalled at the obscenity of what he heard. He desperately wanted to get Yet Mee away from this man. He looked at her 'client' and said, "I will not get you a papaya, but I will get her a papaya. She will need to come and get it?"

The man laughed and pushed Yet Mee toward Isaac.

Isaac walked stiffly down the side of the house into the back garden. Once he was sure they were out of sight, he rounded on her. "That man is an animal. How can you…" he was lost for words. This was not helped by the fact that she looked at him with an expression of scorn and, as hard as it was for him to comprehend, dignity.

"It not real," she said. "It all pretend."

Isaac rubbed his forehead and said in a voice still edged with anger, "What would it take for you to be free of The Suzi?"

Yet Mee snorted with derision. Isaac could not work out if it was directed at herself or at him. "Money. Much money."

Isaac would have given anything to help her get free.

"How much?" he asked.

She waved his question away irritably.

It was then that Isaac had a terrible idea. The idea would never have occurred to him had he not recently been researching the value of amber. He was shocked to learn how much people were prepared to pay for a quality piece… and he was in no doubt that the piece he shared with Sam was a quality piece.

"Stay here," he said.

It was madness, and he was breaking a promise, a covenant with his brother.

Isaac ran inside, trying to outpace his conscience. A moment later, he was in Sam's room. He found the piece of amber easily enough. Sam had put it in his small wooden 'ditty box' that he kept on the dresser.

Part of his soul screamed in protest, but Isaac ignored it. Nothing was as important as securing freedom for Yet Mee. He rushed outside and thrust the stone at Yet Mee as if it was scalding hot. "Here. This is expensive. Use it to help yourself get free."

Yet Mee took hold of the stone with a puzzled expression and turned it over in her hand.

Isaac didn't want to see it. "Put it in your pocket – quickly," he said gruffly.

She raised her eyebrows and obeyed.

Then he led her back out to her client. Isaac was beyond being careful. He said, "There is no papaya." Then he pointed to the Chinese man and said, "You are a number-ten big shit. Go away."

The man sneered at him and said something unintelligible to Yet Mee. The two of them laughed. Then he wheeled Yet Mee around and continued to walk her down to the beach.

"You did what!" exclaimed Sam. He glared at his brother.

In truth, his brother cut a pitiful sight. Isaac was sitting on the end of Sam's bed with his head in his hands. "I wish I hadn't now, Sam. Truly, I do. I just… couldn't bear her being trapped in a brothel."

Sam shook his head. "I still can't believe that you made friends with a prostitute." He glared at his brother. "A prostitute. What were you thinking? You do know what they do, don't you?"

Isaac passed a hand wearily across his face. "Rather more than you do, I suspect." He looked at his brother imploringly. "She is not just a prostitute, Sam. She is so much more… or could be so much more."

"But you said that she just marched off arm in arm with the guy who was using her for sex." He waved a hand in scorn. "Hah. You giving her the amber stone was a completely useless gesture. It won't change her life at all." Sam jabbed a finger at his brother. "And it wasn't just a piece of amber, it was the Scorpion Stone. It was us backing each other up. It was us agreeing to be blood brothers. Did that count for nothing – a few days?" He swung away from his brother in disgust.

He was only slightly mollified to see that his brother's thin frame was now wracked with sobs.

Chapter 6

Isaac was determined to do all he could to win the trust of his brother and to keep to the essence of the covenant he'd made with him. He'd assured Sam of this, but Isaac could tell that his brother was skeptical. Sam was not, however, a boy who was able to maintain a grudge, and after a few days, their relationship was pretty much back to normal. Even so, Isaac wanted to be alert to any opportunity he could use to put things right with Sam.

The boy's standard fallback action when faced with one of life's challenges, was to visit Rosna's *kampong*. There, they were assured of undemanding friendship. As there were still a couple of days left of the school holiday, they decided to go that morning.

Before long, the two of them dodged round a small boy on the highway riding a bike several sizes too big for him, and cut inland up a small dirt track. The path, worn smooth by bare feet, passed through the jungle and passed by the occasional Malay house. At one point it skirted the edge of a rubber plantation. The straight, mottled trunks of rubber trees stood in ordered rows in stark contrast to the overgrown chaos of the jungle. Every two days, workers would trim the diagonal cuts on the tree trunk so that they bled white latex into a little cup wired to the trunk.

At one point, they could see through the undergrowth to rice paddies near the river. Men could sometimes be seen walking behind a plow as it was pulled by a water buffalo. The animals were intimidating with their fearsome swept-back horns. They were unlike the demure bullocks that pulled the bullock carts, in that they could be temperamental.

Today, women were standing in the water, transplanting rice seedlings into the mud. It was their responsibility to plant the rice and do the harvesting. The women always seemed to have their backs bent doing something.

After half a mile, they came to Rosna's kampong. Three houses stood around a clearing. Like all Malay houses, they were built on stilts and had steep, thatched roofs to shed the frequent tropical storms. The communal living area was at the front and had no windows, just shutters. Two sides were usually left open to the elements. It was a sensible arrangement that made for comfortable living in the tropics.

Some boys were in the middle of the cleared area keeping a cane ball in the air with their feet. The dexterity they displayed was amazing. The Malay boys greeted them cheerfully and invited them to join in the game. Both Isaac and Sam did so, and although they had improved their skills significantly over the two years they had lived in Malaya, they remained conspicuously less adept than the locals. No one seemed to mind, however, and there was a good deal of laughter.

When Isaac couldn't bear his incompetence any longer, he waved his thanks and walked with Sam over to Rosna's house. Rosna wasn't at home, but her mother was – along with an assortment of relatives and small children. Rosna's mother was an elegant, gracious woman dressed, as almost all Malay women were, in a colorful sarong kebaya. With typical Malay generosity, she found some biscuits for them.

Having paid their respects, Isaac and Sam left to head toward the rice paddies. Sam carried his dip net with him. He'd made it from mosquito netting, wire, and a bamboo pole.

As they were leaving the kampong, Isaac saw Raahim, Rosna's

brother riding toward them on his squeaky pushbike. Isaac called out to him, "*Selamat petang* (good afternoon) Raahim. How's the fishing?"

Raahim came to a halt and shook his head sadly. "*Tidak begitu bagus* (Not so good). After a few minutes chatting, Isaac said, "Raahim; if my parents said it was okay, could Sam and I go fishing with you one night?"

"*Ya, sudah tentu.*" (Yes, of course).

Sam punched the air in triumph.

Raahim owned a fishing *kelong* just offshore, and Isaac knew that it had been a burning ambition of Sam's to spend a night on it. Organizing for it to happen was his attempt to heal the rift he had caused by giving away the Scorpion Stone.

"When can we come?" said Sam.

Isaac sought to reign in some of his brother's exuberance. "Woah. We need to get permission first."

Sam grinned. "We'll ask mum. She's vague enough not to ask for details. If we ask dad, he'll just worry and come up with an objection."

Isaac conceded that he was probably right.

Provisional arrangements were made to meet at dusk in two day's time on the beach.

Isaac waved Raahim goodbye, and the two of them made their way to the rice paddies. Sam wanted more fish for his aquarium. He needed more fish every two months or so. That was the length of time it took for the Siamese fighting fish to eat all the other tropical fish in the tank.

"You're wasting your time you know," said Isaac as he sat down on the grass.

Sam didn't bother answering. He held the dip net over the water, and then let it sink below the surface onto the mud. Then he rocked back on his haunches and sat down next to Isaac. After a few minutes during which both boys did nothing other than to slap at the mosquitoes trying to feed on them, Sam reached forward and dropped some breadcrumbs on the surface of the water above the net.

Almost instantly, tiny fish of every color and shape darted toward the food source. It was always a fantastic sight to see.

Sam lifted the net out of the water, catching the fish in his net. He inspected them briefly. Isaac held open a plastic bag partly filled with water. Sam tipped the fish into it. "I've got two fighting fish," he enthused.

Isaac grunted. "That's not great news for the other fish."

Later that night, Isaac lay on his bed under the mosquito netting listening to the geckos. There were usually two or three of them on the walls or ceilings. They nodded their heads as they called to each other, 'chirrup, chirrup.' Some of the geckos were so translucent, you could see the last fly they'd swallowed go down their gut.

As he lay there, he reflected on the altercation they'd had with Major Shelbourne two days ago. Even allowing for the fact that the Major was slightly drunk, his behavior had been appalling. Isaac hadn't reported the incident to his father. He could never be sure how his father would react. He too could be quite explosive. Isaac put his hands behind his head and wondered what he should do.

As Sam stepped from the fishing boat onto the crude ladder leading up to the fishing platform, his tee-shirt rode up, showing some of the bandaging on his side. Raahim frowned with concern. He reached forward and touched it lightly. *Awak okay tak?* (Are you okay?).

"Yeah, it's all good," said Sam. Whilst it wasn't quite true, it was near enough.

Raahim had rowed the boys about half a mile offshore to his fishing *kelong*. Sam enjoyed being in his boat. He'd always found the mystique of boats and the sensation of being afloat intriguing.

The kelong consisted of two rows of sticks stuck into the mud in a V shape. The fish drifted with the tide into the ever-closing V until they were caught in the net at the end. The net was lowered down from a fishing platform.

Twilight never lasted long in the tropics, and it was now quite dark. When Sam reached the top of the ladder up to the platform, he was alarmed at how flimsy the fishing platform appeared to be. It was a lot less substantial than it looked from the shore. There was not much decking. Access to the different corners of the platform was by narrow planks, and everything seemed to have been lashed together with rattan. A small hut had been built on one side giving shelter, when needed, from tropical downpours.

It soon became apparent to Sam that in climbing up to the fishing platform, he was not only climbing into another world, but another time zone. Once the net was let down, there was nothing to do other than wait. It was a lazy balmy evening.

The boys sat on a section of planking where the fish were tipped, dangling their feet over the edge. Raahim again asked about Sam's wounded side. This, inevitably, led to talk about the bombing. Raahim knew the details as he'd learned them from Rosna. "Bad fellows," he said. "Which men did it?"

Isaac answered him. "We think it was some Indonesians from President Sukarno. They want to stir up trouble."

Raahim nodded. The features of his face were thrown into sharp relief by the light of the paraffin lamp. He looked as if he'd been carved from ebony. "I have seen Indonesian fishing boat."

Raahim's comment caused Sam to snap his head around. "Really. Where?"

"Here. It came past me at night."

"When?"

Raahim shrugged. "Maybe a month ago."

Isaac frowned. "How do you know it was Indonesian?"

A good deal of hand-signals and broken English followed. At the end of it, Sam was able to deduce that Indonesian fishing boats sat lower in the water and had a sharper prow than Malayan boats. Raahim stressed that the difference was very slight and that only a fisherman would know.

Sam blew out his cheeks. "Wow," he said.

Raahim, however, had not finished surprising them. "I have seen smuggling too. Bad men."

Both boys looked at him in surprise.

"Yes," said Raahim. "I show you." The fisherman got to his feet and ducked into the small hut. A moment later, he reappeared carrying a coconut and a tin can. When he handed the can to Isaac, Sam could see that the can had been attached to the coconut by a length of wire.

"It come floating into my net," explained Raahim.

"What's in the can?" said Sam, craning forward to look.

Raahim reached forward and unscrewed the wide cap on top of the tin. Then he tipped it over, causing some objects inside to rattle to the end.

When he put the can down, Sam was amazed to see bullets lying in the palm of Raahim's hand. The light from the paraffin lamp caused their brass casings to glow with menace.

"Woah!" said Sam.

Isaac nodded. "The can would hang down in the water under the coconut, and no one would see it." He paused. "I suppose another fishing boat would collect them."

Raahim patted the coconut. "But not this one, eh." The fisherman rubbed the stubble on his chin. "What am I going to do with 'im?"

"Take it to the police," said Isaac straight away.

Raahim shook his head. "I don't like police. They make trouble. Maybe I just throw it in the sea."

Isaac sympathized. "Can you at least give me some bullets? I will try and see where they come from. You can throw the rest away if you want."

With some hesitation, Raahim gave Isaac the three bullets in his hand... and then seemed eager to change the subject. "Now we pull up the net, yes?"

The net was hauled up to the platform. When it finally arrived, dripping and swollen, Raahim pulled on a rope and let the net's contents disgorge in a slithering mass onto the wooden planking. A bewildering number of creatures flapped and slid over each other. Sam gave a cry of delight. He could see electric eels, fish that glowed in the dark, and tiny octopuses.

He was in heaven.

Isaac put his pen down and read the letter he'd written.

To Major Shelbourne:

This bullet is one of hundreds found in a tin can that was wired to a coconut. It was found locally. The evidence suggests the bullets were being smuggled.

A local fisherman has also told me that he saw an Indonesian fishing boat come ashore half a mile south of here about a month ago.

I mention these things in case it has relevance to security.

Yours sincerely,

Isaac Hastings

Isaac had signed his name underneath and put the date.

After reading the letter through one more time, he tore the page from his exercise book, exposing the carbon paper he'd put underneath.

He put the letter and the bullet in an envelope and went out to the front carport. There was no sign of Major Shelbourne's Land Rover in the next door driveway. That was good.

Drawing a deep breath, he walked to his neighbor's house and knocked on the door.

When Mrs. Shelbourne opened it, she couldn't repress a start of surprise. Her gaze darted over his shoulder and up the road.

"I'm so sorry," she stammered.

Isaac held up a hand to placate her. "That's quite all right, Mrs. Shelbourne." He handed her the letter.

She looked at it as one might look at a poisonous insect and didn't touch it.

"It's okay, Mrs. Shelbourne. It contains something that the Major might find helpful. Honestly."

Tentatively, she took the letter, but frowned when she felt the weight of the bullet.

Again, Isaac sought to reassure her. "It's just something that is important for the Major to see." The last thing he wanted to tell her was that it contained a bullet.

In the end she nodded, and quickly closed the door.

Feeling that he'd used up all the courage he had, Isaac returned home.

An hour later, when the delicious smell of *nasi goreng* was beginning to waft through from the kitchen, Sam came running into his bedroom. "Major Shelbourne wants to see you. He saw me and Rosna in the carport and told us to get you."

"I'm not going," said Isaac.

"I think it'll be okay. He's on the other side of the fence." Sam swallowed. "And Rosna and I will be there."

Isaac fought his demons, sighed, and got to his feet.

When he got outside, the Major was indeed standing on the other side of the fence. He was partly screened by the bushes and could only be seen from the chest up.

"What's the meaning of this?" demanded the Major. He waved Isaac's letter in the air.

"It should be self-explanatory, sir."

"It is not," said the Major abruptly.

At that moment, Sam stepped forward and stood beside him. That simple action restored some of his courage.

The Major continued. "Where is this can of ammunition you say you found?"

"It was thrown overboard by the fisherman, sir. He was scared."

"And who is this fisherman?"

"I'd rather not say sir. He's a friend, and he's scared enough."

The Major nodded, and then said, nastily. "Then let's just finish this stupid charade, shall we?" He paused. "Did you get the number plate of the taxi?"

It took a moment for Isaac to follow the Major's change of tack. "No sir. It was too far back."

"Of course it was," roared the Major. "We have a taxi that can't be identified; a can of ammunition that can't be found; and a fisherman who can't be named." He crunched up Isaac's letter in his fist and pointed a quivering finger at him. "Don't you waste any more of my time." He turned and stalked away.

Rosna came up to where the boys were standing. She'd stayed

under the carport, too frightened to come further until it was over. Isaac was left in no doubt, however, about how she felt.

She circled a finger around her ear and muttered, *gila babi* (crazy pig). It was the highest insult a Malay could give. Then she put her arms around the boys and shepherded them back inside.

Chapter 7

School had started again after the Christmas break, and Sam was anxious to catch up with his friend, Rohit. He extracted Rohit from a game of brandy and led him across the oval to where Isaac was standing in full sun. Isaac appeared to be looking at the place where the Ferret car had been blown up. People had tidied up the site, but the scarring and the cosmetic gardening that had been done still made the site obvious. Sam didn't like looking at it and wished his brother had chosen another place to meet. But at least it was a place where they wouldn't be disturbed or overheard.

Rohit seemed to catch a sense of the gravity of the situation, because he said, without preamble, "What is the matter, Sam? Are you or your brother in trouble?"

Sam smiled. Rohit's concern was touching. "It may not just be us, Rohit. It might be anyone." He pointed to Isaac. "My brother will tell you what's been happening."

Isaac nodded to Rohit as he approached. Sam noticed that the two boys were the same height, even though Rohit was two years younger. However, the way Rohit carried himself made him look taller. He had an almost regal dignity.

"What's the matter Isaac?" Rohit asked.

"Sam tells me you might be able to help." Isaac passed a hand over his forehead. "Quite honestly, we don't know where else to turn. The Officer Commanding at Batang Tiga won't take us seriously."

"Tell me."

Isaac began by recounting what they had observed on their trip into Malacca, then their experiences on the fishing *kelong*. Finally, he told Rohit about their clashes with Major Shelbourne. "I don't think anyone is going to listen to us," He finished.

"What are you worried about?" asked Rohit.

"I think the community at Batang Tiga are in danger, and Major Shelbourne in particular."

"You think he could be killed... as happened here?"

Isaac shrugged.

Rohit expelled some air from his cheeks. "Wow!" He paused. "What do we know about the killers, assuming they are real?"

Isaac ticked off the details on his fingers. "There's probably more than one. Their use of a taxi indicates that, as does the amount of ammunition Raahim reported finding. That means they are armed with guns and have explosives, probably mines; and they are hiding, possibly in plain sight, in the community."

Sam frowned. Something that Isaac said teased his memory. It was the phrase, "possibly in plain sight." He pinched the top of his nose and tried to think. After a moment's confusion, he made the connection. Sam grabbed Rohit's arm. "Rohit, before the explosion... did you see a *kebun* cutting grass with a scythe. He wasn't far from the Ferret. Do you remember?"

Rohit shook his head. "I don't remember seeing anyone."

Sam shook Rohit's arm in frustration. "He was wearing a conical palm hat and sunglasses."

His brother coaxed him on. "Can you remember anything else about him?"

"No. Hang on... Yes. It was the conical hat. It was held in place under his chin with some red ribbon, probably raffia. Whatever it was, it was definitely red." Sam shrugged. "I can't remember anything else."

Rohit remained impassive, expressionless. Sam was far from sure he was getting anywhere with him. He turned to his brother. "Give him the bullet, Isaac."

Isaac dug into his pocket and produced a bullet. Silently, he dropped it into Rohit's hand. "I don't know if that helps," he said. "But it may tell us what sort of gun it was made for."

Rohit turned it over in his fingers. "My people will know," he said simply, then he put it in his pocket. Then for the first time, he smiled. "I will talk to my father… and we will see what we can do for the people of Batang Tiga."

It was only then that Sam saw the glint of battle in Rohit's eyes.

Sam kept Sir-lettuce-a-lot in the concrete planter box running alongside the carport. He was safely contained there by the lip of the box and was free to roam amongst the plants. Usually, however, the tortoise was content to stay half submerged in the pond Sam had made for him using a sunken glazed pot.

Sam was feeding him last thing at night when he heard the sound of an army Land Rover driving slowly down the cul-de-sac, and then back out again. He couldn't see the details other than to note that it was the long wheel base version.

Sam watched it with a puzzled frown.

It was his favorite lesson at school – woodwork. Sam was delighted when he learned that the Slim School taught woodwork. He was currently making a table lamp and was trying to decide whether he should finish it off with French polish or varnish.

Rohit came up to him at his bench and said. "I have some information. Let's talk at lunch-time."

When the bell went for lunch, Sam and Rohit went off to find Isaac. The three of them headed for the shade where the water faucets were.

Rohit wasted no time getting to the point. "The bullet is a 7.62, and it's made for the Kalashnikov AK-47 assault rifle."

Sam frowned. "Isn't that a Russian gun?"

Rohit nodded. "My father told me that it is used by the Communists. Their insurgents used it here in Malaya."

Isaac looked at Rohit doubtfully. "How can you be sure the bullet is for an AK-47? British assault rifles also use a 7.62 round. Are we getting carried away and being a bit dramatic?"

Sam rose to Rohit's defense, but Rohit shut him down. "It is a good question. Let me explain. The Kalashnikov fires a 7.62mm diameter bullet that uses a 39mm cartridge." Rohit sniffed a sniff that might have been one of derision. "That round is significantly less powerful than the 7.62mm NATO bullets which are fired using a larger 51mm cartridge."

Sam nodded. "So, what does this mean?"

For a moment, no one spoke.

Isaac broke the silence. "At the very least, it means that there are people with Kalashnikov assault rifles in the local area... probably retained secretly after the Malayan emergency. These people are now being resupplied with ammunition, which means that they plan to use them."

Sam shivered. "And that means there are people hiding around here who are not only armed with exploding mines, but who also have assault rifles. If you put the two of those together, you could have a lot of killing."

"Feelings are certainly running a bit hot at the moment." Isaac rubbed the back of his neck. "Malaya's ruling head, Tunku Abdul Rahman, is trying to discriminate in favor of the Malays. It's not been appreciated by everyone."

Sam had long since stopped being amazed at what his older brother knew. But he nonetheless challenged him. "I can't see the connection."

"The Chinese are about 40 percent of the population, but they own almost all of the commerce and industry. The Malays are feeling that they are second-class citizens in their own country."

Isaac paused. "The trouble is; if the Chinese are discriminated against, it's going to cause resentment."

Sam nodded. "So it's a good time for terrorists to cause trouble."

"Yes."

"Come on Isaac. You said you'd help me look for a colugos. It's nearly sunrise, and if we don't look now, we'll be too late."

His brother groaned and turned over in his bed.

"Come on," Sam insisted.

Isaac yawned and stretched. "Do we have to? You've looked lots of times and never found one."

"I'm pretty sure there was one in the jungle strip on the other side of the street two weeks ago." Sam dearly wanted to confirm the existence of the small gliding lemur. The trouble was, he knew it was notoriously shy and usually hid during the day.

Sam towed his reluctant brother out of the house and down the driveway to the cul-de-sac... which was where they saw her, clearly visible in the false dawn of the early morning.

He heard his brother exclaim, "Yet Mee."

A Chinese girl was walking out from the neighboring driveway. She presented a disturbing sight, not least because she had a tear-streaked face and was naked to the waist. The woman was preserving her modesty by clutching a shoulder bag to her chest.

The young woman looked up in alarm at seeing the two boys. She let her gaze rest briefly on Sam, but then turned to Isaac.

"What are you doing here? It is very early." She said. It sounded like an accusation.

Isaac's mouth had dropped open, but a moment later, his face clouded with anger.

"Have you just come from... don't tell me that you've spent the night with..." His brother spun away from the girl in evident disgust. "I don't believe it. With Major Shelbourne!" He sounded incredulous.

Sam looked at the girl, only half understanding what was being said. She was, he had to concede, very pretty. So this was the girl Isaac had given the Scorpion Stone to. He wanted to hate her, but seeing her standing there looking so vulnerable, and in a storm of emotion, he couldn't quite do it.

Eventually Isaac expostulated, "Why Major Shelbourne? He is old, fat, and a brute."

She looked at Isaac with disdain and hugged her shoulder bag more tightly to her chest. "You are a stupid. Where you think I come from the first time I see you?"

Isaac's mouth curled. "I presume the Major's wife is not at home."

She matched his derision with a snarl. "The Major is getting her from Batu Berendam airport at 8:30."

Sam thought it was time for a more practical question. "Where is your top? What happened to it?"

She glanced at him. "It is ripped." Yet Mee turned her attention back to Isaac and said brutally, "The Major rip it off when I with him in Land Rover."

Sam wasn't sure what to say. In the end, he blurted out, "Can you mend it? Our wash amah, Rosna, is very good at mending things." Sam knew it was as stupid thing to say even as he said it.

The woman shook her head. "I no have it."

Sam could see the end of a white sleeve folding over from the top of her shoulder bag and suspected she was lying.

His brother, however, had not seen it. "Where is it?" asked Isaac stiffly.

Yet Mee waved one hand irritably. "It is in Land Rover."

Sam knew about Land Rovers. "I bet you can still get it if you want. The window in the door slides back, and most of the time, they're kept open anyway."

Isaac raised his chin. "I shall get it for you."

Yet Mee's eyes opened wide with alarm. Forgetting her modesty, she put out both hands to stop him. "No!" Her shoulder bag slipped sideways exposing one of her breasts. "No," she said again. "I don't want it."

"I will get it," insisted Isaac.

Sam had the distinct impression he was a voyeur in some sort of weird battle of wills. None of what he was hearing made sense.

Isaac turned and began to walk out the driveway.

"Stop!" screamed Yet Mee.

Isaac turned round, with a puzzled expression on his face.

The girl hurried on. "Stay. I have something for you." As she spoke, she circled round Isaac, stepped backward, and then ducked behind the side wall of the house. For a moment, she was out of sight. A second later, she reappeared. "I have put it for you on top of water tub."

"What is it?" asked Sam. He could make sense of nothing that was going on.

Still looking at Isaac, but speaking to Sam, the woman replied, "It is golden stone."

Sam raised his eyebrows in surprise. "What? The amber stone?"

Yet Mee did not reply. She was still looking at Isaac. For a moment, her face, once stricken with terror, softened for just an instant. "Go with brother and see."

As Sam turned to follow his brother, he noticed a figure on the roadside thirty yards away. He was carrying a scythe and wearing a conical coolie hat. Even from that distance, he thought he could tell with the gathering light that it was held in place with... was it a red ribbon? Sam squinted trying to make it out. "Hey," he shouted out to Isaac.

Isaac ignored him.

When Sam looked round again the man in the hat had gone.

He'd barely begun to puzzle about this when Yet Mee ran past him, naked to the waist, startling him. She sprinted along the front fence to the neighboring driveway and made for the Land Rover. Her shoulder bag lay discarded where she'd dropped it.

He turned to watch her, bewildered.

As he did, he was yanked by the scruff of the neck and hauled backward...

...and the world exploded.

Once the shock wave of the blast had passed, Sam found himself, rather surprisingly, unharmed. The reason for this was not hard to figure out. His brother had hauled him to safety behind the corner of the house and covered him with his own body.

The only damage was to his ears. They had been brutalized by the blast, and his head was ringing.

Isaac dropped him to the ground and lurched back round the corner of the house into the front garden.

Sam pushed himself up on all fours and stood groggily to his feet. When he finally managed to follow his brother back into the front garden, he saw Isaac standing by the fence looking at the carnage in front of him. Sam came up behind him. Yet Mee's bloodied and shattered body lay sprawled fifteen feet from the Land Rover. The vehicle was still standing on its wheels, but the driver's side of the cabin had been blown away. All the windows were shattered and smoke was now drifting lazily from the wreck.

Sam made his way to the end of the driveway to see if any help was coming. One or two people were beginning to appear on the street, shock clearly visible on their faces. He looked up the cul-de-sac toward the brothel. A green and white taxi was parked near the old stone gate. Sam blinked as he watched another drama being played out. He could see a Ghurkha at the door of the taxi. He had his kukri drawn and with one swift jab of its hilt, he shattered the driver's window. Moments later, he'd hauled the driver out, kicked him to his knees, and was holding the kukri to his neck.

Even as he watched, another Ghurkha came into view from the front garden of a house across the road. He had a strange assault rifle over one shoulder and was dragging a body behind him. Sam recognized the coolie hat, now looped round the neck, being dragged with him. In the Ghurkha's other hand was a kukri. Even from where he was standing, Sam could see the dark stain on the blade. Sam thought grimly that the soldier would have no need to nick his thumb before he sheathed his weapon.

Sam turned and made his way back to his brother.

Isaac was still staring, transfixed. "She's dead, isn't she?" he said.

Sam nodded. "She'd have to be."

"She detonated the bomb, so I wouldn't."

Sam hadn't yet managed to think things through, but as he listened to his brother, what he said seemed to make sense. "Yeah. I suppose so."

There was something else Sam needed to say, but he couldn't find the words to do it justice. In the end, he simply said, "Thanks for protecting me."

His brother did not take his eyes off the scene in front of him, but he nodded. "It's what blood brothers do." And then he started to sob.

Chapter 8

Isaac had some sympathy with his parents as they sat in on the interview. The man interviewing Isaac and Sam was a colonel in the military police. He could see his mother's face become increasingly pale. His father became increasingly angry, so much so, that the colonel had to pause the interview so he could have a private chat with him outside the office. His father was quieter after the chat, but still made his feelings clear by glowering and looking aggrieved. Isaac was not surprised when his mother refused to sit in on the second part of the interview. She said it was all too ghastly and that she needed a cigarette.

The colonel positioned a carefully neutral expression on his face, looked at his notes, and said to Isaac, "So you knew this woman, Yet Mee. How did you come to meet her?"

"I met her two weeks ago when she attempted to steal a papaya from a tree in our garden. She said she was hungry." Isaac shrugged. "I helped her get a papaya."

"When did you find out she was a prostitute working at The Suzi?"

"She told me at our first meeting."

"Did she tell you why she was walking down your street?"

66

"Yes. She had spent the night giving sex to Major Shelbourne." He paused. "She said I was stupid because I hadn't realized that was what she'd been doing."

The colonel frowned. "You categorically know that?"

"Yes. Yet Mee told me that when she came out from his home without her blouse, the morning she died."

Isaac chose his words very deliberately. He didn't want there to be any ambiguity.

The colonel leaned back. "Well, that's interesting. Because Major Shelbourne denies he knew the woman or had anything to do with her."

"I reckon a few inquiries at The Suzi will show that he's lying. He drove her from the brothel to his home, presumably because he didn't want people to see her entering his house." Isaac was nursing a visceral loathing for the Major, but knew he needed to keep it under control if he was to visit justice on the man. Isaac's last memory of the Major was seeing him in his underpants on the front porch of his house. It was not a pretty picture.

The colonel put his forefingers together and tapped his lips. "Perhaps you can tell me what you think happened on the morning she died."

"Yes sir. But before I do, can I ask whether you know anything about the type of bomb that exploded?"

The colonel raised an eyebrow, but chose to answer. "It was a simple pressure release mine. It had been wedged between the driver's seat and the door."

"Was the door locked?"

The colonel consulted his notes. "No."

Isaac felt a sense of guilt that he would now need to talk about Yet Mee in a brutally clinical way. In truth, he wanted to scream and rant. Yet Mee had been very human, and her life story was tragic. He drew a deep breath and began to speak. "Yet Mee had been raped as a child and sold to The Suzi in part payment of her father's debts. He was associated with some bad people."

"How do you know this?"

"She told me."

"Did these people have a political agenda?"

"I don't know. But she certainly had strong political feelings."

"How do you know that?"

"She told me that she thought the British were imperialist bullies." Isaac looked at the Colonel. "I'm not real clear about what's going on politically at the moment. Why would she say that?"

The Colonel pursed his lips and then said, "It's only been ten years since the 'Malayan emergency.' The Communists fought a guerrilla war and tried to cause the locals to rise up against our control of this country. Fortunately, we managed to nip it in the bud. The Communists have since fallen out of favor with the locals, but it wouldn't take much for things to change. The Malay Head of Government, Tunku Abdul Rahman, has been stirring up national-istic fervor, and the Chinese don't like it. You've seen all the posters around the place for the local elections. They are never taken down, so politics is always front and center in people's consciousness. That means Malaya is a political tinderbox." The Colonel leaned back in his chair. "Now, tell me all you can remember about your meetings with Yet Mee."

Isaac did so. He concluded by saying, "I believe Yet Mee left the Major's house, planted the explosives in the Land Rover, and then gave the nod to the assassin in the conical hat. I didn't actually see the guy, but Sam did."

"I only saw him briefly," said Sam. "Just before the explosion. He looked like the bloke who was cutting grass near where the Ferret was blown up."

The Colonel jerked his head up. "What?"

Sam continued. "It was the same fellow who was by the Ferret."

"How do you know?"

"He was wearing the same hat, and it was tied under his chin with red ribbon or raffia."

"Are you sure?"

Isaac interrupted. "If Sam sees something, you can be pretty sure about it."

"Why wasn't I told about this man earlier?" said the Colonel, scowling.

Sam shrugged. "No one asked."

The Colonel grunted and then motioned for Isaac to continue.

"Yet Mee would have carried the explosive in her shoulder bag. It was pretty large." Isaac paused as a thought crossed his mind. "Sam tells me he saw part of her blouse poking out from the top of her bag. Did you find her blouse inside?"

The Colonel sighed. "Try and remember that it is me who is interviewing you, young man. But yes, her blouse was in her bag… and it had been ripped quite badly."

Isaac nodded. "I thought so. She wouldn't have wanted to leave any clues about her identity in the Land Rover." Hearing what the Colonel said confirmed what he already knew. She hadn't gone to the Land Rover to get her blouse; she'd gone there to stop Isaac from dying. He'd realized the awful truth seconds before he'd pulled Sam to safety. Yet Mee had lured them behind the safety of the house by placing the Scorpion Stone on the lid of the water tub. Everything she'd done in those final few seconds was deliberate. It had been her gift of self-sacrifice, and Isaac was unable to come to terms with it.

He rubbed his temple as he continued to speak. "I suspect the assassin was waiting for the 'first responders' to the bombing to arrive, so he could open fire with his assault rifle, before escaping in the taxi."

The Colonel looked at his notes again. "Ah yes. You say you told Major Shelbourne about the taxi and the discovery of smuggled ammunition." He looked speculatively at Isaac. "He denies that you told him anything."

Isaac didn't reply. He simply reached down to his school satchel, extracted the carbon copy of the letter he'd written to Major Shelbourne and handed it to the Colonel. As the Colonel read the letter, his face clouded with anger. He pursed his lips and slipped the letter into a manila folder that was in front of him.

Isaac wanted to make sure that Shelbourne could not wriggle out of his responsibility for all that had happened. "What will happen to Major Shelbourne?" he asked.

"That is no concern of yours."

"But it is sir. It is a great concern to me."

Silence hung between them.

Isaac's father growled. "Show the Colonel some respect, boy."

The Colonel lifted a hand in acquiescence. "I suspect that the Commanding Officer will require him to attend a summary hearing."

"And after that?"

"There may be a court-martial."

Isaac nodded. He was satisfied… but couldn't resist adding. "And I doubt that Mrs. Shelbourne is going to be too happy." Privately, Isaac doubted that their marriage, such as it was, would survive.

The ceiling fan was badly balanced and was making a whump, whump, whump sound.

The Colonel leaned back in his chair. "And somehow, you also managed to recruit your own private army."

Isaac managed a smile. "That was not my doing, sir. That was Sam's friend, Rohit Tappit."

Sam butted in. "We couldn't get Major Shelbourne to take us seriously, so Rohit organized with his dad for off-duty Ghurkhas to keep watch at either end of our cul-de-sac."

The Colonel nodded. "Yes, and they were very professional. Evidently, four of them stood watch for four hours, and then were relieved by another four soldiers who stood guard until the morning." He shook his head. "All very unorthodox and completely unofficial."

Sam nodded. "Yeah. They were dropped off in a long wheel-base Land Rover. I saw it, but I didn't know why it was there at the time."

The Colonel leaned back in his chair and tapped his fingers together. His eyes were half closed.

Another silence ensued.

Whump, whump, whump.

After an eternity, he nodded, as if to himself. Then he looked at the boys and smiled. "You've done well – both of you. Thank you."

Isaac and Sam shook his hand.

Isaac knew they may have won the approbation of the Colonel, but that didn't extend to their father. He was now driving them home, glowering and silent. Isaac recognized the signs. Trouble was brewing. It was not unusual.

Once they got home, they had a tense dinner, after which both boys retreated to the safety of their bedrooms. Isaac could clearly hear his father begin to vent his spleen to their mother over all that had happened. If things ran to form, they would be doing so whilst working their way through several glasses of sherry.

Isaac switched his light off and listened to the darkness as he wrestled with a storm of emotion.

He had just drifted off to sleep, but was woken abruptly when his father switched on the light. "Get up boy. Go and apologize to your mother."

Isaac blinked and tried to understand the logic of his father's request. For the life of him, he couldn't, so he risked a question. "Er, yes. Is there anything in particular that you want me to apologize for?"

"Are you trying to be funny?"

"No." Clearly, his father had been stewing over something and could no longer contain himself.

"Apologize to her for not telling her what you've been up to these last few weeks."

Isaac knew better than to argue at the injustice of his demand. "Okay, dad."

He untucked the mosquito netting over his bed and padded over to his parent's bedroom. Sam was already standing disconsolately at the doorway. His father had roused him as well. Sam looked at him imploringly.

Isaac laid a hand briefly on his arm and steered him into their parent's bedroom. He put a knuckle on his forehead and tried to compose the right words. After a moment, he said, "Sorry mum for not letting you know everything that's been happening. We'll both try not to do it again."

If his mother was bewildered by the interruption to her reading, she hid it well. She removed her cigarette and composed her face so that she looked stern. "Very well, boys."

"Now get to bed, both of you," ordered his father. Isaac sighed and suddenly felt very alone. His father was still treating him as if he was eight years old.

He went back to bed, but he did not sleep. Nightmarish images of Yet Mee's shredded body rushed at his face, before backing away, only to rush at him again.

He turned over, punched the pillow, and lay down… but it gave him no solace.

Isaac and Sam should have both been at school, but their father had decreed that in view of all that had happened, they should have a week at home. Personally, Isaac would have welcomed the distraction of school, but his opinion hadn't been asked.

Today, he'd taken himself off to the beach and was sitting with his back against a coconut tree log where there was a patch of sand. He stared out at the dirty sea. Elegant Malay fishing boats sat above their reflection at anchor. They had an overhanging stern behind the deck cabin, and their graceful prow rose elegantly into the air. He could see three fishing *kelongs* beyond them.

Isaac reached into his pocket and pulled out the Scorpion Stone. He turned it over in his hands. Sam had given it to him, with the simple comment, "Yet Mee's dying has really hit you, and so you better have this." That meant he was now custodian of the stone. He conceded that it was probably him who needed the most help at the moment.

A familiar voice, with its distinctive Scottish burr, hailed him from the gate at the head of the beach. It was the voice of the senior chaplain, Hamish O'Brien. "Hi Isaac. Sam said I'd find you here. Do you mind if I join you?"

Isaac thought it strange that an adult would even ask. "Mr. O'Brien! Sure."

The chaplain sat down next to Isaac, grabbed a stick, and started to draw in the sand. He seemed in no hurry to speak. Eventually he said, "I've been talking with Sam, just to see how he was doing."

Isaac nodded. "And how do you think he's doing?"

"Both of you have been in the wars recently – literally, and you've experienced some deeply disturbing things. But I think Sam will be all right. He's tough and he's pragmatic." The chaplain continued to draw in the sand. "But it's you I'm concerned about. You've particularly been through the mill. How are you feeling?"

Isaac frowned. "Did you come all the way from Terendak just to ask me that?"

"Yes."

"Wow." Isaac stared into the middle distance, not really seeing anything. "Um… I'm sometimes numb… not believing what really happened. And sometimes – just sad." He paused. "I'm not sleeping much. And I see… horrible things in my mind."

The chaplain grunted. "That's quite normal given the circumstances."

Isaac looked at him, only half believing him. "Really? I thought I was going mad."

"No you are not. It's the way your mind is trying to cope with things. Sometimes, however, the symptoms can last, and you can continue to have night terrors, have trouble sleeping, and experience difficulty getting on with people."

Isaac coughed a bitter laugh. "Getting on with dad is already difficult."

"Be kind to him. He means well."

Isaac looked at Mr. O'Brien. "Do you understand him… because I certainly don't?"

The chaplain nodded slowly. "A bit. He's had his own demons to deal with in life. He told me that he lost his own father when he was young."

Isaac grunted and was not inclined to be very charitable.

Mr. O'Brien looked at him. "Promise me that you will ask to see a doctor if these symptoms persist."

"That won't be my call. It will only happen if dad thinks I should."

"Well, if he doesn't think it's a good idea, ask to see me."

Isaac nodded. He was conscious that he was no longer feeling quite so alone. "Thanks for coming to see me."

They sat in silence together. Isaac couldn't help but recall the image of Yet Mee, lying dead – discarded by life like a rag doll. His eyes began to well with tears, and he lowered his head.

The movement wasn't lost on the chaplain. "What are you thinking about right now, Isaac?"

Isaac sniffed and turned away. "Nothing."

Mr. O'Brien said nothing and waited.

Isaac could sense the man's care, so conceded that he deserved more than evasion. "I don't know how…" He paused, and tried again. "I don't know how to handle the fact that someone else died to save me." He lowered his head again. "It's not an easy thing to live with."

The chaplain nodded. "It would be an impossible thing to live with, except for one thing."

Isaac looked up at him, questioningly.

"That one thing is this: It was an act motivated by love." He looked at Isaac. "Do please cherish that love. It was Yet Mee's gift to you."

"But I don't deserve it."

"None of us do. When the God of the universe died to take the blame for all the things that would otherwise keep us from him, we didn't deserve it."

"Will… will God have time for Yet Mee? She was a prostitute."

The chaplain laughed. "Read the gospels, Isaac. Jesus had huge compassion for prostitutes." He paused. "Jesus once said that the greatest gift a person can give, is to lay down their life for a friend – just as he did for us, so Yet Mee is in good company."

Isaac was conscious of something heavy in his heart beginning to lift. It was only a slight lift, but it was a beginning.

The chaplain got to his feet and dusted the sand off his shorts.

"It will be most interesting to see what becomes of you, Isaac. I think it could be quite special."

***

Sam enjoyed sweet and sour pork, and Ah Soi cooked it well. The family were at dinner, and he was relishing his first mouthful when his father said, "Boys, I have something to tell you."

Suddenly, the food didn't taste quite so good. "What?" he spluttered.

"Your mother and I have decided to send you to boarding school in England." I'm being posted to the UK next month.

Sam blinked. "Boarding school?" A terrible fear immediately asserted itself. "Will Isaac be going too?"

"He will."

Relief flooded over him – to be followed, in short order, by a thousand different questions. He glanced across to his brother.

Isaac put down his fork and said, "You didn't think to discuss this with us?" The accusation hung in the air uncomfortably.

Their father compressed his lips into a straight line.

Sam tried to rescue the situation. "What school will we be going to?"

"It's a small one in Kent." His father mentioned the name.

His brother kept his eyes down as he asked his next question. "Why did you choose that school?"

"Because I had a nice letter from the headmaster."

Isaac nodded. "A nice letter." He paused. "You didn't do any more research?"

His father said, crossly, "They offer a discount for clergy, and the fees will largely be covered by the army subsidy."

"So it's cheap."

His father lurched to his feet, knocking over the chair behind him. "Get to your room, Isaac," he roared. "And don't come out until you can apologize."

Sam lingered by the doorway to his classroom as his peers filed out for recess. When Doseena came through, he felt himself flush and knew himself to be in unfamiliar territory.

If Doseena was surprised at being approached by Sam, she didn't show it. She smiled shyly.

That simple act was more devastating for Sam than any verbal salutation. He shifted from foot to foot nervously and blurted out, "My dad is being posted to the UK, and I'm being sent to boarding school."

Doseena nodded.

Sam rushed on. "I just wanted you to know."

Doseen waited for Sam to say more. When he didn't, she said, "Will Isaac be going to the same school?"

"Yes." Sam continued. "I just want you to know that I won't forget you."

"That's nice. I don't think I will forget you or your brother either." They were silent for a while, and then a look of sadness crossed her face. She said, hesitantly, "You will remember me as I am now, won't you? When I'm young."

Sam frowned, not understanding what she meant by it. "Why do you say that?"

Doseena lowered her head. "We aboriginal women don't do well in a white man's world."

Sam spluttered his protest. "But you will become a famous writer. You're brilliant."

Doseena smiled a sad smile. "Your brother is brilliant. What do you think he will do after school?"

Sam shrugged. "Oxford or Cambridge, I suppose."

"I think you're right." She paused. "Would you like to know how many Aboriginal woman have been able to go to either of those universities?"

Sam had no idea.

"There have been none, Sam. None. But plenty of white Australian men have gone."

"Perhaps you could change that."

"I think it will change one day. But not in my day." Doseena turned to go.

Sam grabbed her by the elbow. "I won't forget you, Doseena."

She looked at him for a long time. "I think perhaps that's true." Then she eased herself free and walked away.

Two days later, Sam shuffled down the hallway with his hands in his pockets, looking for his brother. He felt out of sorts and didn't know what to think about going to boarding school. Part of him was apprehensive. Another part of him was pleased to be free of his father's grumblings and outbursts. When Sam looked into Isaac's bedroom, Isaac was nowhere to be seen. However, what he did see was deeply disturbing. Doseena's cowrie shell sat on Isaac's card table. The shell was distinctive. It was three inches long and patterned with chocolate and tan speckles.

He looked at it in disbelief. Doseena had given it to Isaac.

Sam put his hand to his chest as if to suppress the pain, then stumbled back to his bedroom.

England, two years later, 1965

Chapter 9

Sophie primped the wild flowers into place in the jam jar she'd placed in the center of the kitchen table.

Miss Chessington sat at the end of the table and steepled her fingers together. Sophie smiled to herself. There were occasions Miss Chessington looked every inch the schoolmistress.

"Today, Sophie, we begin a new adventure." She smiled. "We will begin to explore the thinking of some of the finest minds in history."

Sophie picked up her pen and waited to take notes.

"The greatest debate humankind has engaged in is whether or not the order of the universe is the result of an intelligent mind, or whether it has come about as the result of chance."

"So… God or atheism?"

Miss Chessington nodded. "Things began in 400BC with the Greek philosopher, Democritus. He was called 'the laughing philosopher' because his response to the apparent order of the cosmos was to laugh at the absurdity of its existence. He believed everything was made up from atoms purely as the result of chance."

"He was more of an atheist, then?"

"Yes. The Epicurean philosophers promoted Democritus' thinking, but they soon found themselves in a titanic battle with the Stoics. The Stoics noticed the level of order in nature and saw it as evidence of there being a 'mind' behind creation."

"Who won the battle?"

"The Stoics. The Epicureans died out in 200AD, largely because they crossed swords with three towering intellects: Socrates, Plato, and Aristotle." Miss Chessington smiled sadly. "The thinking since then has been rather less intelligent. With the notable exception of Thomas Aquinas, it has centered more on ridicule than reason…"

At that point, a sharp rap of the front door interrupted her.

Miss Chessington frowned, and rose to answer it.

To Sophie's surprise, she heard squeals of surprise and laughter coming from the hallway. She'd never heard her tutor so animated.

The woman that Miss Chessington ushered into the kitchen brought with her an aura of positivity and laughter that was tangible. Sophie was awestruck. The lady had shoulder length hair with an auburn tinge. Whilst she was only of medium stature, there was nothing medium or average about her personality.

"I've brought scones and an irresponsible amount of jam and cream," she announced. Seeing Sophie, she beamed a smile. "Hello, darling. Who are you?"

Before Sophie could answer, Miss Chessington made the introduction. "Roslyn, this is Sophie Hunter. I'm tutoring her, and like you, she is very bright." She turned to Sophie. "Sophie, this is Roslyn. She was once a favorite student of mine and has continued to be a good friend. Her father is someone very important in the legal service, and she is one of the few people I allow to visit me."

Roslyn shook Sophie by the hand. "Well, Sophie, you have picked a good tutor. She'll have you believing you should rule the world."

Miss Chessington smiled one of her rare smiles. "From what I hear, you are making a fair attempt at it. What are you doing now?"

"I'm currently the events coordinator for the Suffolk agricultural show." Roslyn grinned. "That means scandalizing the events committee and the Women's Institute by organizing all sorts of fun educational things, particularly for kids. I've been booking buses to bring them from schools in Norwich, Sudbury, and Newmarket. We should double the takings at the gate this year." She turned to Sophie. "Put the kettle on, Sophie, and tell me about yourself."

Sophie obeyed dumbly, only managing to stammer, "There's nothing to tell. I live on the farm. Dad looks after the cattle."

"What breed?"

"Red Poles."

"Will you be entering them into the show?"

"Yes. The men enter our stock every year."

"But you're not going?"

Sophie lowered her head. "No. I've never been."

Roslyn grinned. "Well, we'll have to fix that. I'll get you a ticket."

Before long, the three of them were sitting around the kitchen table drinking tea and eating scones. Roslyn made up the scones with levels of jam and cream Sophie thought were positively sinful. Miss Chessington seemed content to allow the ebullient nature of her old student wash over them all. However, after some time, she said, "Roslyn, I wonder if you would teach Sophie some of your particular wisdom, for I'm afraid I cannot." She smiled sadly. "I think she would benefit from your help."

Sophie coughed in surprise as she bit into her scone, scattering crumbs as she did. She wasn't aware of needing any help at all.

Roslyn cocked her head. "You're scheming, Georgina. What, exactly, would you like me to teach?"

"She wants to explore a future in history and politics."

Sophie felt obliged to protest. "Please Miss, I don't think that would be possible..."

Miss Chessington dismissed her objection with a wave of her hand. "Those are choppy waters, so I think she would benefit from your positivity, but I'm afraid that 'hope' is not my strong suit." She paused. "I want her to be able to laugh like you can, when your feet are mired in the pain and complexities of life."

Roslyn looked at her old teacher. "Are the demons still bad?"

"Sophie has helped bring some relief." Miss Chessington managed half a smile. "She has taught me to drink St. John's wort."

"St. John's wort?"

"Yes."

Roslyn turned to Sophie, her laughing eyes now serious. After a moment, she said, "If you are going to keep your heart intact, you will need to learn the difference between joy and happiness."

Sophie looked at her without comprehension.

"Happiness depends on favorable circumstances. But joy, well… that's a different thing entirely. You can experience joy even in the most dire circumstances – but only if you have the right foundation."

Sophie was intrigued, but felt she was now well out of her depth.

"A person can experience joy only if they have a foundation for hope that transcends their current circumstances." Rosyln paused. "And to have that right foundation, you need to know your identity and the destiny you were created for. Without knowing these things, you will be a spiritual orphan, bending to the absurdities and meaninglessness of current opinion."

Sophie stuttered. "I… I don't know much about that."

"Then I think it is time you did." Roslyn wagged a finger. "But there is one proviso."

"What's that?"

"If this foundation is to give you joy, even in the midst of grief, it must be based on truth."

Sophie said slowly, "I'm not sure I understand."

Roslyn passed over the plate of scones. "If you seek it, you will find it." She smiled. "I promise."

As Sophie reached for a scone, Roslyn moved the plate sideways, dodging her hand. She moved it left and right until Sophie finally snared a scone. Sophie laughed in triumph, holding it aloft.

Roslyn put the plate down. "As I said: If you seek it, you will find it."

The attempted rape came five days later.

Sophie was reflecting on what Miss Chessington had taught her the previous day about the extraordinary life of Caroline of Ansbach. As the wife of king George II, she was queen of Great Britain and Ireland. She'd been queen at a time when the significance of women in the affairs of state was minimal. Yet she had unquestionably been the power and brains behind the throne.

Her husband was a boorish Hanovarian. Caroline, on the other hand, was both innovative and intellectual. When smallpox began devastating Europe and Great Britain, Caroline heard the rumor that people who had contracted the mild disease of cowpox were immune to the deadly smallpox. She therefore offered to commute the death sentence for prisoners who agreed to be inoculated with cowpox, to see if it was safe. Having established its safety, she tested its effectiveness on children in an orphanage. When she was satisfied it was effective, she sent a doctor to inoculate her family in Germany, and by doing so, saved their lives.

Catherine surrounded herself with the finest minds in Europe and involved herself in the affairs of state, even in the selection of the next Archbishop of Canterbury.

Sophie lay in the hay and wondered whether such women could exist today. Elizabeth II was currently queen, and she seemed to be a lovely person. But could an ordinary woman amount to anything?

The hay was soft and still smelled of summer. It came from the bales that had broken when being stacked in the corner of the barn. The bales were used to top up the supplies in the stables.

The black weatherboard barn was one of Sophie's favorite places. It leaned to one side, as if on an elbow, tired from the demands of history. Its roof had been tiled centuries earlier with red tiles. They were now mottled with lichen. The colors reminded her of a tweed jacket.

The lofty wooden beams of the barn whispered of days when horses worked the farm. Nowadays, only a few remained in the stables. They were used for recreation and for fox hunting. The leather harness from one of the working horses was still hanging from a peg on one of the beams. It was as if the barn was reluctant to part with its memories. Her father was certainly reluctant. He kept a collection of horse buckles and brasses in a cake tin on the corner of the workbench.

A shadow fell over her.

A young man, perhaps still a boy, was silhouetted against the opening of the barn. He was as thin as a reed and had long hair. Judging from the highlights on the edges, it was fair.

"I've been watching you for some time." The boy's voice was cultured and sounded expensive.

Sophie frowned. "I don't know whether to be flattered or spooked. I think I'll settle for thinking that you're creepy. Who are you?"

The young man lifted his chin. "That doesn't really matter. You're a girl, and I'm a boy. Let's leave it at that."

A frisson of fear began to sound a warning. "I'm not comfortable with that. What do you want?"

"I want to know if you drop 'em." The boy laughed. "Or if you even wear them."

Sophie recoiled in shock. "Why you dirty-minded, foulmouthe..." She tilted her head back and began to yell, "Dad. Dad. Help!"

The young man sneered. "Your father can't hear you. No one's near the barn or the stables. I checked."

He came forward.

Sophie screamed for help again.

A moment later, he fell on top of her, spread-eagled. His hands gripped her wrists with a strength that belied his thin frame.

Sophie fought, wiggled, and screamed for all she was worth. In the process, she managed to bring a leg up sharply and knee him in the groin.

It was enough to slow him down, but no more. He slapped her across the face and groped for her crotch. "Relax," he wheezed. "You'll enjoy it. Everyone is doing it."

Sophie continued to fight like a hellcat.

Suddenly, the boy relaxed his grip. "This is useless," he said.

An instant later, Sophie's sensibilities were shattered by a deafening bang.

The hay beside the boy's left ear quivered and dust hung in the air.

"The next shot will kill you, boy. Get off my daughter right now."

Relief flooded through her. She saw her father come out from behind the tractor holding a double-barreled shotgun.

Somewhat alarmingly, the boy didn't move. Sophie wondered whether he had fainted from shock.

Her father spoke again. "Boy, you'd better move your arse, or I'll blow your leg off. This is a twelve gauge shotgun, and it makes a mess at this range."

Sophie heard the ominous sound of the second hammer being pulled back on the gun. She was now alarmed for the safety of her attacker. "It's all right, Dad. Don't kill him."

She was then amazed to hear the last thing she expected. The young man was sobbing.

Sophie squirmed her way from underneath him. She was greatly assisted in this by her father grabbing the young man by the collar and hauling him over onto his back.

"Blimey," he said looking at the young man. "It's Anthony."

By this time, Sophie was on her feet. She kicked out at her assailant angrily and said, "And who the heck is Anthony?"

"He's Sir Robert Chessington's son."

Sophie's mouth dropped open.

The boy had now rolled into a fetal position and was weeping pitifully. Sophie couldn't understand it. Anything less like a rapist was now hard to imagine. And yet the attack had been very real and very frightening.

Sophie's father hauled Anthony to his feet. The young man's nose was running, but he was heedless of it. "I'm sorry," he said. And then he said it again, and again. "I've never been with a woman. Never wanted to. Never felt the desire. Don't you see," he said pleadingly, "I was trying to see if I could make the feeling come."

Sophie put her hands on her hips. "You don't find love with violence, you idiot."

"I'd settle for…"

"Lust?"

Anthony didn't reply.

"So you're a homosexual seeking to get it on with a woman."

Anthony hung his head.

For an instant, the cruelty of reality for many homosexuals dawned on her. But Anthony had tried to rape her, and she was not inclined to be sympathetic.

Further conversation was forestalled by Sophie's father hauling Anthony by the scruff of the neck to the open barn door. "I don't care what you are, boy. I'm taking you to your father, and then the police."

Germany, two years later, 1967

Chapter 10

The British Airways jet took off from a drizzly Luton airport and bumped its way through the clouds until it emerged magically into blue sky and sunshine. Sam reveled in its optimism and hoped it was a portent for the future. NATO had charted the jet to fly service personnel to Germany. It was also flying a few 'dependants' like himself out to their parents for the Christmas holiday. His father was now a chaplain to the British Forces in Hohne, near Bergen in Lower Saxony.

The stewardesses had judged from Sam's size that he was an adult. He'd learned this when he'd volunteered to help unscrew the cap on a miniature bottle of gin she was wanting for a passenger. She'd smiled when he handed it back, poured the gin with tonic into a beaker, and given it to him. As a result, his head was now spinning.

Sam reflected on his time in boarding school. It had not been an entirely comfortable time, and both he and Isaac initially had trouble fitting in. Having Isaac with him was a huge help. From time to time, they had needed to swap the Scorpion Stone to each other. After all they'd been through overseas, it was difficult to get used to a culture where the thing that most excited his peers was a farting competition. Unlike Isaac, he was a mediocre student, due largely to a restlessness that made it hard for him to commit to anything he could not see the purpose of. Now that he had completed his first term in the sixth form, things were better. He was able to specialize in Biology, Geography, and Physics.

Isaac, of course, had done brilliantly at school. To no one's surprise, he had received a place at King's College, Cambridge, where he was reading English Literature. He had just finished his first Michaelmas term there.

In what seemed to be no time at all, the aircraft sank through the pillow of clouds into the gloom of an overcast Germany and landed at RAF Gütersloh.

Sam's suitcase was barely given any attention in the terminal. As his father had not yet arrived to pick him up, he left his baggage and walked from the building toward the edge of the airfield. He'd seen something intriguing. Against the perimeter fence were the carcasses of two Second World War Mosquitoes. These medium-sized bombers were built of spruce/balsa wood composite that was attached to a steel frame. This made the planes very light and fast. The famous RAF Pathfinder Force had used them during the war.

Sam was appreciating the historically old, when he was suddenly faced with the very new. An English Electric Lightning, the RAF's latest interceptor jet, came trundling down the taxiway. Sam knew enough to know that the jet had massive power and had been built to get up high very quickly. It wasn't a pretty thing. Because one jet engine was mounted on top of the other, it looked pregnant. Its stubby wings seemed to have been added as an afterthought.

The pilot taxied onto the runway and immediately opened up both engines with re-heat. Sam was completely unprepared for the shattering noise. It was shocking and disorientating. Because he was standing behind it, not far away, he experienced its full impact. Flames roared from the engine, and the aircraft hurtled down the runway. A few seconds later, it lifted vertically into the sky. Sam was awestruck.

Once he'd recovered his senses, he massaged his temples and was thoughtful. RAF Gütersloh was the nearest airfield to the

East/West German border… and he'd learned that the squadron based here was currently on 'yellow alert' – ready for trouble. It was not a comforting thought.

"Hey, Sam."

He turned to see Isaac walking toward him.

"Sorry, we're late. Bit of ice on the road. Dad's already got your bags in the car. How are you?"

Sam slapped his brother on the back, pulling him toward him in what might have been a hug. He grinned. "You're certainly looking the part." Isaac had allowed his hair to grow long, and he was now wearing glasses. They were round. He looked every inch the trendy academic.

"What's with the glasses?"

"Too much reading. They don't have to be very strong, fortunately. Don't really need them outdoors."

"When did you get here?"

"Four days ago. I took the ferry from Harwich. Dad picked me up from Hamburg."

"Why didn't you fly?"

"I'm no longer a 'dependant,' so Dad had to pay. Steerage only. No cabin."

"So it was cheaper?"

"Yeah."

They both laughed and began to walk toward the army Morris Traveler in the car park. Their father got out as they approached. "Get a move on, boys. I want to get home while it's still light."

"Hi Dad."

"Oh, Hi." His father shook his hand. It was perfunctory, but it was something.

The geographical feature that attracted the military to the north-eastern part of Lower Saxony was a vast area of heath and woodland known as the Lüneburg Heath. It was a wild and secretive place. Hitler had developed his V2 rocket there. It hadn't taken

NATO long to realize that it made a perfect tank training area. As such, the 2nd Tank Regiment and the 11th Hussars were currently based there. No one needed reminding it was a tank training area. You could hear them. Sam lay on his bed at 11pm listening in the dark. The 55 ton Chieftain tank mounted a general-purpose machine gun that was used to help the main gun to acquire its target. It fired three shots above, below, and at the target, and it's distinctive sound could be heard during the day and during the night – "tat,tat,tat… tat,tat,tat… tat,tat,tat… BOOM!" A night-firing exercise was going on at the moment. It was not quite the standard lullaby, but it was enough to allow Sam to slide into sleep.

Next morning, both Sam and Isaac rugged themselves up and made their way out the back gate of the garden into the woods. No one would have known there was a garden, however, as everything was currently covered with two feet of snow. The branches of the pine trees were dangerously loaded with snow and hung low. After they'd played the usual pranks of banging a branch when a brother was underneath it – rites of passage that signaled the start of another holiday together – the two of them chatted, bringing each other up to date on all that had happened since they'd last seen each other during the summer holiday.

Sam pointed. "Look over here. What do you think that is?"

Isaac looked at the tracks in the snow. "They're pretty big tracks. I reckon that has to be a red deer. It's too big for a roe deer." They pushed on through the hushed world of snow, where everything, including time, seemed to be quiet. The boys came to a small creek. Despite having a thick crusting of ice on its edge, they could see some water moving in the middle. Sam liked visiting the creek, particularly in the summer. He'd sunk some large glass jars into the bank of the creek to see what was around. Quite often, he'd catch a bank vole. They were vicious little creatures. If he caught two, one of them would be half eaten by the time he recovered them.

"What on earth are we going to do to stop ourselves going mad this Christmas?" said Isaac in a muffled voice. Sam could barely see Isaac's face as he was so wrapped up in his scarf and beanie.

"Dunno."

"Mum and Dad will be driven mad if we don't do something. And it's too hard to visit the *gasthaus* for a beer."

It was true. Their local *gasthaus* was in the nearby village of Bergen, and it would be a difficult walk along the forest path in the snow, particularly at night. But there was another reason Sam didn't like to go there. It was a sense that they never felt welcome. The boys were routinely ignored. It wasn't overt rudeness, but it was close.

Sam had spoken to Isaac about it. "Do you feel it too?"

"Yeah."

"Why is it, do you think?"

Isaac had rocked the bottom of his beer glass around and around on the table and looked at the patrons around him. Then he leaned forward and said in a low voice. "You idiot. The notorious Belsen Concentration Camp is only a few miles up the road. You've been there. You know."

Sam shuddered. He had, and the memories of the place, particularly the photographs, still haunted him. It may have been his imagination, but no bird sang in the trees at Belsen.

Isaac continued. "This town was very much complicit with everything that happened there. The Allies knew it and made the townsfolk clean up the camp. So there's not been a lot of love."

"But that was twenty-two years ago."

Isaac smiled sadly. "You're young. That is but yesterday in the bloody pages of history."

The temperature in the room seemed to drop around Sam. He finished his drink. "Let's not come back here."

Isaac nodded. "Suits me fine."

Making that resolution did, however, put certain strictures on their drinking options. Sam acknowledged to himself that the real problem was winter. It shut down a lot of things. By contrast, the summers in Germany were glorious. If they weren't exploring the charming Hanoverian town of Celle, they were living in an army tent at the British Weser Yacht Club. Their parents had discovered the club's existence and suggested the boys go there to learn to sail.

Both boys had agreed with alacrity. As a result, the club had pretty much become their summer home. Sam and Isaac had learned to sail, and then they'd stayed on at the club to teach others. The food was supplied by an army cook, which suited their mother admirably.

Sam had particularly taken to sailing: so much so, that he was pretty sure what he wanted to do for a career.

"Do you remember the *son et lumiere* festival in Nienburg last summer?"

Isaac grunted. "Yeah. It was good."

Sam nodded. It had been more than good. It had been magical. The rescue launch had towed all the dinghies upstream to the town of Nienburg in the early evening. Lanterns had been strung up the stays and shrouds, and the boats looked amazing. Then, as an orchestra played Handel's Water Music on the bank, hundreds of swimmers had swum into the river holding a light above them. They looked like a stream of molten lava.

Sam took a deep breath and said, "I think I know what I want to do when I leave school."

His comment succeeded in getting Isaac's full attention. "Oh yeah. What?"

"I'm thinking of joining the Navy?"

"What? That tool of imperialist oppression!"

Sam punched his brother on the arm. "Seriously. What do you think?"

"I was serious." Isaac paused. "But I suppose it makes some sort of perverse sense. There's action, and you like action. There are boats, and you love boats." He paused again. "It's not great for the love life though."

"How's your love life?"

"A few nibbles, but nothing serious. I want to get established at Cambridge before I indulge that particular fancy."

"What are you going to do when you've finished there?"

"No idea." Isaac sighed. "I don't think anyone's got much of an idea about anything at the moment. Certainly, politically, everything is very uncertain. Is there going to be a nuclear holocaust? Will there ever be freedom and justice? I don't know what I dare hope for."

"Gee, you're a cheerful one. I've never really thought about that stuff much." Sam pointed at his brother. "That's the trouble with you. You think too much."

Sam was rewarded for his comment by a snowball in the back of his head.

Once things had settled down, Isaac said, "Why don't we ask dad to take us over to the officer's mess at Fallingbostel? He doesn't need much of an excuse to have a beer and catch up with people, particularly if we keep out of his way."

Much of the way to Fallingbostel was along concrete roads that had been built to cater for military tanks. Isaac was grateful. The corrugations on the cement gave the car a better grip than on bitumen. With Christmas only a few days away, Northern Germany was deep in the grip of winter, and the presence of 'black ice' posed a real threat.

The officer's mess in Fallingbostel was a stolid stately affair. However, its Germanic demeanor was softened by the presence of a lake that lay beside it. The rumour was that it was stocked with trout, but Isaac and Sam had not yet tried to poach any to find out.

Isaac and Sam followed their father into the mess, and all of them were soon nursing half pints of beer. Their father got into conversation with a group of officers, giving the boys a chance to slip away to one of their favorite places – downstairs to the cellars.

The cellars contained one of the strangest features the boys had ever come across in an officer's mess; a bowling alley.

When they arrived, two army officers were already using it, but they graciously allowed the boys to join them.

The bowling alley was like no other Isaac had ever seen. The wooden floor and the gutters on the edge were conventional enough, but what lurked behind the skittles was a mechanical wonder. Someone could sit in a seat and operate levers that swept the skittles into a basket. From there, the operator placed the skittles into nine metal slots. With another pull of the lever, the skittles were placed upright on the end of the alley. It was ingenious.

Isaac and Sam were pitted against the two Army captains. Sam ventured to ask one of them, "How on earth did the mess manage to get a bowling alley?"

The captain watched his ball knock down six pins. "I'm not sure, young fellah. But the word is you have Hermann Göring to thank."

Isaac furrowed his brow. "What! The German fighter ace who was in charge of the Luftwaffe in the war?"

"The very same. Evidently, he had lots of officers' messes built for his pilots and, for some reason, insisted they all contain bowling alleys."

"Well, I'm grateful to the geezer," said Sam, picking up a ball. This is great. The trouble is, we can't just do this all winter… but there's not much else we can do."

Sam scored a strike.

The army major grunted in admiration. "Why don't you do some skiing? I'm sending a sergeant down to ferry some supplies to our biathlon ski team in Bavaria. You could go with him if you want."

Isaac blinked. "Really? I've never had a go at skiing. Neither of us have. And we don't have skis."

"We can fix you up with skis easily enough, and you wouldn't need to worry about food. The team have got a cook down there."

"Wow. That would be wonderful." Isaac paused. "Can I ask why you suggested it?"

The Major reached for his beer and took a sip. "Do either of you have a driving license?"

"I do," said Isaac.

"Then you can share the driving. In truth, I'd be grateful. I'm sending a Sergeant down with a Land Rover fitted with a spotlight. They need it down there to set up temporary helicopter landing pads. I'm looking for someone to go with him. Otherwise, my chap will be on his own, and it's a long drive. "

Sam broke in. "Where is this place we'd be going too?"

"It's called Oberstdorf, and it's right in the heart of the Bavarian mountains – three miles from the Austrian border."

Isaac looked at Sam, and raised an eyebrow.

Sam nodded.

"Fantastic," said Isaac. "We'll check it out with Dad and get back to you tomorrow. Where can we reach you?"

Details were exchanged.

At the end of the game, the boys took their leave. Isaac had little doubt that their parents would agree to them going skiing. They would be grateful to have both boys out from under their feet.

That night, Isaac again stayed awake long into the night. There were two reasons for this. The first was the exciting prospect of going skiing. The second reason was altogether more somber. He was thinking about the concentration camp at Belsen. Frightful images of the place had tormented him occasionally throughout the day. He tried to think why. And then he remembered. Sam suggesting it was too hard to visit the *gasthaus* for a beer had sparked the memories. Isaac screwed his eyes shut and tried to expunge the terrible memories he had of the place. How he wished he was like Sam – not so sensitive.

He wondered briefly if he was becoming a depressive. That was certainly not a path he wanted to go down. But given all that was going on in the world, it was hard not to be pessimistic. Given the likelihood of nuclear Armageddon, he'd been tempted to surrender to the meaninglessness of Nihilism when at Cambridge. But the outworking of Nihilism, when overlaid with the self-glorifying philosophy of Friedrich Nietzsche, had been Nazism. And that had led to the most appalling atrocities.

Isaac wondered, idly, how the country he was living in and admired so much became capable of such evil. Somehow, the most civilized nation in the world; the nation of Bach, Beethoven, and Brahms; the land that had nurtured the Christian Reformation – had walked away from its Christian heritage and produced the extermination camps of Belsen, Auschwitz, and Treblinka. It was something that bewildered him. The nearest he'd come to an answer was found in a book written by the Austrian psychologist,

Viktor Frankl. The man had survived the horrors of four Nazi concentration camps and written words that Isaac found impossible to forget:

I am absolutely convinced that the gas chambers of Auschwitz, Treblinka, and Majdanek were ultimately prepared not in some ministry or other in Berlin. but rather at the desks and lecture halls of nihilistic scientists and philosophers.

Could it be true? Could educational institutions be so powerful? Would the ambitions of abusive military regimes fail to become a reality, unless a nation's opinion leaders first establish a philosophic climate that removed the sacredness of humankind? The very thought that it might be true had stopped him surrendering to Nihilism at Cambridge. The trouble was, he had nothing to put in its place – nothing really to live for. Life was bewildering.

Eventually, he surrendered to sleep.

It took two days to drive south through Germany to Bavaria, and it was a brutally cold experience. The boys took turns sitting in the back of the Land Rover, protected from the elements only by a piece of canvas. Their journey was hampered by a snowstorm. This necessitated the use of the giant spotlight occasionally to pierce the snow and dark in order to read the road signs. The snow slowed them up so much, that they were obliged to beg accommodation for the night at a German army camp. The upside of this was that they arrived in the beautiful Bavarian mountain town of Oberstdorf late morning the next day. They had needed to fit snow chains onto the wheels of the Land Rover to make the last few miles, as the roads were covered with snow.

The chalet where the ski team were billeted was straight out of a Swiss picture book. It was built of wood and had a decorated balcony beneath a steeply pitched roof. Inside, however, the army had turned it into a utilitarian barracks. The place smelled of men.

Sam and Isaac were given disassembled army stretchers and were told to set them up anywhere there was space. It was somewhat disconcerting for Sam to have a collection of biathlon rifles stacked against the wall near the end of his sleeping bag.

The food, however, was excellent. The cook who prepared it was a wiry man from Glasgow. Perhaps because of his size, he boasted to Sam of his prowess as a middleweight boxer. What was not in dispute was the fact that he was the most foul-mouthed man Sam had ever heard.

One of the officers introduced himself as Geoff. He took the boys outside and gave them an hour's instruction on how to ski. Sam and Isaac had downhill skis, in contrast to the army ski team, who had cross-country *langlauf* skis that were not attached at the heel.

Sam rubbed his bottom ruefully and wondered if he would ever master his skis. He was particularly embarrassed when he fell in an undignified heap near the entrance to the chalet just as a string of soldiers was setting off on their *langlauf* skis.

He looked over to Isaac. From what he could judge, he was faring no better. However, after an hour, both boys had learned the basics. Geoff sent them off to practice, telling them to keep out of the way, and to turn up to the meals on time if they wanted to eat.

The alpine air was crisp and clean, and the views of the mountains were spectacular. Emboldened by the sunshine, the boys set out in the afternoon and proceeded to provide a comedy of errors for those who cared to watch them on the ski slopes. First, they fell off the T bar of the cable lift that dragged skiers up the slopes. Then they found themselves standing on top of a ski run that they failed to notice had been labeled 'black.' They soon found that 'black' meant 'very difficult,' a reality impressed on them by having to come down most of the way on their backsides.

By dinner, Sam was exhausted, aching, and ravenous. He collected his meal and sat with the soldiers at a trestle table.

"Who are these incompetent brats who can't ski?" said an imperious voice.

Sam was shocked to realize that the man asking the question in a plummy English accent was referring to Isaac and himself. He sat there red-faced. Isaac, however, was not so mute. His brother replied evenly. "The two brats are called Isaac and Sam, and though we can't ski, we can recognize good manners."

His comment caused a few chuckles from the men.

Sam had sat himself down next to Geoff. He leaned across and said, "Who is that joker?"

Geoff grunted. "That's Tony Chester-Smith. Don't let him get to you. He's got a silver spoon up his arse. Damn fine skier though. He's the English biathlon champion."

"Which regiment is he from?"

"The 11th Hussars. He's a bit of a prig. His fellow officers in the mess flooded his chest of drawers with a fire hose once, to try and get him to pull his head in." The man smiled ruefully. "I'm not sure it worked. Try and keep out of his way."

Sam nodded. Someone with that accent certainly would be drawn to the 11th Hussars. They were nicknamed the "Cherry Pickers" because of the red trousers they wore on dress occasions. It was a distinguished regiment, famous for the heroic, if misguided, 'charge of the Light Brigade' in the Crimean war. He glanced across at Tony Chester-Smith and was unlucky enough to catch his eye. The man lifted his nose in a sneer.

As the days passed the boys' skiing improved. They also discovered chair lifts that had actual seats, which spared their dignity somewhat. In what seemed a blink of an eye, New Year's Eve was upon them.

It didn't take long for Sam to realize that the Bavarians took New Year's Eve very seriously. Unusually, the boys had decided not to celebrate New Year's Eve together. The reason was purely pragmatic. Sam had vowed never to get into a cold Land Rover again if he could avoid it. He'd chosen to walk down the hill with most of the soldiers who were heading toward the local *gasthaus* for some serious drinking.

Isaac viewed the long walk back up to their chalet with some trepidation and had elected to go in the Land Rover with another group of soldiers to check out the festivities in the nearby town of Alstädten.

Sam entered into the revelry at the local *gasthaus* with enthusiasm. However, it was an enthusiasm tempered with caution. He was sixteen, and although he was already a veteran beer drinker, he knew that he was young and needed to be careful.

The cook from their chalet was, however, not so prudent. As he drank, the man became progressively more abusive. The problem was, Tony Chester-Smith who was nominally in charge of the party, was nearly as drunk and, in his merriment, not inclined to do much about it. In the end, the huge blond German barman hauled the cook to his feet, marched him to the door, and kicked him out into the snow. Some in the bar cheered, and the festivities continued apace.

Sam sat himself down at the table coughing and spluttering. Three German youths had cornered him in the bar and showered him with snuff. They thought it was huge fun. Sam was less sure. He reached for his beer and took a restorative swig. As he did, he saw the young *fräulein* from their chalet enter the bar. Her eyes were darting everywhere, and she was in obvious distress. On seeing Tony Chester-Smith, she rushed over to him and said in broken English. "Your friend, the cook. He is getting your gun to kill."

Chester-Smith hiccupped and sat himself up in his seat. "What? The cook?"

"Yes."

Chester-Smith waved a hand. "Nah. He wouldn't do that."

The woman grabbed the officer's arm and shook it. "Yes. Come. Stop him. Come. Come."

Chester-Smith shook himself free. "Who is he going to kill?"

"The barman here. He told me. Please. Come. Come quickly."

The officer closed his eyes and groaned. When he opened them, he looked blearily across the table. Then, pointing to Sam, he said. "You sort it out," and reached for his stein of beer.

The young girl came around the table and pulled Sam to his feet. Sam couldn't quite believe what was happening. However, he was given no time to think. The young woman tugged and harried him up through the snow to the chalet. Once she got there, she fled to the owner's accommodation and left him alone.

It was not difficult locating the whereabouts of the cook. He was swearing volubly whilst standing at a desk in their dormitory trying to prize open one of its drawers. "Bloody ammunition…"

With some alarm, Sam saw a biathlon rifle lying across the top of the desk.

Taking a deep breath, Sam said, "Hi mate. Can I help you?"

He was told in no uncertain language, where to go.

Sam decided to change tack. "Hey, it's New Year's Eve. It's not a time for getting into trouble. You've had a skinful, so let's get you to bed, eh?"

The cook threw the screwdriver he was holding across the room and swore savagely. He staggered toward Sam. "D'want a fight?"

Sam held up his hands. "No mate. I'm a friend. I just want to help you get into bed so you are safe."

His words seemed to have a mollifying effect, and the cook lurched over to a camp stretcher and fell onto it.

Sam watched him as he might have watched a deadly cobra.

In a few minutes, he was relieved to hear the sound of snoring.

Sam blew air out from his cheeks in relief. He returned the biathlon rifle to its right place and hid the screwdriver under his sleeping bag. He then let himself out of the chalet and trudged through the snow back down the hill to the *gasthaus*.

He was just in time to see the New Year in. Those in the *gasthaus* who were not too drunk were standing outside looking up to where some lights had lit up a ski run on the mountainside. On the stroke of midnight, scores of skiers lit flaming torches and skied down the slope. The effect was spectacular.

Sam shook his head, unsure of what was real and what was not.

Isaac was furious. He spoke through clenched teeth, spitting out the consonants. "Captain Chester-Smith, how dare you send my brother, a sixteen-year old boy, up to the chalet to disarm a drunk man intent on murder – and excuse yourself because you were drunk."

"You can't speak to me like that, you little brat. You weren't even there."

Isaac breathed in deeply. "My brother was certainly there, and he is not someone who exaggerates or lies." He pointed to the captain. "It was you who was conspicuously not there. I checked with others, and they told me you were clearly warned of what was going on. Your response was criminally negligent and irresponsible."

"Boy, you have no idea what goes on in a real man's world. People drink and do stupid things. Those who are wise forget about it in the morning."

"So there is to be no consequence; no apology; nothing?"

"The cook will be put on a charge."

"What for?"

"Drunkenness."

Isaac rolled his eye and scoffed. "Then you might as well arrest the whole British army." He jabbed a finger at the captain. "What actually happened, was the attempted murder of a German national... and an incompetent response from a commanding officer who should have taken responsibility and diffused the situation." He turned away in disgust. "You are simply slapping the cook with a piece of wet lettuce in the hope the real story doesn't get out, and your irresponsibility doesn't get shown up."

It was the evening of New Year's Day, and it had taken all day for Isaac to waylay Captain Chester-Smith and get him on his own. Isaac had finally asked to speak to him in the privacy of the chalet's office. Their conversation was rapidly degenerating into a shouting match.

The Captain roared, "Get out of here you sniveling, long-haired lout."

Isaac drove his finger into the top of the desk. "This is not finished." Then he turned and walked out of the room.

A consequence of Isaac's fracas with Chester-Smith became apparent the very next day. The Land Rover with the spotlight had returned to the chalet to take the boys back to North Germany. As this was the boy's final day on the ski slopes, Geoff, the officer who had first taken them under his wing, suggested that they make use of the Land Rover's spotlight and do some undemanding night skiing after the evening meal.

Captain Chester-Smith surprised everyone when he suggested to Geoff that he take them instead, as he was the better skier, and that night skiing could be tricky. Geoff acquiesced easily enough.

So it was that the Land Rover left the road and began to growl its way up a gentle snowy slope, gripping the snow with the snow chains on its wheels. Once at the top, the Sergeant turned the vehicle round, so that its headlights were shining down the slope. He kept the engine running and then switched on the spotlight.

The effect was magical. It lit up the entire slope.

Sam and Chester-Smith donned their skis and were soon zigzagging down the slope. Isaac, however, elected to stay in the Land Rover with the Sergeant. He had voiced the excuse of being exhausted after a full day's skiing. Whilst that was true enough, Isaac was nursing a lingering sense of unease at Chester-Smith being with them, and he wondered what his motivation was. He didn't believe for one moment that he had Sam or Isaac's well-being at heart.

Sam was skiing well for a novice, but he wasn't anywhere nearly as accomplished as Chester-Smith. The officer had his *langlauf* skis on which he used to good effect to get back to the top and begin his second run. Sam had to take his skis off and trudge back to the top.

When Sam began his second run, Chester-Smith was about to begin his third. As Chester Smith was making extravagant use of the visible ski run, Sam was content to zigzag his way down by the tree line.

Isaac watched with alarm as Chester-Smith speared diagonally across the snow, then hunched down as he barged into Sam causing him to smash to the ground with legs and arms flailing. Chester-Smith came to a stop, waved an apparent apology, and set off again.

Sam, to his credit, got back to his feet, and though obviously winded, began to continue his way down hill.

Chester-Smith, meanwhile, had used his *langlauf* skis to step further up the hill.

With horror, Isaac saw him again spear across the snow and begin to hunch down in preparation for smashing into Sam again.

Isaac did the only thing possible. He reached across and switched off the massive spotlight.

Everything went dark.

A few seconds later, Isaac switched the light back on. He was greeted with the sight of Chester-Smith smashed sideways against a tree. Even from where he was watching, Isaac could see that his right knee was bent at a very unnatural angle.

As he watched, he saw Sam get tentatively back onto his feet. He'd fallen down, perhaps even before Chester-Smith reached him. Whatever had happened, Chester-Smith had been launched into the air into the trees and needed urgent medical help.

England, two years later, 1969

Chapter 11

Tony Chester-Smith… Captain (retired) leaned on his walking stick and looked at the grave. He was in the cemetery of St. Mary the Virgin in the village of Hartfield, forty miles southwest of London. It was the grave of his father, John. He tried to visit the grave every year on his father's birthday. It hadn't always been possible when he was deployed with the army, but since being invalided out of the service two years ago, it was relatively straightforward.

Tony grimaced at the thought of 'relatively.' Nothing was straightforward after his knee had been shattered in Bavaria. His fist tightened around the medal he held in his hand. The medal was the one that he'd won as Britain's biathlon champion. But it was the medal he wasn't holding that truly irked him. He should have been holding an Olympic medal. He closed his eyes. Glory could have been his. As it was, all he could show his father when he visited his grave each year was the medal he'd won as Britain's biathlon champion. It normally sat on the mantelpiece on a tiny display stand that he'd had made. The medal was only ever removed for his annual pilgrimage to his father's grave.

Everything had changed since that accident. Everything. He no longer had the world at his feet. No longer could he seek to expunge the shame of his father ruining the family and putting them into poverty because of his gambling addiction. He looked at the small gravestone with anguish. Until recently, there wasn't even a grave-stone. Tony had only just had one made for him. His father had been buried in a pauper's grave. He'd died, rather conveniently, just after their estate in East Sussex had to be sold. His mother had divorced him ten years earlier, leaving Tony, as the only child, to live with the burden of the shame.

The winter air was causing his leg to ache. He cursed it under his breath and returned the medal to his overcoat pocket. Then he turned and made his way back to his car. There was no car park, and he hadn't been able to park the wretched thing on Church Lane because it was so narrow and overgrown by hedgerows. He'd had to park it at the end of the road where it turned into a dirt track. It was a long walk.

Tony Chester-Smith stared out the window of his ground floor flat at London's streets. A passing shower had doused the city with rain causing the car lights to be reflected in the road. It could have been a cheerful sight, and it nearly was. He was listening to the *Faust Over-ture* by Richard Wagner. The record was quite old, but it was a good recording. He loved Wagner and had never understood the quote attributed to Mark Twain that "Wagner's music is better than it sounds." Wagner's music had complex textures and rich harmonies. Above all, it had drama and savagery. And it was grand. Tony liked grand.

His ground floor flat in Soho was modest but obscenely expen-sive – precisely because it was on the ground floor. His gammy leg did not cope well with stairs, so he'd had little choice. It also required him to use taxis to take him the short distance to the infinitely more salubrious suburb of Mayfair nearby, where he worked. He could have taken the underground to Hyde Park

Corner, but he abhorred trains and the people he was forced to share them with. But taxis were expensive.

There were other things he took pleasure in, in Soho. They were expensive too.

Tony sighed.

He now worked for MI5, where he held a mid-level position. The Security Service was located in Leconfield House, a drab seven-storied building that manifestly failed to do justice to its location – being near the Hilton on Park Lane, close to Hyde Park, just behind Buckingham Palace. The building's first two stories were made of Portland stone, and then the builders seemed to have run out of optimism and settled for red brick.

If the outside of the building was nondescript, the inside was even worse. Everything was dreadfully run down. It was not a place that lifted the soul. Nor was it, he felt, a work place that did him justice.

However, MI5 was a good fit for him. Half of the Security Service was comprised of military personnel, and the rest were civilians. The man in charge was a Vice Admiral who understood ex-military men, like himself. The Security Service was engaged in 'all source' intelligence analysis. In essence, this meant it was responsible for counter-espionage and for formulating military policy in its dealings with the civil population.

Most of the work was mind-numbingly dull, of course. Nonetheless, it had a Machiavellian edge to it. It also had a whiff of power – the power of a cobra to strike from where it lay unseen.

Tony stared moodily at the record player. What he really hungered for was significance – any significance. He, Tony Chester-Smith, wanted to pull the levers of history and strike back at those who had tried to keep him down – and show them. He wanted to prove himself to his father, even though he was dead, and show him that the Chester-Smiths could be great again.

He glanced at his watch and looked out of the window. It didn't look as if it was going to rain again anytime soon. He had time to walk the short distance to the corner pub, "The Coach and Horses." The pub had large windows separated by a row of narrow pillars. It looked dignified and classy, and it suited him. The place had become a popular haunt for the literati who seemed eager to air their opinions about anything, particularly politics.

When he arrived, he found that his friend, Alec Townsend, was already ensconced in a corner booth. Tony didn't know Alec well, just that he was in the book trade. The two of them had met a number of times at the pub. Alec was pleasant, undemanding, and solicitous about Tony's wellbeing. More importantly, Tony could usually beat him at cribbage.

Sophie half skipped and half walked down the laneway that ran past the stables to Miss Chessington's cottage. She wanted to run, but now she was 18, she didn't think it was dignified. In fact, she didn't just want to run; she wanted to dance.

She could see Jimmy Stanground outside the stables, washing and brushing down Sir Robert Chessington's chestnut hunter, Sultan. The horse was clopping on the cobbles and tossing its head, asserting its dominance. Stan was whistling between his teeth – his mouth almost closed to keep the dust from his mouth. He smiled as Sophie approached. "You've got a frolic in your step today, girl."

She grinned and waved a piece of paper in the air. "I've been accepted to Cambridge, Jimmy." She laughed. "I can't believe it."

Jimmy, brush in hand, leaned on Sultan's flank. "Well done, girl. You've always been a bright one."

At that moment, Sir Robert came striding out of the stables. He was dressed in a hacking jacket, cream jodhpurs, and highly polished riding boots. As usual, the gray highlights in his hair made him look very distinguished. Sophie stopped skipping and began walking as demurely as she could. It would be fair to say that Sophie's relationship with Sir Robert – barely existent, as it was – had been strained ever since his son, Anthony, had tried to rape her. Sir Robert had managed to persuade Sophie's father not to go to the police, saying that there was no proof that Sophie wasn't partly to blame for the incident. Her father had been furious, but he wanted to keep his job. The stalemate agreed on was that Anthony was never to show his face at the farm again.

Sir Robert looked at her without expression. "Did I hear you've been accepted to Cambridge?"

Sophie was tempted to lower her head, as she had always done when in Sir Robert's company. But this was her day. She'd been accepted to Cambridge. Sophie looked Sir Robert straight in the eye. "Yes, Sir Robert. I have."

He nodded. "What will you be reading?"

"English and History."

Sir Robert looked at Sophie for some time. For a moment, she thought she saw a hint of grief in his eyes. "I'm sending Anthony to Australia to work as a jackaroo at one of their outback homesteads."

Sophie struggled to find the right words in response. Eventually she said, "I hope he finds himself there and manages to sort himself out."

"So do I." Sir Robert held out his hand. "I wish you well, Sophie." After a brief handshake, he turned on his heel and made for his Land Rover.

She continued on her way, a good deal more thoughtfully, to Miss Chessington's cottage, and knocked on her door. When she shared her news with her mentor, Miss Chessington reached forward and gave her a hug.

Sophie was amazed. This truly was a day of firsts. It was the first hug she'd had from her. "You've made me very happy," said Miss Chessington. She then held Sophie at arm's length. "I can now watch you from a distance, and live my life vicariously through my favorite student."

Sophie laughed. "I thought Roslyn was your favorite student."

"Don't be pedantic. I have two or three favorite students." She sniffed. It might have been to hold back a tear. "I hope that you will stay in contact with Roslyn. You are two of a kind."

"Oh I will," Sophie enthused.

Before long, both were sitting at the kitchen table, drinking tea. Miss Chessington reached for a sugar lump. "I'm delighted for you, Sophie. But I have to warn you; it won't be easy forging a way through a man's world – particularly at Cambridge. Have you thought what it is you really want from life?"

Sophie sighed. "I've just turned 18, and I'm still trying to work out what it means to be a woman – and even more baffling; what it means to be human."

"I can't help you there. But Roslyn can." She paused. "I would be disappointed if you didn't realize your potential as a woman."

"Should I be a feminist?"

Miss Chessington patted her hand. "You already are one, dear."

"Oh." Sophie was silent for some time. "I should hate to undermine the craft of running a home and raising children. I'm not seeking a gray homogeneous form of equality. There are differences that make men and women suited to different roles. But I believe in equal opportunity and equal pay for the same work. It's only just, if we work the same hours and have the same level of competence."

Miss Chessington cocked her head sideways. She always did that when she was about to say something to provoke Sophie. "Does that mean equal financial security? What about child-rearing? Should financial compensation be paid to women rearing children? Or will the desire for a career force them not to put a priority on having offspring? She raised a finger. "What does equality look like for women financially, if you insist on the same pay for the same hours, and the same experience? Can a woman who takes time off to have a family ever hope for equality of pay?"

"As I said, I wouldn't like to deny the craft of home-making – or demean its importance."

"But with so many labor-saving devices, home-making is not the same craft as in the past."

Sophie was well used to these intellectual sparring matches. She fired back: "I think we should close the gap. The industrial revolution has meant that fewer children now work alongside their parents on farms and in cottage industries. Men have become strangers to their children, and wives strangers to their husbands. I think we should do what we can to bring them closer together."

"And…?"

"And the different sexes should be allowed into each other's world more. Did you know that it is the male emu, and the male seahorse, that look after the eggs?'

Miss Chessington leaned back in her chair. "Bravo, Sophie." She turned behind her and picked up a book from the Welsh dresser. "I have a book for you to read. It's *The Feminine Mystique*, by Betty Friedan. It came out a few years ago. She's a leading figure in the feminist movement in America."

Sophie took hold of the book and nodded her thanks. She started to leaf through its pages. "I don't think I shall marry."

"I think it's a bit early to say that, dear. Humankind's eternal quest is for significance. For women, it is to be loved. For men, it is to be honored. Both of these needs meet in the sex drive. And, believe me, that can be a very heady and intoxicating thing." She reached forward and took hold of Sophie's hand. "So please guard your heart well."

"I am very sorry, Tony, but you were not successful in winning prese-lection for East Sussex. But we are terribly grateful to you for throwing your hat into the ring. You doing so shows that the Conser-vative party has terrific depth."

Tony Chester-Smith gripped the telephone tightly and couldn't believe the words he was hearing. He closed his eyes and pinched the bridge of his nose. The urge to scream and hurl abuse was almost overwhelming. "I think you've made a bad mistake, one that you'll come to regret."

"Oh, I don't think we can regret the nominated candidate. He's very good."

"Who is he?"

When Tony heard the name, he was none the wiser. "Who is he?"

"He owns a string of grocery shops."

Tony put a hand out to steady himself against the wall. He'd lost out to a wretched grocer. A grocer! Whichever way he looked at it, it was a brutal slap in the face. The Chester-Smiths were once one of the most distinguished families in Sussex. He had little doubt that the dreadful legacy of his father's bankruptcy was continuing to spoil his life and sabotage his chances. How he hated his father… and yet he desperately wanted to show his father that, unlike him, he could succeed. Without waiting for the man from the Conservative party to stop talking, Tony smashed the phone down onto its cradle.

"Damn, damn, damn, and blast!" he expostulated. "A grocer! I don't believe it."

He continued to lean against the wall, glowering and visualizing the many dark things he would like to do to grocers and to the wretched Conservative party. The British political scene didn't deserve him. It was riddled with elitism and injustice. The irony of what he was thinking barely registered, so great was his seething hatred. Tony glanced at the medal on the mantelpiece. It was the only greatness he'd achieve, and he should have achieved so much more. He would have, if the loathsome Hastings boys hadn't conspired to wreck his life. He drove a fist into his hand and swore to himself that he would one day have his revenge. He wanted revenge on the Hastings boys, and revenge on the British political system. "Damn them all!"

Tony looked in the mirror above the mantelpiece. He was not greatly impressed by what he saw. The superb fitness he'd achieved before his knee had been shattered was a distant memory. His body was soft, and he was starting to run to fat. Tony's hairstyle had also changed. His blond hair, once cut to regulation army length, now fell over his collar. He never allowed it to get longer, however, and regularly visited his barber.

He limped over to one of his two armchairs and sank into it. The *Siegfried Idyll* by Wagner was still on his record player, but he had no heart to listen to it again… and everything on TV was crass.

When he could bear the weariness of his resentment no longer, he hauled himself to his feet and shrugged himself into his camel-hair coat. In deep dudgeon, he made his way to "The Coach and Horses".

Alec Townsend was just finishing a half pint of beer when he arrived. He glanced at Tony. "You look as if you could do with both a beer and a whiskey. Sit down, and I'll get them."

Tony nodded his thanks and slumped into a seat, not bothering to take off his coat. He still had it on when the drinks arrived. Alec raised an eyebrow. "What's eating at you?"

Tony leaned his head back and sighed. "Everything."

"Everything?"

"I hate the political system of this country. I hate being passed over by the privileged class. And I hate not having enough money."

Alec looked round the pub at the other patrons sitting at the tables. "This place is full of intellectuals, some of whom are distinctly left wing. So you can probably get away with saying that here. But you might have to be careful saying it elsewhere. Didn't you say you worked for the government?"

"Yes, I do. But I rarely do anything significant." Tony passed a hand wearily over his forehead. "I'd love to do something to put the privileged prigs in government in their place…"

Alec finished Tony's sentence. "…and make things fairer and more equitable for ordinary people?"

Tony nodded, although he hadn't quite been thinking that.

Alec looked into his beer mug and said, very deliberately, "Would you consider working subversively for a foreign government whose ideals are more closely aligned with your own?"

Tony frowned. "Do you mean, be a spy, or something like that?"

"Someone who could make a difference to history; someone who really would 'stick it up' the ruling class."

"Would I be paid?"

Alec kept his voice carefully neutral. "I hear Kim Philby is being paid eight times the national average wage in Russia."

"The British traitor?"

"Philby wouldn't call himself a traitor. He would say he is a Communist who, because he was born into the ruling class, was recruited, quite fortuitously, by an arrogant and lax British Security Service."

Tony grunted. "Serve the bastards right." He paused, and then said, "So I'd be spying for Russia?"

"I'm not saying anything concrete." Alec smiled. "It's just that in this place, you get to know people who know people, who know people… if you get my drift."

In that moment, a new world of possibilities began to open up to Tony. The idea that he could do things in secret, things that his boss and those in power knew nothing about, gave him a sense of superiority that was delicious. Perhaps he could, after all, become someone significant in history.

Alec looked him straight in the eye. "How seriously do you want to pursue this?"

Tony met his gaze. "Very seriously."

"Then I shall talk to someone."

Six months later

Chapter 12

Tony's Russian handler sat down on the park bench beside him. Today, the man had a Pekinese dog on a leash. He usually had some prop with him that deflected people's attention from his real identity. On one occasion, he'd had an elderly woman on his arm. Whatever he did, was never repeated. His disguises were good. Once, he'd even built up the height of one shoe so that it caused him to limp.

Without preamble he said, "We want you to go for the Cambridge job."

"What Cambridge job?"

"You will find out this week."

Tony knew better than to ask how a Russian operative could possibly know what was about to happen inside Leconfield House and MI5. The idea of being an MI5 operative in Cambridge did not appeal to him at all. If you weren't an academic, Cambridge had little to offer. Certainly, it was a long way from the fleshpots of Soho. Tony despised the academic elite. He wrinkled his nose. "What will my role be?"

"Your MI5 role will be to keep an eye on foreign operatives seeking to recruit the more radical students in the university to spy for them." The man smiled. "Your actual job, of course will be to recruit them."

"So my official role will be to prevent another debacle such as the Cambridge five."

"Yes, the spies who worked for us – Burgess, Maclean, Cairncross, Blunt, and Philby."

"My cover will have to be good."

"We will give you some sheep to lead to the slaughter – people we don't really want. Don't worry. You will be seen to be fruitful in your role." He smiled. "You might even get a promotion."

Tony loved the excitement and duplicity of the role. He would be changing history. So this was what power felt like. He had the power to change a person's life – or even end it, if he so ordered. It was a heady feeling, and he liked it. Only one thing bothered him, and that was the fear of being discovered to be a double agent. If the truth were known, Tony had little sympathy for Marxist ideology – unless it meant returning more power to himself. He actually liked the idea of being part of an elite. Tony had little doubt that the foibles of humankind would always result in an elite of some sort existing, whether it was capitalist or Marxist. In fact, Tony had once toyed with the idea of double-crossing his Russian handlers, and earning kudos for himself in the process. That idea had quickly been dispelled when his Russian handler had leaned forward and deliberately allowed his coat to gape. Tony found himself looking at a shoulder-holstered pistol. His handler then passed across a newspaper folded to the page telling the story of a man who had been murdered. "You will keep breathing for precisely as long as I decide. One hint of a double-cross, and you will be liquidated. Is that clear?"

Tony had nodded dumbly; appalled at the high stakes game he was now playing. But the game was thrilling.

His handler lifted the Pekinese from his lap and stood up to leave. Then he said in a low voice, "And there is another reason you should enjoy Cambridge."

"What's that?"

"One of the brothers you hate, Isaac Hastings, is doing his final year at Cambridge."

Tony's head jerked up, and a surge of bitterness rose up within him. He could taste its bile. "Hastings?"

"Yes."

"How do you know this?"

"Because we're grooming him to become an agent..." His handler smiled. "Unfortunately for him, he will be an agent whom you will uncover and report to MI5."

This time, it was Tony's turn to smile. He rubbed his hands together. Tony would take a good deal of time working out how he would destroy Isaac Hastings. He resolved there and then that Hastings wouldn't simply be reported to MI5, Isaac Hastings would experience exquisite suffering before that particular *coup de grâce*.

Chapter 13

I n the last nine months, the man had been slowly self-destructing. She'd watched it from a safe distance, wary as she was of men. She was watching him covertly now.

Sophie was sitting at a table in 'The Baron of Beef.' It was a popular pub with Cambridge students, as it was located between St. John's College and Jesus College. She didn't often go into pubs, but one of the two girlfriends she was with was celebrating her birthday.

The three of them had cycled from Girton College into town. Girton was the only college for woman undergraduates. It was situated a pious two miles northeast of Central Cambridge – stuck out on a limb in case its emancipatory ideas were contagious.

Sophie had greatly enjoyed her time at Girton. It was a handsome redbrick Victorian affair built on two levels, with dormer windows above. Girton may not have had the history of the more illustrious colleges in the center of town, but it still looked good. It helped that it was situated in fifty acres of mature woods, parkland, and gardens.

The College was organized around a series of spacious courtyards, and the undisputed jewel of the college was opposite the main entrance. It was the dining hall. The walls were held up by flying buttresses, and its lofty interior featured wooden beams holding up a magnificent arched roof.

Nothing much was holding up the young man on the other side of the pub who was slowly getting drunk. He was wearing round glasses and a leather mariner's hat – reminiscent of that which a revolutionary might wear. All that was missing was the red star. He'd once interrupted everyone's conversations by standing up and shouting, *"Viva la revolución,"* before collapsing back into his seat.

Sophie knew the young man slightly. She'd even admired him once. He was doing the same course as her, reading English and history, but he was two years ahead. However, in the last six months, he'd barely attended a lecture. She'd first seen him in a tutorial that had been shared by different year groups. He'd impressed her with his piercing questions and his obvious passion for social justice. She'd only seen him in a few lectures since. Sophie shook her head sadly. Seeing him now, he was a wreck. The ideological rabbit hole he'd crawled down was slowly destroying him. Isaac Hastings had made no secret of his growing Marxist convictions.

He was currently in the company of a young woman. She had jet-black hair, but her skin was very white, almost translucent. There was no denying the fact that she was striking to look at. The thing that roused Sophie's attention was that the woman had twice bought Isaac a drink. Even by today's egalitarian standards, that was not normal behavior.

Sophie wasn't surprised when the woman helped Isaac to his feet and shepherded him out of the pub onto Bridge Street. He'd certainly had enough for the evening.

She sighed. She too had had enough. One Babycham and several glasses of water were enough for her. She could not bring herself to indulge in any more extravagance. Miss Chessington may have trained her to be an educated lady, but she was still a herdsman's daughter at heart.

Sophie rose to her feet. "I'm off, girls. I've got to finish an assignment."

The girls protested. "Oh Soph, you're always weeks ahead in your assignments. Stay and let your hair down for once."

Sophie smiled at the reference to hair. She very often had her hair down. It was a habit she'd cultivated over the time Miss Chessington had tutored her. Miss Chessington always had her hair down. "No. I'm off. Promise that you'll not enjoy yourselves too much without me." With a wave, she made for the door.

Sophie had parked her bike in the alleyway beside the pub. It had been built under the neighboring shop. She'd never bothered to find out where it led to. Suddenly, she heard yelps of pain and muffled thumps. The noise came from just ahead of her. She reached into her shoulder bag for her flashlight, switched it on, and aimed it down the alleyway.

The light picked out two men who were punching and kicking someone lying on the ground.

"Hey!" she shouted instinctively. "Get off him."

One of the men glanced up in surprise and started to run away. His companion was soon hot on his heels.

Sophie ran up to the body lying on the cobblestones. She recognized him immediately. It was Isaac Hastings. She glanced around. There was no sign of the woman who had accompanied him out of the pub.

Isaac's face was badly bloodied, and at some stage, he'd vomited down his front. He lay groaning on the floor.

Sophie squatted down and rolled him into the recovery position. She then got to her feet and tried to think what she should do next. "Call the police," she said, half to herself.

She was staggered to hear a weak voice coming from Isaac. "No. No police. Please." Then his head collapsed back down. He looked as if he had lost consciousness.

What should she do? Where could she go for help?

Then she had an idea. She checked Isaac was still safely in the recovery position, and then ran back onto Bridge Street to the nearby phone box. Sophie didn't need the directory to dial the number. She rang the Rector of her local church.

The Rector answered straight away. Sophie suspected he'd been working at his desk. She explained the situation she found herself in.

With a masterful economy of words, the Rector said. "Give me your number in the phone box and stay there. I'll get back to you."

Three minutes later, the phone in the call box rang. Sophie snatched up the handset and pressed it to her ear. "Yes, I'm here."

"Ah, Sophie. Good. Listen carefully. Two parishioners of Church, Judy and Adrian, will pick you and the young man up and take you to their home. Do you know them?"

Sophie smiled involuntarily. "Yes. They're great."

"Good. We'll assess the situation once we have your man at their house." The Rector paused. "Are you sure you are okay?"

"Yes, I'm fine."

Sophie put the phone back on its cradle, amazed at how quickly the Rector had been able to mobilize help. The thought came to her that it was probably not the first time he had needed to deal with emergency situations.

Brown hair, beautiful hair, hair with lighter honey highlights hung down to him. A strand of it brushed against his face. He attempted to move, but every part of his body felt broken. Isaac blinked and tried to focus on the room he was in. It was a strange room, a room he'd never seen before. Bandages pulled on his skin as he moved.

The hair, and the beautiful face in the middle of it, lifted up. "Try not to move too much. You've been badly bashed about."

But Isaac was not so easily dissuaded. "You're beautiful," he said.

"You're drunk. Which college are you at? We've got to get you back."

Isaac's throat was coarse and raw. He ignored it and waved a hand in protest. "No. Don't take me back."

"Which college," the voice said insistently.

"What's your name?"

"My name is Sophie." The woman had her hands on her hips and was looking at him scornfully. "You'll be driven back to Kings so that you won't bother these good people anymore."

Isaac moved his head and saw a young couple standing by the dresser. The woman came over to him and pulled the bedclothes back over him again. "The doctor has been and you've been patched up. He's also given you an injection of Clindamycin."

Isaac had no idea what Clindamycin was. "My throat is raw," he complained.

Sophie, the girl with the long hair, pointed at him. "That's because you've had my fingers down your throat encouraging you to throw up. There was no way I wanted you to be sick in the car or in the home of these lovely people."

Isaac blinked. "Where did you learn to do that?"

"I practiced on calves on a farm. Now lie down and rest until we bring the car back round to the front."

Isaac shook his head. Then wished he hadn't. It hurt abominably. "No, no. Don't do that. I can't go back to my digs. The porter will see me, and I'll be rusticated."

"You'll be what?"

"Sent down, expelled. I'm already on my final warning."

"What on earth did you do?"

Isaac grinned foolishly. "I honored the founder."

"You did what?"

"I honored the founder. I walked across the sacred turf in the Front Court of Kings to the fountain, and I honored our venerable founder."

Sophie knew the fountain. She'd often seen it in when attending evensong at King's College chapel. She frowned. "No undergraduate is allowed to walk on that lawn."

Isaac waved a hand dismissively. "Elitist nonsense." He slurred his words. "I pissed in front of King Henry VI on top of the fountain, and I even had enough in me to piss in front of the statues to religion and philosophy built in to the base of the pediment."

Sophie rolled her eyes and turned to the older couple in the room. "I'm so sorry about this. Is there any way he can stay here until the morning, when we can take him back to college?"

The woman looked at Isaac briefly. "I actually don't think he should be going anywhere for a day or so. He's in no fit state to look after himself. The trouble is, my husband and I both have to go off to work tomorrow." She bit her lip and looked at Sophie. "Would you be able to look after him if we made up the bed in the spare room."

The woman called Sophie looked shocked, and said slowly. "I suppose so."

Isaac smiled and closed his eyes.

Sophie held out a beaker of water. "You need lots of fluid. Drink up."

It had been 2am before Sophie got to bed the previous night, and she'd slept fitfully. There were a number of things about the previous evening that had puzzled her.

Now that she was up again and attending to Isaac Hasting's needs, she voiced one of them. "Where did the woman go who was with you last night?"

"What woman?"

"The woman who was getting you drunk – the one you left the pub with."

Isaac screwed up his face in concentration. "Ah. The lovely Helga. Only met her two weeks ago." He smiled. "Not as pretty as you. "Why do you ask?"

"Because I think there's a good chance she set you up."

Isaac frowned. "Why would she do that?"

"Well it wasn't a robbery. The men were beating you, not robbing you. Could it have been a jealous boyfriend?"

"Nah. Helga told me she wasn't married… and that she didn't have a boyfriend."

"Well, whoever she was, I advise you to keep well clear of her from now on."

Isaac reached for Sophie's hand. "Now that I've got you, I will."

Sophie snatched her hand away. "Oh please," she said rolling her eyes.

He looked at her with a frown. "Don't I recognize you. I've seen you before somewhere, haven't I?"

"Yes. We've shared some tutorials. I'm doing the same course as you, but two years behind. Not that I'd expect you to remember. You so rarely turn up these days."

"Ah yes. The quiet one. You always sit at the back."

"I'm amazed you noticed." She looked at him scornfully. "There is probably no more privileged education a person can dream of, than being educated at Cambridge. And you just piss it all against a wall and discard it without thought; without a care. I despise you."

"You despise me?"

"Yes. Yours are the actions of a spoiled brat. My father is a herdsman on a farm, and I can tell you, no one from a poor background would treat the privilege of being at Cambridge so carelessly."

"But I want to fight for the working class. I want to invert the class system and bring justice to the poor."

"I think the world has seen quite enough of your justice. "How many millions did Stalin murder and starve to death?"

Isaac lay back on his pillow and lifted an arm, parodying an orator giving a speech. "Let me quote the great man himself. 'If only one man dies of hunger, that is a tragedy. If millions die, that is only statistics.'" He tried a lopsided grin.

Sophie was furious. "You can smile at the murder of millions?" She snorted, "I wash my hands of you, Isaac Hastings. You are morally bankrupt."

He put out a hand to stop her leaving the room. "No. Don't go." He frowned as if trying to marshal his thoughts. "You are my moral compass… or your moral crutch."

Sophie shook herself free. "Well, I refuse to be your moral compass. If you have no heart to find truth, meaning, and morality yourself, then you can stew in your own vomit."

Unfortunately, Sophie was obliged to go back into the room Isaac was in at lunchtime. She brought a mug of soup for him.

Isaac's hands trembled slightly as he took the mug. "Thank you," he said meekly.

She turned to leave.

"Please don't go," he said.

Sophie paused, and much against her better judgment, sat down on the end of the bed.

He smiled. "It seems as if I'm always asking you not to go."

Sophie said nothing.

Isaac held the mug in two hands. "I've actually been doing a bit of thinking this morning – mainly because of you."

"Thinking of another way you can debauch and waste your life, I suppose."

He lifted a finger and said. "Well, that's the question, isn't it? You cannot waste a life, if a life has no meaning or purpose. If we are the result of a monstrously cruel act of chance, then nothing is wasted. Everything is absurd." He paused. "Will you marry me?"

Sophie shook her head. "I don't give my heart to someone who has borrowed their identity from Trotsky. I need someone who has it together enough to know who they are."

"Oh, Sophie, you cause my heart such pain."

"Then I advise you not to go there again, or you'll get another pain – a thump in the ear."

He closed his eyes. "How many weeks are left this term?"

"Five."

"So I've missed seven weeks of lectures."

"Yes. You're heading for a fail."

He smiled. "Nah. I've got distinctions for my essays so far… except the last one. That was a fail. Hardly surprising really, I wrote it on toilet paper."

"How on earth did you manage that?"

He grinned. "I used hard toilet paper and typed it. Lots of carriage returns."

Sophie put her hand to her forehead. "I don't believe it."

Isaac eased himself into a sitting position. "Whose home is this?"

It belongs to Judy and Adrian. I know them because they go to my church. They are good people." She pointed to him. "So don't mess them around."

"Church!" he said incredulously. "You go to church?"

"It's a good thing I do, because none of your Marxist comrades volunteered to look after you. I'm serious. Don't mess them around."

He gave a mock salute. "Yes sir."

For a while, all Sophie could hear was the sound of traffic humming past outside.

She was surprised when he said, "Tell me about your family. Do you have any brothers or sisters?"

"Er, no. I'm an only child,"

"Is your father really a herdsman?"

"Yes." Sophie remembered the day her parents had driven her to Cambridge for her first day. Dad had borrowed the estate car. Her mother had fussed over her. "You're a lady, now," she sniffed. "Go and show 'em what you're made of."

"Yes mum."

Her father had dressed up in his best trousers and jacket. Both were now several sizes too small for him. "You can always come home girl if this education thing doesn't work."

She'd kissed him on the cheek, not trusting herself to reply. "Bye, dad."

Sophie brought herself back to reality. "What about you? Do you have any siblings?"

"Yes. I have a brother. He's currently finishing officer cadet training at Dartmouth."

"He's joining the navy, then."

"Yes. He's becoming an imperialist lackey."

Sophie looked at him speculatively. "But you are proud of him."

"It's perverse, isn't it? Yes, we're quite close."

Sophie nodded and got up to leave.

Again, he held out a hand to her. "Sophie."

"Yes?"

"Something of your *bourgeois* tirade has actually reached me. Please don't think I'm a lost cause." He inclined his head. "I'm lost, sure, but I hope I'm not yet a lost cause."

Sophie looked for signs of insincerity and failed to see any.

"Well, that's good. What are you going to do about all those lectures you've missed?"

Isaac leaned back on the bed and closed his eyes. "You've been to them all, I suppose."

"Yes."

"Then I can borrow your notes, and make notes from yours."

She looked at him scornfully. "There is no way I'm entrusting my folder to an irresponsible idiot like you."

Even as she said the words, she knew with utter conviction that Isaac was very far from being an idiot.

Isaac waved a finger at her. "Now, now. Where is your Christian charity?"

Accusations and obligations hung in the air uncomfortably.

"All right, then. This is how it will happen. I'm not letting my folder of notes out of my sight. Therefore, you and I will spend several afternoons and evenings in Trinity College Library, where I can do my work, and you can update yourself with my notes. The library is open seven days a week."

Even as she made the offer, Sophie was conscious of a slight lift in her spirit.

Chapter 14

"Hastings. A moment of your time please."

Isaac was in a line of students jostling to leave the lecture theater at the end of a tutorial. He turned back immediately and made his way to the bench at the front of the room.

The professor looked him up and down. Isaac had the uncomfortable feeling of being a prisoner in a courtroom. "Yes Sir."

The professor grunted. "You've finally cleaned yourself up."

"Yes sir. I realize I've been a bit lax this term. I'm sorry about that. But I've decided to buck up my ideas."

"It's good to actually see you turn up to a tutorial."

"Yes sir. Is that all, sir?"

"No it isn't. I didn't get your last essay. Up to this point, your essays have been good. Distressingly so, for such a smart-arse. So, where is it?"

Isaac's mouth dropped open in surprise. "I assure you sir, I handed it in. I put it on the pile at the end of this bench a week ago with all the others."

"Well, I haven't got it. So, explain yourself."

Isaac shook his head. "I can't explain it sir. I just know I queued up with the others and put it on the pile at the end of the lecture."

"Was it the first or the last essay on the pile?"

"No sir. About the middle, I'd say."

"Then it is highly likely it didn't drop out." The professor fixed him with a steely eye. "You are not messing me around are you, Hastings?"

"Definitely not, sir."

An uncomfortable silence hung between them, and then Isaac clicked his finger. "Sir, as you might know, I always type my essays, and I use carbon paper to keep a copy. I can have the carbon-copy to you within the hour."

The professor raised a bushy eyebrow. "Can you now? Well that changes almost everything."

"Almost, sir?"

The professor sighed. "I and some of my colleagues have had an anonymous letter." He paused. "They all say the same thing."

A prickle of unease ran up Isaac's spine. He waited for the professor to continue.

"They all accuse you of plagiarism."

Isaac was dumbfounded. "Plagiarism?"

"Yes."

"Oh no, sir. I've never plagiarized. I wouldn't dare."

The professor sniffed. "I don't like anonymous letters. But I dislike plagiarists even more. Do you understand me?"

"I don't plagiarize, sir."

"Well let me spell it out for you, Hastings. Nothing will ruin an academic career more completely and utterly… and bring you shame, than claiming other people's work as your own. Do you understand me? It will be ruination."

Isaac stuttered. "I… I understand perfectly sir, but I assure you I have never plagiarized. I'm not yet sure of what I want to do with my life, but one of the options I'm keeping open is a career as an academic."

The bushy eyebrows twitched. "So you can mark essays typed on toilet paper by smart-arse students."

"Yes sir. I'm sorry sir. It won't happen again."

The professor grunted again. "I actually read the essay, and it was quite good. I failed you on principle."

"Yes sir."

"Don't do it again."

Isaac stood with Sophie in front of the imposing entrance to Trinity College. A statue of King Henry VIII stood above the gate. He was holding a golden orb in his left hand. In his other hand, where the scepter should have been, was a chair leg. Some students had swapped it over some years ago, and no one had the heart to change it back.

He pointed to it. "One of our better pranks."

Sophie looked at him scornfully. "You just like it because it makes a political statement."

"Do you know; I never feel quite as much a Communist when you're around."

"Is that an invitation?"

Isaac nodded. "It could very well be."

"Gosh, you sure know how to knock a girl off her feet."

Isaac smiled. He wasn't sure where the conversation was going, or should go. So he said, "I think the best prank was when some engineering students put an Austin Seven on the roof of Senate House."

Sophie looked at him in amazement. "Did they really?"

"Yes. In 1958. No one's quite sure how they did it."

They walked through the gate, crossed Trinity College and passed on through to Nevile's Court. The sun was beginning to set, and its light was warming the Western flanks of the court. Isaac couldn't remember being so much at peace for a very long time. As if by common consent, they made their way to Wren's Library – one of Sir Christopher Wren's architectural masterpieces.

Sophie sighed. "This is one of my favorite places."

Isaac looked around as if seeing it for the first time. He had seen it before, but his vision then had been masked by derision. Today, it looked totally different. He rubbed the back of his neck. It was extraordinary.

Wren's Library had huge windows and beautiful proportions. A black and white checkerboard floor ran the length of the library between the bookcases. At the end of each bookcase was the bust of a famous writer. The biggest statue, however, was a full-sized one of Lord Byron. His immorality had banished him from Poet's Corner in Westminster Abbey, and he now sat, apparently at ease, against the end wall of the library.

Once they had soaked up the ambience of the place, they made their way to the library's annex, found a table, and began to work.

Isaac was charmed at reading Sophie's notes. She had a neat, clear hand. He could almost hear her talking.

Sophie only interrupted him once. He'd looked up and seen her studying him. "What?" he said.

She shook her head. "I can't believe the speed you are reading and writing."

Isaac put down his pen and stretched. "It's just a habit… lot's of practice."

"Well, I don't think it is 'just' anything. You must have a very fine mind."

"Looking at this," he pointed to her notes, "yours isn't bad. You just need to sharpen up your logic and ask more questions."

"You cheeky blighter."

After another hour had passed, Isaac screwed the top on to his fountain pen. "I'm done for tonight. How about we walk along the river, and I buy you a drink at 'The Anchor?'" This was the first time he'd asked Sophie for anything social. He found himself holding his breath.

'The Anchor' was a popular pub for tourists, so Isaac had not been there often. He did, however, remember that it had a fabulous view across the river.

They found a table by the window, and Isaac went to order the drinks – a half of cider for Sophie, and a pint of Double Diamond for himself.

When they'd settled with their drinks, they gazed across the water to Darwin College. Wooden punts were moored both sides of the River Cam, and all was still. The quirky Old Granary at the northern end of Darwin College was now in shadow, but the white balcony that hung over the river could still be seen clearly.

Sophie pointed to it. "Did you know that Darwin College was the first college to admit women to Cambridge University?"

"I thought that was Girton College, where you are."

"They were the first to admit undergraduates. Darwin only accepts graduates."

"Just the really clever ones. Very classist."

"No. It has to do with talent." She prodded his arm with a finger. "I'll tell you what is unjust; and that is the fact that there is only one college for women undergraduates in Cambridge. You ought to be protesting about that, if you have any social conscience."

"Wow. There is some Marxist blood in you after all." He changed the subject. "Old Charlie Darwin certainly put the kibosh on the crap you Christians believe. He studied here, you know."

"I do know. And I know the subject he studied."

"And what was that?"

"It was theology. He was training to be an Anglican priest, after failing at medical school in Edinburgh."

"But he became an atheist when he found biological evidence for evolution."

Sophie shook her head. "No. He always believed in God. Darwin once told a friend that he'd never been an atheist in the sense of denying the existence of God." She looked at him. "Did you know that?"

Isaac opened his mouth and was nearly going to lie, but in the end, he simply said, "No." Then he rushed on. "But you've got to admit, the Bible is just myth, isn't it – albeit a myth some people find helpful."

Sophie looked at him reproachfully. "That's both patronizing and untrue."

"Untrue?"

"C.S. Lewis doesn't think the gospel stories are myth."

Isaac gave a cough of derision. "You're not reading that old polemicist, are you?"

"That 'old polemicist' happens to be the foremost authority on myth literature in the world. Until he died in 1963, he was one of both Oxford and Cambridge's most distinguished professors."

Isaac held up his hands. "I surrender." He grinned. "But I reserve the right to reengage in the battle at any time in the future."

Sophie laughed. Then she looked at her watch. "I'd better get back to my bike. I've left it at Trinity. I'm going to be late getting back to Girton."

"I'll walk you to your bike."

It was eleven o'clock by the time Isaac finally got to the newly built accommodation block for King's College. It was called 'The Keynes Building,' and it was a brutal modernist thing built of concrete. It seemed that the world no longer had the inclination to build anything as elegant as the 18th century "Fellows Building" that graced the far side of the Great Court. The upside, however, was that each student at Keynes had a room to themselves which had its own bathroom. The other upside was the bar. It was just underneath him.

He was just about to enter the lobby when a figure detached itself from the wall. "Hello Isaac. I've not seen you for a week or so."

Isaac recognized the voice. It was his old drinking partner, Stan Wincup. Stan was a writer and a freelance social commentator. Isaac had been impressed with his sophistication and his conviction that society could, and should, change. Stan dressed much like any student at Cambridge, although he must have been at least ten years older than most. "Hi Stan. You're up late. What's up?"

"I dropped by to ask the porter if you were okay. I haven't seen you for a while." Stan smiled. "I miss your political insights and passion. They give me hope."

"Hope?"

"Hope that things might change – if we have the courage to pursue it."

Isaac passed a hand wearily over his face. "No, I've not seen you for a while, Stan. I've been preoccupied with other things. And to be quite honest, I'm not feeling the passion like I used to. I've got too many questions." He shrugged. "I'm seeing too many things in a different light."

Stan's face creased in a frown. "You're not going soft on me, are you Isaac?"

Isaac patted him on the shoulder. "No Stan. I'm just waking up from a dream." So saying, he pushed past his friend and entered the building.

Chapter 15

Sam always felt good hearing Isaac's voice at the end of the telephone. It was a sense of connection, or at least, connection with something that wasn't Naval. For the last thirty months, the Navy had owned him, both body and soul. His training had been relentless and grueling. But now it was over. He had graduated.

In truth, he had loved his training. There was something about the lore of ships that intrigued him. Even the sensation of being afloat, of being suspended in a clear liquid, fascinated him.

He heard his brother's voice. "So, you are now Midshipman Hastings, a junior officer."

Sam chuckled. "You've got no idea how junior that is. I will be regarded as a snotty-nosed jerk for a year or so."

"Well, congratulations." Isaac paused. "Why didn't you tell me about your graduation. I would have come."

"I knew you had quite enough on your plate trying to catch up at university. I didn't want to stop the momentum."

Isaac grunted. "I don't suppose Mum or Dad…"

Sam laughed. "Of course not. And I wouldn't have expected them to come." Their father had been posted to Fort Stanley in

Hong Kong. "You're sounding brighter these days and less abusive with your Communist rants. What's happened to you?"

"I've caught an acute case of sobriety, occasioned by the attentions of a good woman."

"You're kidding me."

"Nup."

"What's her name?"

"Her name is Sophie. But she is just a friend. Nothing more."

Sam digested the information with a degree of pleasure. However, what he heard Isaac say next caused him to be instantly alarmed.

"Sam. I think I've got a problem."

"A problem?"

"Four things have happened to me that I can't explain, and together, they point to the possibility that someone is trying to ruin my life."

Sam pressed the phone closer to his ear. "Tell me."

"I think someone stole an essay of mine before it could be marked."

"Go on."

"Then someone wrote an anonymous letter to my History and English professors accusing me of plagiarism."

"Is that bad?"

"It would be disastrous if it were true. It would wreck my academic ambitions. No one would take me on."

"The third?"

"I got beaten up by two thugs in an alleyway beside a pub – and it wasn't an attempted robbery."

"Good grief. Why didn't you tell me this earlier?"

"Because I didn't want to ruin your final week at Dartmouth."

"What happened next?"

He heard Isaac sigh. "That happened yesterday when I was with Sophie. I was standing next to her at the traffic lights on Bridge Street, when someone in the group waiting to cross the road tried to push Sophie in front of a truck. I only just managed to haul her back to safety in time."

"Did you see who did it?"

"No. When I asked the people there if they saw anything, they said they saw a man in a hat and coat. When I looked around, there was no sign of him."

"Have you told the police?"

"Not yet."

"Wow."

"Wow, indeed."

For a long moment, neither of them spoke.

In the end, Isaac broke the silence. "The thing is Sam, I'm going for the 'Norsworthy Prize,' and I've made no secret about it. If anyone wanted to wreck my career, sabotaging my submission would do it." He paused. "So I'm feeling a bit vulnerable."

"What's the Norsworthy Prize?"

"It's an in-house thing in my department aimed at final year students. Nothing is formally published, but the winner can expect to be invited to stay on at Cambridge as a tutor if they want to go on and do a PhD."

"And is that what you want?"

"Very much."

Sam thought furiously. "When do you have to submit?"

"In two weeks."

"Right. I'll be with you tomorrow."

"What?" You're kidding."

"Not at all. I've got a month off before I join my ship in Portsmouth."

"Where will you stay?"

"I'll find somewhere. Cambridge has probably got a Royal Naval Association place somewhere. They sometimes have accommodation. If not, I'll doss down in the nearest military mess. They're pretty accommodating about officers waiting to join a ship."

"I've got to confess, Sam. It would be good to see you."

"Right, that's settled then. Oh, and Isaac…"

"Yes."

"I'll be bringing the Scorpion Stone."

Isaac clattered down the stairs and opened the door to the porter's lodge. Jenkins, the porter, pointed to the man sitting on the corner of his desk. Sam smiled, and the two of them embraced.

Isaac then held his bother at arm's length. "Wow. Look at you. You look wonderful, distressingly fit, and horribly institutional." Indeed. Sam did. His brother was wearing jeans, Hush Puppy shoes, and a white shirt. He'd thrown his old school sweater over one shoulder. His hair cut and bearing, however, marked him as a military man.

"Have you managed to find a place to stay?"

"Yes. All organized."

"Good. Come upstairs and see my place."

When Sam looked around Isaac's bedsit, he nodded his head in admiration. "This is a lot better than my dormitory at the Britannia Royal Naval College I can tell you." So saying, he put his hand in his pocket and gripped hold of something in his fist. When he took it out, Isaac saw that Sam was holding the Scorpion Stone. He placed it in Isaac's hand. "Right," said Sam. "Let's get down to business." He sat himself down in Isaac's desk chair.

Isaac sat in his armchair, slightly amused by Sam's military brusqueness. "I'm all ears."

"There are two presenting issues as I see it. The first is the need to protect your academic future – and in all probability, that means protecting your Norsworthy essay."

Isaac nodded.

"The second is to protect you from physical harm." Sam looked up at him. "Have I got that right?"

"Yes. And you'd probably need to throw in the need to look after Sophie as well."

Sam grunted. "Let's look at protecting your Norsworthy thing first. Have you got the instructions for the competition?"

Isaac rifled in a drawer of his desk, found a folder, and handed Sam the entry requirements. He hadn't looked at them for some time because he was already familiar with them.

Sam put it on the desk and started to read.

Once he'd finished, Isaac saw him start to read it again.

Eventually, Sam said: "It says here that you are allowed to enter previous work, and that you are even encouraged to do so in order to develop a theme further. Is that right?"

"Yes. A normal academic essay here is 4,000 words. But the Norsworthy essay has to be between 8 to 10,000 words."

"Wow. That's a lot."

"It's the normal length for an article in an academic journal."

"Hm." For a long while, Sam said nothing. He stared at the wall behind the desk, tapping a finger against his lips.

After five minutes had passed, Sam spun round in his chair. "Right," he said. "This is what we'll do."

A long discussion followed. Isaac couldn't help but be impressed with Sam's clarity of thinking and the decisiveness of his actions. The Navy had done very well to secure his services. "What will we do now?" he asked.

Sam looked at his watch. "What time do you normally go out drinking?"

"When I can afford it, about seven."

"Good." Sam got up to leave.

"What are you going to do?"

"I'm going to look around and buy a few things before the shops close."

"And what do you want me to do?"

Sam smiled. "I want you to get slightly drunk. What pubs do you normally drink in?"

"The college bar downstairs and 'The Baron of Beef' on Bridge Street."

"Right. Your job is to drink and shout your head off in both places, saying that you've finished writing your Norsworthy essay, and that you plan to celebrate your achievement by having a leisurely punt on your own in two days time – on Thursday evening. Tell everyone you need another day or so to check your essay through."

"Why would I go for a punt?"

"I dunno. Be creative. Maybe to center yourself in reality again. Your real purpose, of course, is advertise the fact that you will be on your own, so that anyone wishing to harm you is likely to follow you in the punt." Sam paused. "Do you think you can manage that?"

Isaac grinned. "The drinking part is easy."

Sam nodded. "And one more thing: I want you to buy a garden gnome."

"What?"

"A small one. You can call him Ralph."

Isaac rolled his eyes. "And why do I need Ralph?"

"Ralph's job is to guard your essay. He's the paperweight on top of your essay."

Isaac furrowed his brow.

Sam continued. "We want to make it easy for people to find it." He stood up from the seat and stretched. "I'll see you tomorrow night."

Sam bought a haversack, a basketball, and dog's feeding bowl. Then he went in search of a vehicle repair shop. It didn't take him long to find one. Inside, he bought a can of spray paint and an extendable car radio antenna. The radio antenna was for plan B. He very much hoped he wouldn't need it. An extended radio antenna could inflict terrible damage when wielded by a determined man. And there was no doubt about it, when it came to Isaac's safety, he would be determined.

Sophie chained up her bike and made her way through to the lounge of 'The Anchor.' She was far from sure what to expect, but it was enough for her to know that Isaac would be waiting for her. It had been two days since she'd seen him.

As she threaded her way through the bar, the beauty of the view across the Cam struck her again. The river became a large pool outside 'The Anchor' after two arms of the river rejoined having passed either side of an island. Wooden punts crowed the shore like leaves blown to the side of a puddle.

She nearly missed seeing Isaac because he was with another young man. Sophie looked at the strange man appreciatively. He was obviously superbly fit, and his square chin and aquiline nose made him very handsome. Unlike Isaac, he had short hair and was neatly groomed.

Isaac saw her and got to his feet. The other man gallantly did the same. "Hi, Sophie." Isaac gestured to the young man next to him. "This is my brother, Sam. He's staying in Cambridge for a while."

"Ah. You're training for the Navy, I understand."

Sophie was aware of Sam inspecting her with a strange expression – it was almost one of disbelief. For whatever reason, it took him a moment to find his words. "Yes, ma'am. I've just finished training and have a month off before I join my ship."

Sophie laughed. "Please call me Sophie. Ma'am makes me sound like a duchess."

"Yes, ma'am." Sam shook his head. "Sorry. Yes, Sophie."

Soon, drinks had been organized, and they were sitting together at their table. They couldn't get one by the window this time, but it was still near enough to afford them an excellent view.

Isaac spoke up. "Sam only got here a minute or so before you, Sophie, so I'm bringing him up to speed." He turned to his brother. "I'm pleased to report that Ralph is now guarding the essay."

Sam nodded. "And you will be away from your room most evenings for the next week."

"Yes."

Sophie was curious. "Who's Ralph?"

Isaac grinned. "Ralph is a garden gnome."

She laughed. "Where on earth did you get a garden gnome."

"I stole one from a garden."

"You can't do that!" she expostulated.

"Don't worry. I put a garden stake in its place, with a note."

"What did the note say?"

"It said, 'Off to visit the relatives. Back soon.'"

Sophie laughed. "And what essay is Ralph guarding?"

"My essay for the Norsworthy prize."

"You've written it already?"

"Yes. I wrote it yesterday."

Sophie scoffed. "You can't write a 10,000 word essay in a single day. It's impossible."

"It's 8,500 words, actually, and I typed it."

Sophie shook her head and wasn't sure what to believe. One thing was for certain, she wasn't being told the whole story. She bowed her head, ostensibly to study her drink. In reality, she was watching Sam under her long eyelashes. He had taken over the conversation.

"We're working on a plot to keep Isaac and you, Sophie, safe. Isaac has been beaten up, and I understand you were pushed into the path of a truck."

Sophie looked up at him, and she caught her breath. The horror of the moment suddenly replayed itself in all its rawness. "So you don't think it was an accident either."

"No."

She lowered her head.

Sam continued to speak. "The important thing is for you to keep your head down, Sophie, and for Isaac never to be alone. I'll be able to help with that in the coming days."

Isaac toyed with his drink. "It would mean you attending a few lectures."

"Would anyone ask any questions?"

"I doubt it."

Sophie put both hands on the edge of the table. "What are you two up to?"

In the next ten minutes, Sophie found out.

When Sam had finished, she didn't know whether to laugh, scream, or cry. In the end, she settled for saying, "Can I help?"

Sam rubbed his chin. "It would be handy to know if you spot anyone following Isaac. Would you be able to wave a white handkerchief or something from a bridge?"

She nodded. "I'll sort something out."

Isaac leaned back. "This all happens tomorrow evening. The days are drawing out so it won't be dark until very late. I'll be at lectures until mid afternoon. What shall we do until 6:30?"

Sophie smiled. "Why not do what many good Christians do at the end of the day? Let's go to church. Let's attend evensong at King's Chapel." She smiled. "You know the Cambridge aphorism: 'Study at St. John's; live at Jesus; and worship at King's.'"

Isaac shook his head. "No one will believe I went to church."

Sophie smiled. "Then you can bet that no one will be looking for you there."

He acknowledged the truth of her statement with a nod. Then he sat up straight. "One of my drinking friends at Kings is a chorister. He's a rampant homosexual, sings bass, and has a fine intellect. I'm pretty sure he'll get us a place beside the choir stalls, away from the *hoi polloi*."

"I thought you were a Marxist," said Sophie, laughing.

"You see how you've ruined me. I'm joining Enoch Powell's fan club next week."

Chapter 16

Tony Chester-Smith banged the table with his fist. He was sitting at an ugly cement picnic table in a park. He wanted to destroy the man who'd been speaking to him. The 'academic look' seemed to advertise the man's sense of superiority.

Tony spat out "Do you mean to tell me that after toadying up to Hastings for almost a year, we've got nothing to show for it? Dammit man. I thought you said he was radicalized enough to commit."

The man sitting opposite him failed to give any sign of having been rebuked. That, as much as anything, infuriated Tony. The man was safe in the knowledge that Tony was not his boss, nor did he outrank him. Tony shook his head. There were times he dearly missed the army.

The man called Stan leaned back and stared at him with his bleak eyes. "Nothing is certain in our game," he said.

"Well, I want it to be certain." Tony closed his hand into a fist. "I want this man. What's the reason you've not managed to get him over the line?"

Stan lifted his chin. It was a gesture of defiance, and Tony knew it. "It would seem that Hastings has got himself involved with a woman." Stan shrugged. "I can only think that she has had a moderating influence on him."

Tony groaned, and for a long while said nothing. Finally, he sat himself up. "You've been in the game longer than me. Is there any chance this woman can be neutralized?"

Stan didn't answer, and after a few seconds, he got to his feet. Without saying a word, he ambled his way down the footpath through the park. Some children were kicking a ball to each other on the grass. One of them kicked it wide so that it dribbled out in front of Stan.

He smiled and kicked it back to the children.

Tony wanted to scream.

Isaac had never been to a service at King's Chapel, although he had occasionally gone inside. He'd certainly never sat in the ancient wooden stalls next to the choir and heard them sing. He was completely unprepared for the experience of hearing one of the finest choirs in the world.

Candles guttered in the brass and glass holders, whilst high above him, the radiating fingers of the world's largest fan vaulting showed off their glory. Isaac shook his head. The building had been finished in the time of Henry VIII, and he doubted whether humankind had managed to build anything as beautiful since. The building was a symphony of stained glass, held together by a filigree of stone. The late afternoon sun splashed colors on the pillars and the floor.

The day thou gavest, Lord has ended. The words of the choir were hauntingly beautiful. He glanced at Sophie beside him. She seemed to be very much at peace. So was Sam who was seated next to her.

He sighed. Here was peace, and he didn't understand it. All he knew was that a rampant homosexual was singing in the choir; a once avowed Marxist was in the congregation… and God seemed to smile. It was very confusing.

The feeling of peace followed him when he left the chapel. He savored it. Then thoughts of nuclear war, revolution, and girls being blown up by bombs, shattered the moment. "Do you think there will ever be an end to war?" he said to no one in particular.

Sophie glanced at him. "You know what the Spanish/American philosopher, George Santayana said, 'Only the dead have seen the end of war.'"

It wasn't the most comforting of replies, but it was enough to put him on edge and prepare him for what he must do next.

———————

Both Sam and Sophie escorted Isaac to the water's edge outside 'The Anchor' and saw him safely off in his punt. Sam noticed idly that Isaac seemed quite adept at poling the flat-bottomed vessel along. He'd obviously done it a few times.

Sam turned to Sophie. "Stand on Silver Street Bridge and see if anyone follows Isaac. If you see them, wave a white handkerchief. Isaac will look back at you from time to time, apparently admiring the scenery. If no one is following him by the time he gets to that crazy wooden Mathematic Bridge, you can be pretty sure no one is following him. If that's so, just go home."

Sophie looked at him nervously. "What will you do?"

"I'll be well up ahead on King's College Bridge. If he gives me a wave – apparently brushing away an insect, I'll know someone is following."

"What will happen next?"

Sam smiled. "Things will get interesting."

"Will anyone get hurt?"

"I hope not." He waved Isaac's student pass. "I've got to use this to make my way through the colleges and get well downstream. See you later." He jogged off, feeling the backpack bounce as he ran.

After a lot of ducking and weaving through different college courtyards, Sam arrived at King's College Bridge. It was an arched stone footbridge that linked the lawns sweeping down to the River from King's College, to 'The Backs,' the grassy Western bank of the River. From where he stood, he was able to see the iconic view of King's College Chapel. Something had moved in his soul in that building and disturbed him. He hoped he might talk to Sophie about it some time.

He forced himself to attend to the matter in hand. Sam rummaged in his backpack and put the dog bowl in the center of the parapet. Then, he placed the basketball on top of it. Both the dog bowl and the basketball had been spray-painted gray. Finally, he took out half a brick – and waited.

The sun was still strong, although it was edging nearer to the horizon. The dappled light through the treetops danced and laughed on the grass and the shadows were getting longer. Isaac would be hard pressed to get his punt back in time to avoid paying a penalty for being late. Sam shook his head. It was stupid the things you thought about when there were more important things to consider.

He thought about Sophie. Wow. She'd taken his breath away. He wondered whether…

Stop it! He told himself.

The sight of Isaac coming into view put paid to further ruminations. More urgent things now required his attention.

Isaac was punting downstream with easy fluid motions – lifting his pole forward and dropping it to the riverbed, before driving it backward. From time to time, he paused to swat away the midges. Sam had seen clouds of them dancing in the summer sun.

Sure enough, a punt was following Isaac. A man, who was considerably less practiced in the art of punting than his brother, was propelling it. The punt contained two men, both wearing hats and coats. Sam grimaced. You could hide a lot under a coat. One man lay sprawled, apparently at ease, in the center of the punt, whilst his colleague stood on the rear deck and wielded the punt pole.

Isaac came closer and closer. Just before he glided under the bridge he favored Sam with a smile.

Two minutes later, the two men in the following punt

approached the bridge. The man holding the punt pole had a look of grim determination as he tried to keep his punt midstream.

They came closer and closer.

Just before they came to the bridge, Sam called out to them. "Hey guys! Do you want to watch the sinking of the Titanic?" So saying, Sam heaved, with apparent effort, the stone ball decorating the center of the bridge's balustrade, so that it rolled along the parapet directly above where the punt would pass. A dreadful sound of stone crunching on stone could be heard. Sam was dragging the half-brick along the inside edge of the parapet.

The front of the punt disappeared under the bridge.

"Bombs away," yelled Sam as he dropped the ball over the side.

By this stage, the man in the center of the punt was on his feet. He put his foot on the edge of the punt and dived overboard, tipping the boat alarmingly as he did. The tilting was enough to throw his colleague with the punt pole off balance. He too ended in the water.

Sam wasted no time. He ran across the bridge to the riverbank the two men were splashing toward. Both were attempting to scramble up the slippery bank when Sam took out his Kodak Instamatic 100 and started to take a rapid series of photographs. "Congratulations," he yelled. "Your ugly mugs will make the front page of the Student Union magazine. Everyone will see it." He waved. "Thanks for giving us all a laugh."

Sam was dimly aware of a stream of invectives being directed at him as he scampered back to the bridge. He put the brick and the dog bowl back into his backpack and jogged away.

Tony Chester-Smith looked at his Russian handler much as someone would look at a deadly spider.

The spider, however, gave every appearance of being at ease. Today, he was wearing a shabby tweed jacket over which he'd thrown an academic gown. He looked every inch a Cambridge don.

"It's a beautiful walk from Cambridge along the river to Granchester."

Tony nodded and tried to keep the sourness he was feeling from his expression. He hadn't been able to walk anywhere. His walking stick was leaning against the trestle table that the proprietors of the Red Lion had managed to squeeze between their thatched, whitewashed pub and the High Street. The sun was out, but Tony was not feeling its optimism.

It didn't take long for him to learn that his pessimism was well founded. His handler spoke softly, with a perfect, southern counties accent. Tony had learned that it was the tone he adopted when he was at his most dangerous.

The man gazed down the High Street, apparently half-distracted from his own conversation. "Ours is a dangerous game; one in which we show our head as rarely as possible." He smiled as if his words were humorous. It was all an act. "Our resources are also thinly stretched and must be used with the utmost care, and with the greatest caution."

Tony stared at his pint of beer. He hadn't yet had the stomach to drink it.

The man continued. "This private vendetta you have against Isaac Hastings has gone too far." He smiled. "I would have allowed you one attempt to destroy him, purely to motivate you to move to Cambridge, but that is all. As it is, you have used my staff to burgle, to physically attack, and to attempt a murder – and all to no avail, I understand. And now, following your recent attempt to use my men to attack Mr. Hastings, I have to assume that their photographs will appear in a student newspaper that will not only be read in Cambridge, but which will find its way to every corner of England. Our men now have to be retired."

Tony was far from sure what 'retirement' meant, but he said nothing.

His handler continued. "So as of now, you will cease your vendetta. Is that understood?"

Tony put his hand around his beer and said sulkily. "Yes.

However, I do have one more project currently underway which has yet to play out. It will be too late to stop it now."

"Will it involve any of my staff?"

"No. Everything has been set in place. It is only a case of waiting."

The man nodded. "Very well, then." He smiled. "Let's turn to other matters. Your recruiting has not gone as well as we'd hoped."

Chapter 17

Two days later, Sophie was again in the annex of Trinity library with Isaac. He had just finished making notes from her lecture files and was now leaning back in his chair with his hands behind his head, apparently very pleased with himself. When Sophie retrieved her folder from him, she discovered that the wretched man had used his red pen to make comments in the margin of her notes. What really irked her was that his comments were insightful and warranted. Isaac obviously had an extraordinary mind. But the blatant cheek of the man! She gave expression to her anger by starting a fight. In truth, Sophie was on tenterhooks. Both she and Isaac were waiting for Sam to join them, hopefully with the photographs he had taken at the river. She was worried. Had they done enough to frighten off those who posed such a danger to them?

Sophie chose to react when Isaac mentioned he was reading the modern French philosopher's Jean-Paul Sartre and Paul-Michel Foucault. Isaac had been relishing their trashing of all forms of morality and truth.

"They are heralding a new era," he said. There was a slight

touch of mischief in his eyes. Sophie suspected he was deliberately trying to provoke her.

She took up the challenge.

"Jean-Paul Sartre is self-indulgent sex addict who, although he doesn't realize it, is giving momentum to Marxism's deconstruction of Western civilization." She scoffed. "He's simply tried to give meaning to his meaninglessness with big words to hoodwink people like you."

Isaac smiled. "Perhaps he's shining a light into the future."

"It's not a future I want to be part of. No meaning, no morality, and no hope – I can hardly wait."

"Good things can come from deconstruction. There can be real reform."

"Oh really." Sophie tossed her head derisively. "I've heard more persuasive arguments in children's sandpits. Just where has reform worked well when it has trashed the Judeo-Christian ethic of justice and care for the vulnerable?"

"Foucault says…"

Sophie threw up her arms. "Oh, Foucault – a suicidal man over-taken by the macabre and sexual perversions. What a fantastic role model he is. He's a real beacon of hope."

Sadly, the full force of her derision was blunted by the arrival of Sam.

He looked good, and he was smiling. "Listening to you two squabble is like hearing kids in a playground. It's hilarious."

"Have you got the photographs," Isaac asked.

"I have. And they're great."

Sophie leaned forward on her chair. "Show us."

For the next few minutes, they passed the photographs around to each other. Sophie had to admit they were good. Two very bedraggled men, with furious expressions on their faces, were trying to hide their faces from the camera, whilst simultaneously attempting to climb up the steep riverbank. The pictures showed them not being very successful at either.

"Good enough, do you think?" asked Sam.

Isaac grinned. "They're perfect. I'll get them to the editor of the

Student Union rag straight away." So saying, he scooped the photos into their pouch, picked up his study folder, and headed toward the door.

Sophie called out to him. "When are we catching up again?"

Isaac turned. "Exam week begins on Monday. We won't have time for socializing until they are over. I'll give you a call." He waved and turned toward the exit.

Sam stretched his legs out and leaned back in his chair. He was trying to kid himself that he was at ease. In reality, he was not. Isaac had left, and now, for the very first time, he was alone with Sophie. She had filled almost every idle thought in his head, but now he had to navigate the infinitely more dangerous world of reality. He watched with some dismay as Sophie packed up her shoulder bag. He didn't want her to leave.

He swallowed, and said, "What is it that you two keep arguing about?"

Sophie gave an apologetic laugh. "I'm sorry. We must sound like squabbling siblings." She placed the shoulder bag beside her chair. "We argue about truth and meaning – big things. But I'm afraid we do it very poorly."

"You sounded pretty convincing to me."

Sophie cocked her head and ran her eyes over him. "Are you a thinker, Sam?"

He laughed. "Not really. I was either going to be a zoo curator or join the Navy." He shrugged. "I'm young and stupid, and need a bit of action. So I chose the Navy."

"I don't think you are stupid at all."

Sam raised an eyebrow. "What am I?"

"You are both similar to, and different, from Isaac."

"In what way?"

"Isaac is terrifyingly clever, passionate about justice, and nicely flawed by a strong streak of mischief."

"But you don't agree with him?"

Sophie sighed. "He can be ideologically blind, sometimes."

Sam looked up at Sophie. "Then what am I?"

"You are principled, easy to underestimate, and a natural leader." She smiled. "And you have the same Hastings predisposition for mischief."

"I'm not an academic, though."

Sophie laughed. "Then you might just qualify to be human." She paused. "Have you read any philosophy?"

"Barely. I read a bit of Bertrand Russell – just to get another perspective on life."

"Another perspective?"

"Our Dad is a chaplain in the Army. We had to go to church a lot as kids." He shrugged. "I thought I'd read what an atheist had to say."

"And what do you think?"

"Honestly?"

"Yes."

"Russell is clever, but I didn't recognize the Christians he attacks. He paints them as extreme. So I'm not sure how honest he is."

Sophie inclined her head. "Very perceptive." She smiled. "I suspect that underneath all his cleverness, Bertie was a child kicking against the Presbyterian strictures of his grandmother. He saw them as an impediment to his sexual appetite. He wanted to be a free-thinker like his father, who died when he was young." She smiled sadly. "However, his atheism came at some cost to his peace of mind.

"How so?"

"Hang on. I've got some notes here somewhere." She pulled a folder from her bag and began leafing through its pages. "Ah, here it is." She cleared her throat. "Knowing that he was near the end of his life, he wrote a poem to his fourth wife Edith. In the first stanza of it, he said:

Through the long years
I have sought peace,
I found ecstasy,
I found anguish,

I found madness,
I found loneliness.
I found the solitary pain
that gnaws the heart,
But peace I did not find.

When she finished, Sam nodded slowly. "That's a very sad epitaph."

For a while, nothing was said. There were so many things Sam wanted to say, but he felt unable to voice them.

Finally, Sophie rescued him. She lowered her head and asked, "Do you think one of the two men in the punt pushed me in front of the truck?"

It took a moment for Sam to reorder his thinking. "Um, yes. Unless the entire British underworld is ranged against you, it's likely that these two are the men who are attacking you and Isaac."

"But why?"

Sam sighed. "That's a very good question – one that I've been asking myself a lot."

"Do you have any ideas?"

"None that answer all my questions."

Sophie looked at him. He could see the pleading in her eyes. His heart skipped a beat. He so much wanted to reassure her, but was far from confident that he could. "Isaac has, as you know, a passion for justice, and he's pretty voluble about it here in Cambridge. He's seen as a radical." Sam shrugged. "He may have rubbed some people up the wrong way."

"But they also attacked me."

"Yes. You, or your influence on Isaac, is being seen as a threat."

"But I'm no threat to anyone. I'm not a radical."

Sam folded his hands together on the table, wishing that he didn't have to say the words she had to hear. "That may be the problem, Sophie. Perhaps some people want Isaac to be radicalized."

Sophie's mouth dropped open. "You're kidding me?"

Sam shrugged. "I've been mulling it over for ages. It's the only thing that makes sense."

Sophie lowered her head so that her gorgeous hair fell forward. He could see the chestnut highlights as it cascaded down in front of her. Sam swallowed.

She said, in a soft voice. "Do you think the danger is passed now that we're publicizing the pictures of the two men?"

"I think some danger has passed, but we still haven't got to the root of what is going on."

"So, I'm still in danger."

"I don't think so. Unless there is a very good reason for doing so, you won't be attacked again. If you are, it will be seen for what it is."

"An attempted murder?"

Sam didn't answer.

Sophie stood up and put her folder back into her bag.

Sam stood up with her. How dearly he wanted to protect this girl. Before he'd realized it, he'd blurted out the question he really wanted to ask. "Just so that I know; are you and Isaac romantically…" his words trailed away.

Sophie finished his question. "…together?"

"Yes."

"We fight and, perversely, I have become very fond of him. But no. We are not officially boyfriend and girlfriend – although he did ask me to marry him."

"He what?"

She laughed. "He was drunk at the time and won't remember."

"So you two are not an item?"

"No."

Sam was conscious of a feeling profound relief. "Can I walk you to your bike?"

She smiled at him. "I'd appreciate that very much."

"The ax has fallen." Isaac was sitting on the chair of his desk, and had his head in his hands. He groaned. "I'm not sure I can face this."

Sam was lying on Isaac's bed. He had his eyes closed and was tapping his fingertips together. If he'd kept them still, he would have looked like a man in prayer. "When do you have to see them?" he asked.

"At 2pm tomorrow."

"Where?"

"At the faculty of English at Sidgwick."

"Where's that?"

"It's in an old Victorian villa across the river – not far from here."

"Did you ask if you could have a support person with you?"

"Yes. They were a bit put out about it, but relented." Isaac paused. "I was told that both the Head of English and the Head of History will be there." Isaac groaned again.

Sam swung his legs off the bed and stood up. "Well, we've evened up the odds a bit."

"Where are you going?" demanded Isaac.

"We are going downstairs to the bar, and I'm going to buy you a beer."

———————

As intimidating rooms go, Sam had to admit that the one they were in ranked fairly highly. In the rare places there wasn't a bookshelf, the Victorian room was lined with wood paneling. A heavy oak desk sat toward one end. The afternoon was overcast, so there wasn't much light coming from the windows. A green banker's light on the desk was switched on. Its light highlighted the stern expressions of the two professors seated behind the desk.

The two academics aimed their grim expressions first at Isaac, and then at Sam. It was hard not to feel like a ten-year-old standing in front of a headmaster.

Sam resolved immediately to take at least some control over what was going on in the room. He stepped forward with his arm outstretched. "How do you do? I'm Sam Hastings, Isaac's brother. I've come as his moral support."

The two professors appeared nonplussed but were gracious enough to lever themselves out of their chairs and shake Sam's hand, before seating themselves again.

One of the professors steepled his hands together and looked sternly at Isaac. "Kings has had a long and distinguished heritage of scholars; the first Prime Minister of Great Britain, being one of them." He gestured toward the professor sitting beside him. "My colleague and I had some hope that you, Isaac Hastings, might have continued that tradition." The professor sniffed. "But it appears that you have sullied it."

Isaac, with commendable calm nodded. "In what way, sir?"

"In what way!" the professor expostulated, "by blatant plagiarism."

Sam was glad that Isaac was still holding it together. Isaac replied evenly, "Perhaps you could tell me the details, sir."

"What? What! You know damn well. It's your Norsworthy essay. It's plagiarized – almost every word."

"I don't think so, sir."

"Don't be impertinent, Hastings. This is no small matter. What you are looking at is the end of any academic ambitions you might once have held. This matter will have to be reported to the Dean of Studies, and you have to expect he will expel you from the university."

Sam decided to diffuse the atmosphere. "May we sit down, sir? I can see two spare chairs by the window."

"What?" The professor frowned. "I suppose so. Bring them across."

Sam and Isaac did so. As they did, Sam was thinking furiously. He sat down and risked asking a question. "May I ask, sir: what is the evidence for this alleged plagiarism?" Sam emphasized the word 'alleged.'

The professor reached forward to the desk and picked up a piece of paper. "This was sent to me by the Dean of Studies. He was concerned that the grades given for the Norsworthy essays were in line with those given in previous years. So he sent me three essays that had been previously entered to assist us in our moderation." He looked at Isaac. "One of them is your essay, almost word for word, but with the name of another student on top; a student from two years ago." The professor threw the paper he was holding back on the desk.

Sam got to his feet and held out a hand. "May I look at the letter from the Dean, sir."

The professor was now clearly irritated. He waved a hand. "If you must."

Sam picked up the letter. It was embossed with the university crest and looked authentic in every respect – except one.

Sam cleared his throat. "This letter has the details and name of the Dean of Studies, but it hasn't actually been signed by him."

The professor scowled. He grabbed the paper from Sam, scanned it briefly, then put it back on the desk. "That is just an over-sight. The Dean probably dictated it to his secretary and told her to send it off."

"I don't think that is an accident sir. I believe this letter is a fake, and that someone is trying to set Isaac up."

The other professor sat bolt upright in his chair. "What makes you think that?"

"We've had a suspicion that someone has being trying to discredit Isaac for some time." Sam paused. "Evidently you were both sent an anonymous letter claiming Isaac was a plagiarist."

Sam was gratified to see the first hint of uncertainty in the eyes of the professor leading the interview. He pressed on. "Isaac was so concerned, that he made me aware of it, which is one of the reasons I came to Cambridge."

The professor put his elbows on the desk. "Just what are you suggesting?"

Isaac took over from Sam. "I realized someone might try and cause me mischief over the Norsworthy essay. I'd made no secret of the fact that I was entering an essay and was in some hope of winning."

The professor grunted. "Go on."

"So I submitted an essay I'd already written three years ago, with some small modifications, corrections, and improvements."

The professor's eyes were now wide open. "And just where is this essay?"

Sam picked up a journal that he'd placed beside his chair. "You'll find it in here sir. It's Isaac's first published work."

"What's that?"

"It is from your history library sir. It's the 'Journal of Military History,' an edition from three years ago. I understand it is a prestigious American journal." Sam turned to the inside pages. "The index is here, and the information about each contributor is also given." Sam read aloud: "'Isaac Hastings is a young scholar who has just been accepted at Cambridge University. This is his first paper heralding what promises to be a distinguished career. He is uniquely qualified to write about the subject of his paper because he lived in Malaya during the recent Indonesian confrontation as a child.'"

"Give me that," said the professor.

Sam handed the journal across to him.

The professor turned to the article. "The Indonesian Confrontation… from the Perspective of a Prostitute." He raised his eyebrows. "It's got a different title – an arresting one, I might say." Then he started to read. After a few seconds, he smiled, leaned back in his chair, and took off his glasses. "Well," he said. "That changes everything." He smiled. "I cannot tell you how relieved I am to see this. Quite honestly, I can now tell you that the alternative was breaking my heart." He jabbed his glasses toward Isaac. "You have had your ups and downs, but it's been obvious to us that you are a good student. We don't want to lose you." He turned to his colleague. "What do think, Claude? Have we heard enough?"

The other professor frowned. "So, you are suggesting that someone burgled your apartment and photographed your essay?"

"Probably, sir. Yes."

"And then someone retyped the essay and got it to us with a fake document?"

"Yes."

The professor shook his head, but it was in wonderment rather than disbelief.

The lead professor repeated his question to his colleague. "Are you satisfied, Claude?"

The other professor nodded. "I'm quite satisfied." He looked at Isaac and smiled. "You and your brother have hatched an extraordinary scheme, and I'm sorry that you needed to do so. For our part, let me assure you that your essay will be accorded all due respect."

Sam had no idea what that meant, but he nodded his thanks.

"However," continued the professor, "This dreadful business does raise a host of other questions. Who is doing this mischief, and why? And how have they managed to do what they have done?"

Sam had been wrestling with the same questions for some time. "All that we can say, sir, is that we rather suspected something was afoot. That's why Isaac was very public about having written the essay – even saying that it was being guarded by Ralph."

"Who is Ralph?"

"A garden gnome, sir. We wanted people to find it."

The professor didn't smile. "So these people, whoever they are, have the means to gain access to private accommodation in the college and…" he waved the alleged letter from the Dean of Studies, "have the ability to forge letters from the Dean." He shook his head. "Whoever they are, they are not to be underestimated. I think we should call the police."

"So do I sir. Any publicity caused by the police being involved should slow them down." He paused. "I just ask one thing."

"What's that?"

"I don't want the reporting to reflect badly on Isaac in any way."

The professor nodded. "I'll do all I can to keep his name out of the press." He pushed himself out of the chair and extended his hand.

As they all shook hands, the professor continued to speak. "You've made me a very relieved man – both of you. And rest assured, Isaac, we'll now be guarding your back – at least from the academic angle. I'm just sorry I didn't smell a rat when we got the anonymous letters about plagiarism. My apologies." He waved them away. "Now go and enjoy yourselves. Goodness knows; you deserve it."

Chapter 18

S ophie squeezed herself into the call box in the hallway of Girton College and dialed a number she knew by heart. To her intense relief, it was answered. Roslyn was quite often away on some project or other and was not always able to be contacted.

"Hi Roslyn, it's Sophie."

Roslyn's energy came surging down the phone line. "Hello, lovely one. Wonderful to hear from you. Are you still wowing Cambridge with your brilliance?"

Sophie laughed. "There are rather a lot of brilliant people here, so my star is not so easily seen."

"Rubbish. You're fabulous. What can I do for you?"

Sophie drew a deep breath. "Doesn't your dad do something really important in the legal world – things to do with the Civil Service?"

Roslyn replied cautiously. "Yes. Why do you ask?"

"There have been some disturbing things going on here in Cambridge that I think should come to the attention of the Security Service. But I don't know how to get hold of them, or who to trust."

There was silence on the end of the phone for a while. After a few seconds, Roslyn's voice came back. "Are you safe, Sophie?"

"I… I'm not sure."

"Tell me."

"Someone tried to push me in front of a truck."

"What!"

"And more stuff has happened."

"What's going on?"

"Well, that's it. I don't really know. But it's been suggested that it may be because I've been keeping the company of a Marxist student, who, mercifully, is coming to his senses." She paused. "The student's brother has suggested that I've been targeted because I'm steering his brother away from Marxism." Even as she said it, she could hear the catch in her own voice. "Roslyn, lots of crazy stuff has been happening."

"You've told me enough, Sophie. I'll call Dad straight away. Expect to hear from him, or someone, in the next hour or so." She paused. "Sophie, you will be dealing with people who live in a very strange world. They can do things that are a little odd. Keep on your toes."

Sophie was far from sure what she meant, but those few words told her that there was a great deal about Roslyn and her father that she didn't know.

"Thanks, Roslyn. I knew you'd come through."

After the phone call, Sophie stayed in the common room so she could be in reach of the phone and tried to read. She was plowing her way through Arnold Toynbee's '*A Study of History*,' volume II.'

Forty minutes later, a student came into the common room and called out to her. "Someone's on the phone for you Soph."

She made her way to the call booth and tentatively picked up the receiver. "Sophie Hunter speaking."

A woman's voice answered. "Good evening Miss Hunter. Thank you for your application for the position we advertised. Miss Roslyn, or her Managing Director will be available to interview you at Ely, midday tomorrow at the tearooms by Babylon Bridge."

For a moment, confusion swirled its giddy way through her brain, but she picked up enough of its essence to reply. "Ely. Tomorrow?"

"Yes. Can you make the interview?"

The small city of Ely was only fourteen miles to the northeast of Cambridge. "I can."

"Good. I'll schedule you in. Oh, and Miss Hunter, please bring with you any documents you need to support your case."

The phone then went dead.

———

Sophie elected to take the train rather than the bus to Ely, and she was glad that she did. The train journey was pretty. For the most part, the train carried her through the water meadows and willows near the banks of the River Cam, which eventually flowed into the River Great Ouse – the river that wound its way through Ely.

Sophie loved Ely. The medieval cathedral town had been built on an island surrounded by marshland. The marshes had since been drained and become the most fertile agricultural land in England. Ely, however, seemed to be stuck in a time warp. It was a small city nestled in the shadow of the cathedral, and its medieval petticoat could still be seen. Places such as 'the almonry' and 'the grange' still existed.

She was in good time, so she walked to Babylon Bridge and took in the view over the water basins where a motley collection of narrow boats was berthed. The tearooms were just the other side of the bridge. Sophie found a table and sat down. She'd not brought any paperwork with her, because she had none, other than an envelope of photographs.

"Miss Hunter?"

Sophie looked up with a start. A middle-aged man with a pencil mustache stood by her table. His dark hair was brushed backward over his scalp, and he was dressed in a blue pinstripe suit. He was, in every way, unremarkable. However, the searching directness of his gaze gave warning of significant intelligence. She smiled. "You are Miss Roslyn, I presume?"

"I am. But I also go by the name of Oliver Tremain. How do

you do." His handshake was firm and brief. "Shall I order tea, or would you like an early lunch?"

"Tea is fine."

He sat himself down and asked Sophie to tell him about herself. She could almost hear him calibrating her in his mind, assessing every detail. Eventually, he nodded. "Now tell me, Miss Hunter, why do you wish to speak to me?"

Sophie put her teacup down with exaggerated care. "Before I say anything, Mr. Tremain, can you tell me who you are?"

"Certainly. I am a personal friend of Roslyn's father and have worked with him occasionally in a professional sense. He told me that you were pushed in front of a truck. Would you like to call Roslyn and mention my name?"

Sophie shook her head. "No, I don't think that is necessary." She paused. "I take it that you work for the Intelligence Service, or something like that?"

He smiled. "Yes, something like that."

Sophie spent the next twenty minutes sharing all that had transpired in Cambridge concerning Isaac, from the time he was first attacked. When she'd finished, Mr. Tremain stared out of the window for a long time, saying nothing. Eventually, he said. "Do you have the photographs?"

"Yes." She handed the envelope to him.

He took them out, inspected them briefly, and then put the envelope away inside his jacket pocket.

"On the surface of things, there seem to be two narratives going on." He ticked them off on his fingers. "First: there is evidence of someone harboring real malice toward Isaac. Second: there is evidence of persons unknown, who are not keen that you de-radicalize Isaac." He looked up at her. "Have I read that rightly?"

"Yes."

He interlaced his hands and tapped his forefingers on his lips. "What is your take on it?"

"What concerns me is that these people are persistent, trained in unconventional skills, and are well resourced." She looked at Mr.

Tremain. "That suggests this should fall under your brief. But, to be quite honest, I simply want Isaac, Sam, and myself to be safe."

Mr. Tremain nodded. "I will make inquiries and see what I can do." He fished in his wallet and handed her a card. She read it with a smile. 'Oliver Tremain, Professional Career Counseling Services'. A telephone number followed the words. No address was given. Sophie wondered how many other cards he had, that listed different 'professional services.' He continued to speak as he tucked his wallet away. "Ring that number at any time. The answering service will ask for your number. Give it, and then hang up. You will be called back within the next five minutes."

Sophie heard the instructions with a growing sense of disbelief. She shook her head, only half believing the strange world she'd chosen to walk into.

"Will you have time to stay and look at the cathedral?"

Sophie shook her head. "I should be getting back." She sighed. "Which is a pity, because Ely is probably my favorite cathedral. It seems so light and airy, particularly the Lady Chapel. It's such a peaceful place."

Mr. Tremain nodded. "Peace can be hard to find." He smiled. "May I drive you back to Cambridge? It's on my way to London."

"There's no need. I have a return train ticket. But thank you for offering." In truth, the thought of spending another twenty minutes with the deeply unsettling Mr. Tremain was more than she could bear.

He nodded and stood up to leave.

Sophie shook his hand, and Mr. Tremain walked away, as silently as he had come.

Tony Chester-Smith listened to the record-player: shhhh click; shhhh click; shhhh click. The wretched automatic switch-off was not working again. He winced in pain as he heaved himself out of his chair and limped over to the player. The grand music of Wagner, that had once lifted his soul, was beginning to fail in its magic. He lifted the playing arm onto its cradle and put the record back into its sleeve.

He plumped himself back down in his seat and stared moodily at the mantelpiece. His British biathlon medal was still there, reminding him of what might have been… of what should have been. He reflected back on the last month. It had not been a good one. The biggest change was that he had been recalled to London and was now back in his old flat. At first, he'd been terrified that people were suspicious he might be a double agent, but nothing sinister had transpired. There had been no grilling. His manager at MI5 had thanked him for giving him the names of two students who had allowed themselves to be radicalized – two who, in reality, had been supplied by his Russian handler. However, they were small fry. MI5 had visited both young men and frightened them enough with the reality of treason, that they'd both folded completely and told everything they knew. Tony very much suspected that both would soon be residents of London's commuter belt and be busying themselves accumulating stocks and shares. He did, however, take credit for one spy that had been recruited for Russia, even though Stan had done the work. But secretly, Tony was doubtful about the quality of even this recruit. He'd lived long enough to know that ideology can trickle away, like good intentions, in the young who have not yet been tested by life.

He banged his right thigh in irritation. It was an action that did nothing to dull the pain in his leg. Whilst he was at Cambridge, he'd gone to Addenbrooke's Hospital in the desperate hope that some new research might improve the mobility of his leg. They told him it was impossible. The doctor had tried to cheer him up with some black humor. "Just hope that we have another war. That's when we really get funds to research broken limbs."

Tony hadn't laughed.

He was under no illusions, however. Things were dangerous. It was time to pull his head in and lay low. He'd gone too far in pursuing Isaac Hastings, and he knew it. And all he'd achieved was to raise suspicions. He pursed his lips. Suspicions in his game did not fade away easily. The real curse was that he'd nothing to show for it. Tony hadn't managed to land a killer blow on Isaac Hastings. His frustration at this failure had been further fueled when he learned that Hasting's brother, Sam, had played a key role in thwarting his plans.

Damn them both.

But if the pain of living had taught him anything, it was that opportunities came to those who were patient.

And so he resolved to wait.

Chapter 19

Cleopatra leaned her raised bow into the spiteful waves and sent spray sizzling across the foredeck. Her forward 4.5 inch gun gleamed wet in the dim light of an overcast day.

Sam was on Starboard Watch and they were currently on duty, guiding *Cleopatra* amongst the islands of the Hebrides, the rugged islands off the west coast of Scotland. She was doing what she did best – hunting. *Cleopatra* was on patrol looking for Russian submarines.

Midshipman Sam Hastings was on the bridge of the frigate trying to keep out of everyone's way. It hadn't taken him long to learn that he barely registered on the food chain when it came to significance on an operational ship. He was there to watch and learn, which in essence meant being a lackey to any officer who barked a command. He was on the bridge with the Second Officer who had the ship. The coxswain, a petty officer, had the helm. Behind them, the navigating officer hovered around the large chart table. Although the bridge was set down low on *Cleopatra's* flush deck, its front and side windows afforded excellent visibility.

The rating standing on guard at the top of the companionway

into the bridge came smartly to attention and barked, "Captain on deck."

Commander James Holman swung through the companionway with practiced ease. He nodded to the Second Officer and growled, "Keep the ship, Number Two." Sam had learned to judge the captain's mood over the weeks they had been at sea and gauged the captain to be in good spirits. This wasn't always the case. Holman was sufficiently close to 'Colman,' the famous maker of mustard that the captain was referred to as 'Captain Mustard' behind his back. He didn't suffer fools gladly.

The Second Officer was holding binoculars to his eyes. "We are steering, 010. Wind 18 knots at 085. The Wasp is twenty miles to the northeast. He's just reported a contact."

The captain grunted. "Patch his comms to the bridge. Let's hear what he has to say."

Cleopatra had flown her lightweight helicopter, a Westland Wasp, off from her stern. It was currently dropping a sonar buoy down on a winch, listening for trouble.

Sam overheard the encrypted voice on the intercom. "Stag 02. Confirmed contact. Wait. Out."

The captain moved to the front consul. Sam could see the glint of battle in his eyes. "What's the latest from Benbecula?" he barked.

Benbecula was a low, flat island squeezed between the islands of North and South Uist. Amongst other things, it housed a tracking station. The Navigation Office spoke from behind them. "They've plotted five Russian subs ringing Scotland. They suspect more."

The captain picked up a pair of binoculars. "If the sleepy citizens of Britain only knew." He stared out across the starboard bow. "Can you see the Wasp?"

The Officer of the Watch shook his head. "No sir."

"Damn. I hate waiting." The captain turned to Sam. "Mid. Get me a mug of cocoa."

Sam clattered down the companionway to the galley. Hot water was always available for drinks, so his mission didn't take him long.

Cleopatra was a comfortable ship. She was sea-kindly and air-conditioned. She'd been air-conditioned, as had all the Leander class frigates, to improve her nuclear, biological, and chemical defense. There were no portholes.

As Sam made his way back on to the bridge, the speakers came to life. "Stag 02. We have the signature of a big submarine."

"You've interrogated the 'friend or foe?'"

"Affirmative. No friend. Contact is 300 feet long."

The First Mate whistled. "She's big."

The tinny voice from the helicopter continued. "We can confirm signature. She is a Russian Yorsh. Repeat: a Russian Yorsh."

"The captain swore under his breath. "Russia's latest nuclear powered submarine. What's her tonnage?"

Sam knew the answer, so he dared to speak. "5,000 tons sir. Twice our size."

"Thank you, Mid." The captain picked up the handpiece. "Depth and position?"

"Eight nautical miles due west of Tiree. Stationary on the sea floor at 230 feet."

"Damn and blast his impertinence. He's well within British Sovereign Waters." The captain banged the consul with his fist. Then he turned and made his way to the navigation chart, grabbed a wax chinagraph pencil and ringed the submarine's rough position on the Perspex covered chart.

Sam followed him like an obedient puppy, still holding the captain's cocoa.

"Damn, damn, damn. What to do? Is he poised to attack one of our nuclear subs coming out from Clyde, or is he simply testing us?"

The Second Officer joined him at the chart table. "Sadly, we can't torpedo him, sir, without starting an international incident."

The captain scowled. "Dammit. We are a warship, Number Two. We can't just sit idly by in a militarily aggressive situation, singing kumbaya. Ask for the submarine's exact position and recall the Wasp."

The speaker came alive, giving the red, blue, and green numbers of the Decca positioning system.

By this stage, the captain was back at the consul with the navigation officer. As no one was doing anything with the position fixing,

Sam picked up the chinagraph and plotted the exact position of the submarine on the chart.

When he'd finished, the captain and navigation officer came up behind him. "So what do we do, Mid?" He clapped Sam on the shoulder. "Do we start a war, or do we advertise our impotence? These are the decisions you will have to make if you get your own command."

The Navigation Officer said, "We could call Fleet Command, sir."

"Damn-it, George. This incident is going to be over in fifteen minutes. We don't have the time."

Sam had been using the last few minutes to think about what he would do, and so he felt emboldened to say, "I have an idea, sir."

The navigation officer growled. "Keep it to yourself, Mid."

The captain laughed. It wasn't quite a laugh of derision, but it came close. "Tell me your idea, Mid."

"I'd recall the Wasp. It can carry either a torpedo or a depth charge. I'd load it with a depth charge set to explode at twenty feet, and drop it on top of him."

The captain frowned. "What's the lethal zone for our depth charge?"

"It's rated at 100 feet sir." Sam was grateful that he knew the details. "Although we have to assume it is less for a new nuclear powered sub."

"Why explode it at twenty feet?"

"The sub is sitting at 230 feet and probably stands 60 feet tall. A depth charge could be lethal at 100 feet. Allow an extra 50 feet for safety."

The captain furrowed his brow, then nodded. "That's a good idea, Mid. Where did you learn that?"

"Sam grinned. "I used to put fire-crackers down rabbit holes. It frightened the rabbits out of the other holes which I'd netted."

"Well it's a damn fine idea." He called to the Officer of the Watch. "Call the Armament's Officer. I want the Wasp loaded as soon as it lands." He rubbed his hands together. "Captain has the ship."

Perhaps it was his imagination, but *Cleopatra* seemed to have a spring in her step. Her pennant, F28, streamed stiffly from the yardarm as she surged through the Scottish waters.

Sam listened to the commands as they came through the intercom with both excitement and trepidation.

"Tell the Armament's Officer that he will be riding in the Wasp with the Load Master. They are both to verify that the depth charge is set for twenty feet, before it is dropped." The captain was now pacing up and down the bridge – all thought of a cup of cocoa now forgotten.

Sam kept out of his way and stood by the chart table.

The speaker came to life again. "Stag 02 ready for take off."

"Stag 02; QFE 1010; wind 085 at 20 knots. Cloud base 1,500 feet. Happy Hunting."

The sound of the Wasp's beating rotors could be heard faintly on the bridge, and then quickly faded away.

It only took a few minutes for the Wasp to be on station. "Stag 02 overhead target."

The captain lifted the handpiece to his mouth. "Loadmaster. Check twenty feet: Two-zero: on the depth charge."

"Two-zero confirmed, sir."

"Armament Officer. Confirm two-zero on the depth charge."

"Two-zero confirmed, sir."

"The explosion is shallow, so move to safety immediately after engagement."

"Wilco."

"Acquire target."

"Target acquired."

"Fire when ready."

There was a pause.

"Depth charge away."

"Move to safety but stay on station. Drop the sonar and monitor."

"Safety; stay and monitor."

The captain was looking through the binoculars. "Dammit. I can't see anything. What about you, Number Two?"

"Nothing sir."

An eternity seemed to pass. Then the communication speaker came to life. "The Yorsh is moving. Confirm movement. Turning west and accelerating."

More minutes passed. "The pilot from the Wasp spoke again. "Target moving west into the Atlantic, now at thirty-two knots."

The Second Officer let out a mild expletive. "Thirty-two knots. That's quick."

The captain laughed. "That's sent him packing – hopefully with a headache. Set revolutions for twenty knots and make for Clyde. It's time to go home." He turned round to Sam. "Mid. Where's my cocoa?"

"I'm afraid it's gone cold sir. Can I get you another?"

The watch had changed at midday, but as they would be in port within a few hours, no one off watch sought out their bunks. The First Officer now had the ship. Sam saluted him as he came onto the bridge. "Permission to stay on the bridge, sir."

He received the usual reply. "Stay out of the way."

"Sir." Sam stepped away.

The captain also stayed on the bridge. He was in a good mood. "Damn shame the Navy has just abolished the 'up spirits' eh, Number One. The ship deserves a tot of rum."

Indeed, the British Navy had just abolished the 400-year-old tradition of metering out a tot of rum for all hands each day between 11am and noon. The old hands, particularly, did not appreciate its abolition. Sam, however, thought it was probably a wise decision. Ships were now highly technical, lethal machines, and sailors needed all their wits about them.

Cleopatra's engines were driving the ship along at a comfortable 20 knots. She could, of course, go a lot faster. Her two Babcock and Wilcox boilers fed steam turbines capable of pushing the ship along at 27 knots. But she'd come to the end of her two-week deployment amongst the Hebridean Islands and was now heading to Her

Majesty's Naval Base, Clyde, which was sited at Faslane on Gare Loch.

Clyde had become the home of the navy's four nuclear submarines, all of which had recently been armed with Trident missiles. This corner of Scotland had therefore become an area of key strategic interest. Sam looked out of the windows of the bridge. Whilst the grim game of nuclear brinkmanship was being played out in these waters, Sam had to admit that the area was breathtakingly beautiful. Both sea and land pierced each other with long sea-lochs and mountainous mulls.

Cleopatra made her way around the Mull of Kintyre, around the Isle of Arran, and up into the sheltered waters of the Firth of Clyde. Forested hillsides gave way to gorse and heather on the higher ground – all now partly shrouded in mist.

The First Officer had the binoculars to his eyes, looking for the channel markers. "Revolutions for 12 knots. Steer 335."

The coxswain turned the wheel. "Twelve knots; 335."

The frigate swung into the long narrow confines of Gare Loch.

Sam was so absorbed in watching everything; he was startled to hear the captain say to him. "How would you bring her in, Mid? You've got two boat lengths of wharf running due north, and a strong easterly wind trying to blow you off it."

Sam's mind worked furiously. "I, er, would drive in at a shallow angle, bow first, and drop a forward spring. Once that is attached, I'd push forward gently, so the ship would swing in. Then I'd make fast both bow and stern lines."

The captain turned to the First Officer. "What do you think, Number One? Is he a sailor?"

"Pretty close. I'd also have the helm hard over to port when we push forward."

"Make it so, Number One. You have the ship." He turned to Sam. "Midshipman; watch and learn."

An hour later when the ship's engines had stopped and all was made shipshape. Sam headed to the gangplank. To say that he was feeling euphoric, was probably an overstatement, but he was nonetheless delighted with all that had happened during the morning, and the part that he had played in it all.

He didn't really notice the Royal Naval Policemen standing on the dock beside the gangplank. Both were Warrant Officers.

He smiled when he saw them. "Good afternoon, gentlemen."

They did not smile back. "You are Midshipman Sam Hastings?"

Sam furrowed his brow. "Yes."

One of the Warrant Officers reached forward with a pair of handcuffs. "Midshipman Hastings; you are under arrest."

Chapter 20

S am sat alone in one of the most depressing rooms he'd ever been in. It had a small window with wire reinforced frosted glass in it. It was set high in order to let in as much Scottish light as possible – and light was never at much of a premium in Scotland.

The interior wall had been painted khaki green to shoulder height. Above that, it was a dirty cream. Four chairs sat around a tubular steel table. The room reeked of despair.

He'd been there thirty minutes before the door opened and let in four men. One was a Royal Naval Policeman. He stayed by the door. The only man he recognized was the naval lawyer who had been tasked to represent him. Sam had met the man the day before, but had not yet had a chance to talk to him. The lawyer sat himself down next to Sam. The other two men sat opposite. They introduced themselves as Lieutenant Carstairs, and Petty Officer Machin.

Carstairs took out a folder, opened it and scowled at Sam. "Do you own a light blue, portable, manual typewriter," he looked at his notes "...made by Brother Industries?"

Sam looked at him cautiously. "Yes." Two years earlier, Isaac had complained about Sam's poor handwriting so much that he'd finally bought the Japanese typewriter and taught himself to touch-type.

"And did you catch the train to Helensburgh for some R and R just prior to your deployment on *Cleopatra* 17 days ago?"

"Yes," said Sam. He was now slightly irritated. "These facts can be easily verified. "What exactly am I accused of?"

Carstairs sucked in his lips and took his time replying. "You are accused of recklessly endangering national security by gross negligence and carelessness."

Sam scoffed. "I don't know anything that is of the remotest interest to those threatening our national security. What are you talking about?"

Carstairs reached down into his briefcase and extracted a sheaf of papers held together in one corner by a clip. It took a while for Sam to recognize it. It was his own study notes, but the sheaf of papers had been badly water-damaged. From the splattering of the ink, Sam could only assume it had been rained on. "Hey," he said. "They're my notes on telecommunications and RT procedure. How did you get them?"

"You confirm, then, that they are yours."

His lawyer tried to whisper in his ear, but Sam was having none of it. "Of course it's mine. Where did you find it?"

"Did you realize it was lost?"

"No. I can't see how it could have been."

Carstairs put on a pair of latex gloves and began turning the pages. It obviously wasn't the first time he'd opened them because the pages showed signs of having been forced apart after being stuck together with water. "Let me draw your attention to page five of your typed notes."

Sam watched with bewilderment as the pages turned. The first thing he noted was that half way down the page, someone had typed. 'TOP SECRET' in capitals and in red. Carstairs cleared his throat and started to read.

The encryption equipment used by NATO is made by Crypto AG. The word is that this Swiss company – located in Steinhausen – is part owned by the CIA, and they have engineered their cipher devices so they can listen in to conversations through the back door. There is a strong suspicion that the CIA has done this in partnership with BND (the West German Federal Intelligence Service). Certainly, the Russians and the Chinese don't trust it, and neither, I suspect, should we.

Carstairs tapped the document. "Forensics tells us that this was typed on your typewriter."

Sam's lawyer leaned forward to speak to Sam, but Sam forestalled him. "This is the first time I've seen that paragraph – or that 'top secret' bullshit. I didn't write that."

His lawyer leaned back, apparently satisfied with Sam's answer.

Carstairs pursed his lips in obvious disbelief. "It was written on your typewriter. How do you explain that?"

"I can't."

Carstairs nodded slowly. "Writing this sensitive information wouldn't have been so damaging had not this folder been found behind a bus stop in a sodden mess at Helensburgh. One of our seamen saw it and handed it in, when a local citizen pointed it out."

Nothing was said for quite some time. Then Carstairs continued. "Needless to say, this sort of information could cause incalculable damage if it got into the wrong hands… and it may have already got there."

"But it's not my information. I've never heard of Crypto AG."

Carstairs sighed and put the folder back into his briefcase. Then he nodded to Sam's lawyer. "I'll leave him to you," and stood to leave.

Sam called out in alarm, "What happens now?"

Carstairs paused halfway to the door. "I very much suspect, Midshipman Hastings, that unless something spectacular happens, you will be facing a court-martial in *Cleopatra's* home port."

Sam was aghast. "What? In Portsmouth?"

"Yes."

Tony sat in his armchair, conducting the orchestrated version of *Wesendonck Lieder* with his fountain pen. It was amazing how much better his leg was feeling since his trip to Scotland. He smiled to himself. Things couldn't have gone better. What made things even sweeter was that he'd done it all himself. He'd not needed to call in any favors from his Russian handler, whom, he was very sure, would have given him no help at all.

He'd found out that Sam Hastings had been sent to HMNB Clyde in Scotland for a training course. His own ship was due to join him later, taking him away from his course for two weeks on a brief deployment to the west and north of Scotland. Hastings would therefore retain his room in the accommodation block of the shore-based wardroom for officers. The lout would be away from his private quarters for fifteen days.

The only tricky bit of the entire operation had been gaining access to Hastings' room in the wardroom. In the end, he'd secured the use of a Commander's naval uniform from the entertainment industry, of all places. He'd found out which room was Hastings', then approached the Officer-of-the-Day on duty at the wardroom, a lowly first lieutenant, and asked for the spare key to his room, saying, he'd locked his keys inside.

It was as simple as that.

After that, the plan was simple. He donned gloves and typed the incriminating paragraph on a section of notes where he felt it might best fit in. Tony then returned the key and changed back to baggy tweeds in a public toilet.

After catching the train the short distance to Helensburgh, he'd had to stand in the rain at the bus stop for ages until he saw a sailor about to cross the road to the station. "Hey wee laddie. "Ganen yourself over 'ere." He'd pointed to the rain-soaked document. "Och, it's one of ye sailor mannie's writings. Confidential, I'm thinking. Can ye fetch it home, laddie?" Then, tipping his hat, he'd limped away on his stick.

Tony smiled at the memory of the broad Scottish accent he'd put on. He was good with accents.

And now, it was just a case of waiting to see how things worked out. It was difficult to conceive of anything other than the complete destruction of Hastings' Naval career. The drivel he'd typed about

Crypto AG had only been partly true. He'd simply voiced a suspicion the Russians had, but it was only a suspicion. And the Russians were always suspicious. It couldn't really be true, could it?

The CIA Station Chief in London leaned on the Admiral's desk with both hands and glared at his MI5 counterpart. "In the name of all that is…" the Chief was quite unable to get his words out. He tried again. "Just how did this information get out? Tell me that."

The Admiral picked up his pen and studied it. "We are not at all sure that it has got out, Adrian. His exact words were: 'The word is.' In no way can that be construed as definite."

The Station Chief banged the desk with his fist. "Well sounds too damn definite to me. Where did this man; a midshipman, for goodness sake; find out?"

"We don't know."

The Station Chief stood up with a grunt of exasperation and looked moodily out the window. "We are talking about the greatest secret of Western intelligence."

"I'm fully aware of that, Adrian. Do try and stay calm."

"Calm!"

For a long while, only the sound of traffic nosing their way down Curzon Street could be heard. The Admiral leaned on his elbows, still apparently inspecting his fountain pen. "We could try and turn this affair to our advantage?"

"I don't see how."

"Just think for a moment. What would be the greatest win for Western intelligence?"

"Tell me."

"It would be Russia choosing to use Crypto AG technology."

"And just how would we do that now that this blasted midshipmen has told them we might be looking at their information through the back door?"

The Admiral lifted his chin and stretched his neck. "We do it by making it obvious that we want them to think we can look at their information through the back door. Let's make it clear to them that we are desperate for them *not* to use Crypto AG technology."

The CIA Station Chief frowned and slumped in a chair. "Tell me more."

"If we make the trial of this midshipman a bit of a show trial – not making it too obvious of course, the Russians will smell a rat." He paused. "We can also give a bit of information to the Russians through one of their spies."

The CIA Chief raised an eyebrow. "Do you know any of their spies?"

"Of course. We have one of them working here at Leconfield House."

"How on earth did you find out?"

The Admiral smiled enigmatically. "We have, as you Americans say, a spook for our spooks, and he's very good – if distressingly principled. Let's leave it at that."

"This show trial thing: You realize that we would have to find the young midshipman guilty."

"Yes."

The autumn leaves were beginning to fall, patterning the footpaths with the last sigh of summer. Isaac was walking with Sophie along Bridge Street. They'd agreed to meet at the square by Magdalene Bridge and walk into town together. Isaac was a bit late as he'd stopped to collect his mail. He was pleased to see a letter from Sam. It was now in his jacket pocket waiting to be read.

Sophie wheeled her bike as she walked beside him. Their conversation had mellowed over the years and was now one of real friendship. Isaac could tell, however, that Sophie was nervous of romance, but at the same time, was courting its possibility. She was slowly opening up like a flower. Isaac reflected ruefully that theirs had been a long and slow courtship. Sophie was now beginning her final year, and Isaac had just started the second year of his PhD. He was paying his way by tutoring. It was a privilege not given to many, and Isaac was fully aware of it. He suspected that it was due, in no small part, to the professors trying to make amends. Isaac's life had changed. He spent longer on his own, reading and researching. Isaac's revolutionary persona was gone, although he still retained the round glasses. He was now cleanly shaven, and, if he wore a hat, it was a French-style beret.

When they reached the junction with St. John's Street, Isaac started to head down it, but Sophie dragged him twenty yards beyond until they were standing in front of The Round Church.

"Have you ever been inside?" she asked.

Isaac shook his head. "It's not really been on my bucket list."

"Come and have a look. It's amazing. The church dates from 1130. Just imagine that."

Isaac allowed himself to be pulled inside the church.

The inside was, indeed, remarkable. A row of massive Norman arches stood in a circle. A second row of small arches stood on top of them. The central tower above let in light through small clerestory windows. Despite himself, Isaac was enchanted. The church was simple and stolid… and reeked of history.

The two of them sat down in some chairs that had been left out, and for a long time, said nothing.

"It's lovely," conceded Isaac. "But I'm still not sure Christianity is my thing."

Sophie didn't respond immediately. She seemed to be soaking in the soul of the place. Eventually, she replied. "The real issue concerning Christianity is this: Is it true? Nothing else really matters. If God really has revealed himself through Jesus Christ, then God is worthy of our full commitment. If God has not, then Christianity is worthy of nothing."

"But what about the church's abuse in history – the inquisition and the Crusades?"

Sophie waved a hand. "The bad behavior of fallible church institutions is irrelevant to the central issue."

"But surely, hypocrites…"

"Are irrelevant. And whether or not you believe you can live a moral life without being a Christian; is irrelevant. And saying that

Christianity is boring or inconvenient to your lifestyle, is similarly irrelevant. The real issue is: Is it true? That's what you need to check out."

Isaac held up his hands. "Okay. I'll check it out." Seeking to change the subject, he said, "I got a letter from Sam this morning."

"Great. How's he going? What did he say?"

"I haven't read it yet."

Sophie shook his arm. "Then read it."

Isaac took out the letter, opened the envelope and started to read. As he did, he felt the blood drain from his face. He couldn't believe what he was reading.

Sophie looked at him with concern. "You look as if you've seen a ghost. What's the matter?"

Isaac frowned and looked at her without comprehension. "Sam says that he is confined at Her Majesty's Naval Base, Clyde. Evidently, he's facing a court-martial for recklessly endangering national security." He shook his head. "I don't believe it. That's not Sam at all."

Sophie had her mouth open. She managed to blurt out, "Neither do I. What on earth's happened?"

Isaac got to his feet. "There's a telephone number on the letter. I'm going to call it now. The phone box is just down the street."

"I'm coming with you," said Sophie.

After a long wait, and feeding endless coins into the phone box, Isaac heard Sam's voice. Isaac thrust a five-pound note at Sophie who was squeezed beside him in the phone box. "Sophie. Can you get me some more coins?"

She nodded and left the phone box.

Isaac gripped the phone with two hands. "Sam, how are you? What on earth has happened?"

He was both relieved and devastated to hear Sam's tired voice at the end of the phone. Sam gave him the details of his situation with a masterful economy of words. His voice sounded flat and dispirited.

Isaac came to an instant decision. "I'm coming up there so we can have a decent talk."

Sam coughed a laugh of derision. "No. You can't do that. You've got tutorials and things."

"Sam, I'll find a way. I'm coming." He paused. "And I'll be bringing you the Scorpion Stone. It's my pledge to you."

"No Isaac. Don't bring it. It will only be confiscated. I'm a prisoner here."

"Well, my being there will be me fulfilling our vow. How do I get there?"

Sam told him.

Sophie returned in time for Isaac to push more coins into the phone box and keep the connection. Isaac nodded his thanks and said to her, "Sophie, can you take two tutorials for me, Thursday morning and Friday evening? I've got to catch the train to Scotland."

She shook her head. "No. I'm an undergraduate. I'm not qualified."

Isaac shook his head and grabbed her by the hand. "You are the most intelligent, sensible, and competent person I've ever met. You'll have my notes. They are typed and easy to read. Please say yes."

Sophie looked him in the eyes for some time, and then said "All right. If you get your notes now and prep me, I'll do my best."

After some more talking, Isaac hung up. Then he turned to Sophie, put his arms around her, and started to weep. He wept at Sam's despair. He wept at the brutal unfairness of life. And he wept at his own impotence to do anything to help.

Chapter 21

Isaac entered one of the most miserable rooms he'd ever been in. His brother was the only occupant.

Sam was standing by the wall under a small window. He was dressed in his naval uniform. Its crisp neatness was at odds with his surroundings. Sam's face was pale and pinched, but he managed a smile. "You've lost the Marxist look."

Isaac nodded. "Marxism didn't bring the civility and justice I'd hoped for."

"Sophie's influence?"

"My own decision, but Sophie made me look at the evidence honestly."

"Honestly?"

"I'd got pretty good at shouting into my own sound shell – only hearing words I wanted to hear from similarly minded people."

"And where is the evidence leading?"

Isaac drew in a deep breath. "To a place I least expected."

For a moment, the two brothers looked at each other. Then Isaac stepped forward and embraced his brother. For a few seconds, Sam remained as stiff as the uniform he was wearing. But then he folded his arms around Isaac and clung to him fiercely, as if for support. He buried his head on Isaac's shoulder, an action that didn't quite fail to suppress a sob.

Once decorum was restored. Isaac sat down in the chair on the opposite side of the table. He put his hand in his pocket and pulled out the Scorpion Stone. He toyed with it for a moment before putting it on the table in front of Sam.

Sam picked it up and turned it around so that the light turned the stone to gold. "How on earth did you manage to get that through security?"

It occurred to Isaac that if Sam's case really did involve national security, then there was a chance that the Spartan table or chairs might have a hidden microphone. He held up a finger to caution Sam, then spoke up in a loud voice: "For the benefit of those listening, I am now giving my brother a piece of ninety-million-year old petrified tree sap. It is a piece of amber, and it signifies my commitment to helping my brother clear his name of these ridiculous charges."

Sam smiled. "Did that make you feel better?"

"Only slightly." Isaac drew in a deep breath. "Now tell me, as carefully as you can, everything that has happened."

For the next fifteen minutes, Isaac listened intently, only occasionally interrupting to get clarification on something. Once Sam had finished, Isaac said nothing. He picked up the scorpion stone from the desk and massaged it in his hand. After a few minutes, he handed it to Sam.

Sam took it dumbly and waited for Isaac to speak.

"As I see it, we need to investigate four things."

"Which are?"

"First: Is the language that was typed typical of what you write?" He looked up at his brother. "Have you got the text that was inserted into your notes?"

Sam nodded and fished out a piece of paper from his jacket pocket.

Isaac nodded his thanks and continued to speak. "Second: Have forensics had a really close look at what fingerprints are on the typewriter keys. Thirdly: We need to interview the two officers who stood Officer-of-the-day at the wardroom in the two weeks you were gone, to see if they remember anything."

Sam nodded. "And fourthly?"

Isaac pushed his spectacles up on his nose. "Someone needs to talk to the sailor who picked up your dossier at Helensburgh. We need to know a lot more about this local who drew it to his attention."

All too soon, the half-hour allotted to Isaac to speak to his brother was over. A naval police officer abruptly entered the room and said, not unkindly, "Time's up, boys." He looked at Isaac. "It is time for you to go, sir."

Isaac nodded, and both boys got to their feet. As they embraced, Isaac whispered, "You have the Scorpion Stone. You know what that means."

He received an almost imperceptible nod.

Isaac turned and left the room.

Sophie stood by the phone booth outside the common room in a welter of indecision. She tapped Oliver Tremain's business card in her hand. Finally, she could bear it no longer. She stepped forward and took the phone off the hook. Then, looking at the business card, she dialed the number. It was 8pm, but the no-nonsense voice that answered her, almost straight away, sounded as bright as if it was morning. "Good evening. May I have you number please."

Sophie gulped. "Er, yes. I'm calling from a call box." She gave the number.

The voice on the phone said, "Thank you, madam. Good night."

Feeling slightly surreal, she put the phone back on the hook. It then occurred to her that she would need to guard the phone until Tremain rang back – if he rang back. Plenty of students used the phone in the evenings. She lifted the phone back to her ear but kept a finger pressed down on the cradle.

Four minutes later, the phone rang. She lifted her finger and spoke straight away. "Mr. Tremain."

The unmistakable voice of Oliver Tremain came through – cool and measured. "Good evening, Miss Hunter."

She frowned. "How did you know it was me?"

"Every client has their own number. We have a database."

"Oh," she said weakly. "I was wondering if we might talk again. There have been more developments concerning Isaac Hastings' brother, Sam."

"What is your concern?"

"He's been accused of a terrible crime… and I'm afraid I don't know the details. But I suspect he may have been set up."

"What do you want from me?"

"Isaac is currently making his way back from Scotland on the train. He should arrive in Cambridge late tonight. I was hoping both of us might be able to talk with you sometime, soon afterward."

"What can you tell me about the nature of the trouble Sam Hastings is in?"

"It has to do with national security. That's why I thought of you."

There was a pause at the other end of the phone. "How time-sensitive is the situation?"

"Nothing critical at the moment. But there is a court-martial fairly soon."

After a moment's delay, Tremain came back. "Let's meet at 'The Chequers' pub in Wrestlingworth on Monday at 11am. It's fifteen miles southwest of Cambridge. Can both of you make it?"

"I can, and I'm pretty sure Mondays are one of Isaac's research days. So, yes."

"Good. Call me and leave a message if anything changes."

The phone went dead.

Sophie looked at the motorbike with suspicion. "There's not much room. Is it safe?"

Isaac slapped the petrol tank. "It's as slow as old Harry. Only 125cc. But these BSA Bantams are reliable." He handed her a motorbike helmet. "Here, put this on. It will keep your head warm, if nothing else."

"Haven't you got a helmet?"

"I've only got one helmet. You take it. I'll be okay. I've got my beanie." He looked her over. "I'm glad you've dressed warmly, though. It's cold on these autumn mornings. Climb on and put your feet on the foot pegs."

Gingerly, Sophie did so, and in no time at all, they were off. "Isaac yelled out as he took off, "Hang on tight and lean with me when we go round the corners."

A number of things surprised Sophie. The first was how physically intimate it was, riding pillion on a motorbike. She was squeezed up behind Isaac and was forced to have her arms around him. Sophie could feel his body-warmth. Rather guiltily, she enjoyed the sensation. In fact, it awakened in her a feeling that she'd been trying to repress in recent months. It was primal hunger.

She was not wearing goggles like Isaac, so she pressed her head behind Isaac's shoulder. Some of his dark hair had escaped the beanie and whipped against her cheeks. She liked the sensation.

Isaac did not know it, but when he had wept on her shoulders five days ago, she had not just stroked the back of his neck, she had kissed his hair as she'd comforted him. At the time, it was the most natural thing in the world to do. Feeling him in front of her now, she wanted to kiss him again, but not on his hair.

Thoughts of love were temporarily put on hold as they puttered along to the little village of Wrestlingworth. The wind was bitterly cold and succeeded in cooling her ardor. By the time they arrived at the ancient mustard-colored pub pressed hard up against the High Street, Sophie was frozen.

Isaac led her inside, and although the pub had just opened, she was glad to see that a warm fire was already burning cheerfully in the fireplace. So cold was she, that she was only dimly aware of

Isaac removing her duffle coat and scarf. He rubbed her arms and stood her in front of the fire. It was a good feeling.

Momentarily, he laid his hand against her cold cheek. Before she'd realized what she was doing, she'd taken his hand, and kissed it.

Isaac looked at her questioningly, delight plainly evident on his face.

Having got this far, it seemed entirely natural for Sophie to stand on tiptoe and kiss him on the cheek.

Isaac appeared to be transfixed. He touched his cheek tentatively and said, huskily, "I'm looking forward to many more of those."

They were, however, in a public place. It was eleven o'clock and other patrons were coming into the bar.

Isaac went off to order a port and lemon for Sophie to warm her up.

As he was at the bar, Oliver Tremain entered the pub's snug. He was wearing a gray double-breasted suit that looked completely out of place amongst the other patrons. They were wearing knitted sweaters and shapeless Tweed jackets. He saw Sophie and made his way toward her, ducking below the low oak beams that had been decorated with horse brasses. She forced her teeth to stop chattering and pointed to Isaac. "Isaac is getting me a drink to warm me up. Introduce yourself and ask him to buy you what you want."

He smiled his thanks. "I will have a small sherry. But I will pay. I suspect student finances don't go very far." Sophie watched him turn to the bar, where he shook Isaac by the hand.

In short order, all three of them were ensconced at a table close to the fire.

Tremain took a delicate sip of his sherry. "Tell me what has happened," he said.

Oliver Tremain knew exactly how many patrons were in the pub, and had, in the first few milliseconds, assessed all of them. He judged all of them to be locals except for Sophie and Isaac.

Sophie and Isaac were a good-looking couple, and there was an undeniable chemistry between them. He'd taken particular notice of Isaac in the first few minutes. There was now no hint of the Marxist radical. Instead, Isaac presented as a generous-spirited academic who was already developing a slight stoop – probably as a result of his study.

Oliver knew a great deal more about Isaac than the boy could possibly guess. He made it his business to know.

When he'd first met Sophie in Ely, she didn't know it, but she had passed a number of tests. She was on time. She was motivated enough to travel to Ely. Sophie was careful, needing to be assured of who he was. And she had spoken clearly, giving a concise picture of all that had transpired. It was as well she did, for he wouldn't have got involved at all unless Roslyn's father had asked him to investigate.

As it transpired, it was just as well he had. Things had been going on in Cambridge that the agency had no knowledge of. Given the debacle that had occurred fifteen years ago with Philby, Burgess, and Maclean, the agency's ignorance of events was a concern. The activities going on in Cambridge had shone a light on Tony Chester-Smith. The man didn't know it, but he had been red-flagged as either being incompetent or, more likely, a double agent. Oliver had had him recalled to London, where he had been given safe boundaries to operate within. He would be played like a trout to tease out any others who were part of his network. What Oliver had yet to establish was whether there was a link between Chester-Smith and the Hastings boys. It was a loose end, and he didn't like loose ends.

In a low voice, Isaac recounted all he had learned from his visit to his brother in Scotland. Oliver tapped his fingertips together as he listened. It was a remarkable story that raised all sorts of questions.

When Isaac had finished, Sophie leaned forward. "Don't you

think it is just too much of a coincidence that this accusation against Sam has followed a string of incidences aimed at destroying Isaac?"

Oliver frowned. "That was a year-and-a-half ago. But I take your point." In reality, he saw the point very clearly and had already made the connection. "Tell me again, Isaac, what were the four issues you felt needed investigation?"

Isaac told him.

Oliver was impressed with the boy's clear thinking. It was enough to cause him to debate with himself whether he should involve Isaac and Sophie in the plans he was formulating in his mind. "Do you have a copy of the text that your brother alleges was inserted into his notes?"

Isaac fished inside his bomber jacket pocket and produced a piece of paper. He handed it to him.

Oliver read it quickly. "Is this just a rough recollection of what was written, or is this accurate?"

Isaac smiled. "When it comes to detail and noticing things, Sam is pretty unique. I think you can take that as the exact words that were written."

"Can I keep this?"

"Yes. I have the original piece of paper Sam gave me at the college. I brought that for you, in case you wanted it."

Oliver nodded and put the piece of paper away in his pocket. "There is no way that you will have the authority or opportunity to question the sailor who retrieved your brother's file. Nor will you have the authority or opportunity to question the Officers-of-the-Day on duty at the wardroom. And you certainly can't make inquiries into the forensics of the typewriter."

Isaac was looking forlorn. Oliver noticed that Sophie slipped her hand into his.

"However," said Oliver, "I do."

Isaac's face brightened straight away. "You will help, then?"

"I will do what I can. But I want you to do something as well. I want you to scrutinize the text your brother says was inserted, and examine it for words, or sentence structures, that are not typical of your brother's writing. Do you think you can you do that?"

"Of course."

Oliver drew a deep breath. "There's one more thing. I'm going to tell you a name, and I want to know if that name has any significance for you."

"What's the name?"

"Have you had any dealings with a person called Tony Chester-Smith?"

The Admiral handed the CIA Station Chief a glass of single malt. "It's a Glenmorangie."

The Station Chief nodded his appreciation. He was lounging in a chair in front of the Admiral's desk.

The Admiral stayed on his feet and looked out of the window. "The Hastings boys are bright. We have to be careful."

"How do you know?"

"One cheeky blighter left us a message, assuming we would have the room bugged."

"Hardly convincing."

"No Adrian. You should have heard them asking questions about the evidence surrounding the trial." He took a drink from his crystal tumbler.

"So we don't have much time to waste."

"No. I've had the trial moved as far forward as I dare." The Admiral grimaced. "You mess with the British judicial system at your peril, but I think I've got things in hand."

It was only a short distance from the barracks where he'd been confined to the courtroom, but the Navy had nonetheless thought to deliver him by car.

Sam, in full naval uniform, stepped out of the car with a sense of unreality and impending doom.

There, sitting in all her glory in a dry dock, was Nelson's flagship, *HMS Victory*. She'd been a 104-gun ship of the line, and had had an illustrious career, bringing Nelson victory in the Battle of Trafalgar in 1805. What was not commonly known was that she was the oldest ship in the world still in commission… and one of her functions was to host court-martials – such as his own.

A gangway took him up to the quarterdeck. Above him, Sam could see the soaring masts, all crossed with yards. A bewildering web of lines and stays all ran to their allotted task.

Sam was escorted aft past the ship's wheel and under the poop deck into the captain's quarters. A marine stood by the door reminding him, if he needed reminding, that he was a prisoner about to face trial. Two warrant officers stood with him in the captain's cabin. Both were in their finest uniforms and both studiously avoided Sam's eyes.

After what seemed an eternity, Sam was marched to the steps that led down to the Admiral's cabin where the court-martial was to be held.

He entered the room with a sense of giddy disbelief. The room was full of people, but the three men who would determine his fate were difficult to see. They were seated behind a long table directly in front of the nine sloping stern windows. As such, they were in silhouette. Only a diagonal black and white checkerboard floor covering separated him from them.

On a normal occasion, Sam would have been in awe of the massive curved deck beams, and intrigued by the quarter doors that opened to the outside balcony. But this was no ordinary day.

A chief petty officer barked, "The court is now in session."

Sam's dreams of being made up to Lieutenant after thirty months and becoming an Officer of the Watch after another thirty months, now hung in the balance. The next two days would decide.

Chapter 22

The tip of the sword pointed directly at him.

Sam stared at it in disbelief. The court had found him guilty. Guilty! He couldn't believe it. His navy sword, like that carried by all commissioned officers, had a white fish-skin grip and a brass pommel forged in the form of a lion. He'd been praying that he would see that pommel pointed at him. But it was the tip of the sword that was pointing its accusing finger at him. In line with naval tradition, the sword of the accused was placed on the table with either the sword tip or pommel pointing to the prisoner when they re-entered the courtroom to hear the verdict. It signified whether the accused had been found guilty or innocent.

Everyone in the main cabin looked severe. It was too much. Sam closed his eyes. Various people intoned both the verdict and the consequences of it. The only bright spot came when the Captain of the *Cleopatra*, James Holman, Commander, DSO, DSC and BAR, asked permission to speak. He didn't mince his words.

"I don't know what sort of tomfoolery is going on here. But what I can tell you is that Midshipman Sam Hastings is one of the most promising young officers it has been my privilege to have aboard my ship." He glared at all those in the room. "I've said this in my written submission. But I just want to say it again in front of you all."

The Captain received a mild rebuke for disrespecting the court, but his comments were noted.

Perhaps the captain's submission carried weight, because Sam's sentence was simply that he be discharged from the navy – effective immediately. Crucially, he did not receive a dishonorable discharge. Had he been given that, it would have cast a shadow over his entire life. Nonetheless, it was a nightmarish end to a nightmarish saga.

Oliver Tremain was not surprised to see the Admiral at the court-martial. Given the nature of the trial, he had expected him to be there. He rather suspected, however, that the Admiral would have been surprised to see him. Neither man had spoken to the other either during or after the trial. Oliver didn't mind that the Admiral had seen him, because he wanted it to be known that was taking an interest in the case. In truth, Oliver was disturbed and had been very thoughtful as he left the *Victory*. He felt that the defense council for Sam left a lot to be desired. They had not been at all rigorous. Indeed, he couldn't help but feel that Sam would have fared better if his brother had conducted his defense and asked the penetrating questions Oliver had heard him voice. Something didn't smell right.

He didn't like bad smells because he had an implacable hatred of evil. He hated evil in all its forms, and had done ever since an intruder had murdered his pregnant wife. It had occurred early in their marriage, before they had had a chance to have any children. Oliver had been on a crusade against evil ever since, working first with the police, then for the government in more clandestine roles.

In Oliver's opinion, Sam had been on the receiving end of a monstrous miscarriage of justice. To his mind, Sam's guilt had not been satisfactorily established. Not only that, he didn't believe the alleged offense warranted a court-martial. Sam had not endangered his ship, disobeyed a critical order, or failed to engage the enemy – which were the usual grounds for a court-martial.

He walked down the gangplank of the *Victory* a troubled man.

Isaac was not allowed to attend the court-martial. But wild horses wouldn't have stopped him from being on hand for his brother. He'd booked himself into the George Hotel, on Queen Street. It was a small hotel that had been built outside the brick walls of the Portsmouth Naval dockyards. Evidently, it had a long maritime tradition. Isaac couldn't have cared less. He just wanted to support his brother as much as he could.

For the most part, he stayed in his room in the hotel, trying to work on his thesis, but his heart wasn't in it. He'd let a number of cups of tea get cold and was in the process of making another when there was a knock on the door.

It was Sam, and he was dressed in civilian clothes. He simply said, "I've been found guilty, and I have been discharged from the Navy. He hung his head and fingered the lapel of his jacket. He tried to laugh. "This is my new uniform."

Then Isaac held him as he burst into tears.

Once things had settled down. Isaac realized that a number of things had to happen. "Where are you spending the night?"

"No idea."

"Well, that's easy. Spend it here with me here at the George. Where's all your kit and belongings?"

"I'm allowed to keep them in a temporary store for 48 hours at the dockyard."

"And after that?"

"No idea."

"Good grief. We haven't much time, then." Isaac removed his glasses and pinched the top of his nose. "I'll call Sophie. She's well connected with Christian organizations around the place. She might be able to suggest something. Have you had any dinner?"

Sam shook his head. "I couldn't eat anything."

"You should." He shepherded his brother to the door. "Go

downstairs and get yourself a meal. I'll join you after I've spoken to Sophie."

Sam left reluctantly.

Once Isaac had closed the door behind Sam, he leaned against it, letting the full force of the grief he felt for his brother rise to the surface. What he'd heard was appalling. It was unjust and wrong. In every way, it was wrong.

Once he had his emotions back under control, he picked up the phone and asked for an outside line.

Ten minutes later, he joined Sam in the dining room. The man had only managed to eat a prawn cocktail and said he couldn't eat anything more. Isaac deemed that a walk, followed by a stiff drink was in order, so the two of them stepped out onto Queen Street and began making their way in the general direction of Old Portsmouth. It was a charming place, rich in maritime history, full of cobbled streets, and crucially, pubs.

They wound their way through the streets until they came to an old pub, 'The Still and West.' Isaac conceded that it may not have been the best pub they could have chosen, because it had a commanding view, even at night, over Portsmouth harbor. Naval ships, decked with lights, could clearly be seen. Sam would no doubt see them and feel a knife turn in his heart.

Inside, the pub was noisy and anonymous – the perfect combination Isaac felt Sam needed. The walls of the pub contained photos of Robin Knox-Johnson, who last year, had become the first man to sail solo non-stop around the globe in his tiny boat, Suhaili.

Sam paused to look at them. Then he shook his head. "It makes you wonder, doesn't it. What will I be remembered for?"

Sam cut a desperate and forlorn figure.

Next morning, the two brothers dawdled over a late breakfast, partly to allow the excesses of the previous night to dissipate; partly to share each other's company; and partly because they had nothing else to do.

The waitress approached them with the coffee pot and a message. "There's a call for Isaac Hastings. You can take it in the foyer or up in your room."

Isaac got to his feet. "Thank you. I'll take it in my room."

He was not surprised to hear Sophie on the other end of the line. He'd rung her the previous evening. She asked straight away, "How's Sam doing?"

"Not well. I poured a few drinks into him last night, but I'm not sure it helped. I'm afraid it's going to take a long time for Sam to get over this."

"It's appalling and so unjust." She paused. "But I have some good news. I've managed to find Sam some short term accommodation – if he wants it."

Isaac shook his head in amazement. "Where is it?"

"Not far from you. It's at the YMCA in Portsmouth. You'll find it on Penny Street. The guy in charge sounds a lovely chap and he's expecting to speak to Sam some time today."

"Wow! I'm amazed you've managed to organize things so quickly?"

"I fully expect to amaze you with all sorts of things, Isaac Hastings."

He grinned. "Gee, I like the sound of that."

"When are you coming back?" she asked.

"Tonight, if I can. I just want to get Sam settled somewhere first."

"Yes. Understood."

Isaac said his farewell and made his way back downstairs. When he entered the dining room, Sam looked at him enquiringly. "Who was that?"

"That was your guardian angel, Sophie. She's found a place for you to stay. It's an easy walk from here, so get on your feet."

Sam conceded that the YMCA suited his purposes very well. It not only provided accommodation, but also served breakfast and dinner in its dining hall. The building itself was an unspectacular modern brick affair with blue paneling under its windows. It was, however, in a wonderful location on the seafront. Unfortunately, his room was on the ground floor at the back, so he had no view to speak of. He therefore contrived to spend as much time outside the building as possible. From what he could judge, most of the other people in the building seemed to be students at Portsmouth Polytechnic. He hadn't attempted to fraternize with them.

He'd now been at the YMCA for five days. All his worldly belongings were stowed away into one cupboard and some drawers. It was profoundly depressing to see how little he had. He sighed. So this was what his life had amounted to – nothing.

Sam felt for the Scorpion Stone in his pocket, seeking its comfort. It didn't seem to help, so he made his way out through the foyer onto Penny Street.

The remains of the Royal Garrison Church stood on the opposite side of the road. It had no roof, having been a casualty of World War II. The old church now stood on neatly clipped lawn as a memorial to those terrible days when Portsmouth was bombed to within an inch of its life.

He made his way to the sea wall and looked out across the Solent to the Isle of Wight, three miles offshore. Even as he watched, he could hear the noisy buzz of the hovercraft dashing its way from the island to Portsmouth.

It was a fresh, sunny day. A brisk southwesterly breeze was sending clouds scudding across the sky. Sam stood in the wind, hoping that it would cleanse him from the grief he was feeling.

The view from the sea wall was spectacular. He could see two round forts sitting offshore. They had been built to protect the maritime entrance to Portsmouth harbor during the Napoleonic wars. The Solent was busy with sailboats, ferries, and occasionally, a naval ship. Even as he watched, a black submarine was making its way into the harbor, seeking its home in Gosport, across the harbor from Portsmouth.

Sam walked along the sea wall to the old fortifications near the harbor entrance. He passed the place where Nelson took his last walk down the steps of the Sally Port to the ship's boat that took him to his flagship, *Victory*.

Victory, where everything had happened. The knife turned again in Sam's heart.

He felt very alone. Sam laughed bitterly to himself. He'd lost everything. He'd once entertained some hope of a romance with Sophie, but the strictures of naval life had sabotaged those hopes. That was one downside of joining the navy. It was brutally unkind to lovers, wives, and families.

Sam made his way back to the YMCA via the High Street. On the way, he passed the cathedral. It was a modest affair for a cathedral, quite unlike any other he'd seen. Its tower had a small wooden cupola on top that looked as if it had been transplanted from a naval signals tower. Sam thought it was probably quite appropriate.

When he arrived back at the YMCA, the porter on duty called out to him. "Mr. Hastings. There's a gentleman to see you. He's waiting for you in the café area."

Sam frowned and couldn't think who it could be.

He walked round the corner to the café, which was currently closed, and saw a neat looking man in a blue pinstriped suit. He was playing patience with a deck of cards.

Sam approached him. "I'm Sam Hastings. I understand you are looking for me."

The man laid a king over a queen, looked up and smiled. "I am." He stood up and shook Sam by the hand. "My name is Oliver Tremain, and I work for the civil service."

"And how can I help you, Mr. Tremain?"

"I rather hope that I can help you." He indicated a chair. "Do sit down."

Sam did so.

Mr. Tremain then surprised him by saying. "Your brother Isaac and Sophie Hunter both send their regards." He smiled. "They have been in communication with me concerning your, er, unfortunate situation."

Sam closed his eyes. So that's what the ruination of his life was – an 'unfortunate situation.' He waited for his visitor to say more.

"You have three problems, as I see it."

Sam suddenly became fully alert.

The man continued. "You have no permanent place to live. You have no job, and the mystery surrounding your court-martial remains unresolved."

"I'm not sure it can be resolved. It's all over."

Mr. Tremain shook his head. "I doubt very much that it is over." He smiled. "Your trial was simply the opening salvo in a much bigger affair."

Sam frowned with incomprehension.

Mr. Tremain laid down the ace card. "Your brother tells me that you have a history with a certain Tony Chester-Smith." He looked up. "Do you recall the name?"

Sam certainly could. "What? Do you mean the man whose knee was broken when he was in the army, skiing in Bavaria?"

"Yes."

"Don't tell me he's involved in this. How is that possible?"

"That is something I am investigating. At this point, I don't think there is anything to be gained by pursuing the subject. Just be aware that it is being investigated, and that it is happening under the strictest of confidences – which I will ask you to respect."

Sam nodded dumbly.

"Good. That brings us to the next issue, your employment. Tell me, Sam, how much do you know about Trinity House?"

Sam opened his eyes wide. "What – the mob in charge of maritime buoyage and lighthouses?"

"The same."

"Very little."

The man leaned back in his chair and folded his hands together. "Trinity House is a remarkable organization. It is presided over by The Master of the Corporation, which is now an honorary title. You might be interested to know that Samuel Pepys, William Pitt the Younger, and the Duke of Wellington once held the role. However, the real governance of the organization comes from a court of thirty-one Elder Brethren who are presided over by a Master. The Elder Brethren are appointed from three-hundred Younger

Brethren who act as advisors. They are appointed from lay people who have maritime experience – retired naval officers, ship's masters – anyone with significant maritime experience."

"What are you suggesting?" said Sam.

"I'm suggesting that you apply to become a lighthouse keeper with Trinity House." It will keep you away from trouble, and it will use many of the skills you have already been trained in." Tremain smiled – and you would be doing me a service."

"And what is that service?"

"I'll tell you about that later. But first tell me, would you entertain the possibility of working for Trinity House?"

Sam was given no time to think. "I, I… think so," he stammered.

"That's good, because I've provisionally organized for you to have an interview."

Sam raised his eyebrows. "Really? When?"

"This afternoon at three o'clock."

"Where?"

"At Trinity House, on Tower Hill in London."

"But how on earth…"

Tremain scooped up all his playing cards. "I'll drive you to London… and you can make your own way back by train."

Chapter 23

S am got out of the car and gave a nod of thanks to Tremain.
Tremain sketched a wave and said, "Good luck," before driving off along Tower Hill.

Sam looked south across the park beside the road. The Tower of London, with its iconic roofline, could be seen clearly. He couldn't help but think of those who had been condemned and imprisoned there. What did his future hold?

Sam crossed the road and looked up at the building in front of him. Its architecture reminded him of a mausoleum – or perhaps it was just his mood. The building had arched windows at ground level and a neoclassical pillared frontage with tall Georgian windows above it.

Taking a deep breath, he passed through a gate in the iron railings, and mounted the steps.

When he was conducted to the interview room, Sam nearly laughed at the absurdity of the room. It was massive and would have done justice to any ballroom. It was also, he had to concede, beautiful. The huge Georgian windows let in a lot of light. A long table had been placed near one of the windows, and three men sat behind it.

They rose to their feet and introduced themselves. Two of the men wore beards and had an unmistakable nautical look about them. The third looked more like a lawyer than a mariner, but Sam had learned that looks could be deceptive. He could just as easily have captained the Queen Elizabeth. He was dressed in a black suit. The man introduced himself as Jason Stains and said that he would be leading the interview. He pointed to a chair on the opposite side of the table and asked Sam to be seated. Sam quickly realized that this meant that those interviewing him were largely in silhouette – just as the judges aboard the Victory had been.

He shivered.

Stains cleared his throat. "Mr. Hastings; just to put you at ease, we have here a reference written for you by Commander James Holman. It is very complimentary."

"I'd no idea he'd written it, sir."

"Well, he has."

"One of the bearded men gave a chuckle and said, "Do they still call him Colonel Mustard?"

Sam smiled, "Yes sir."

The man grunted. "He's not a man to hand out plaudits lightly." He nodded to his colleague indicating that he should continue.

Stains adjusted the spectacles on his nose. "We can certainly use a man of your experience. You already know the shipping rules of the road, radio protocol, signaling, and basic seamanship." He looked up at Sam. "I assume you are also trained in basic first aid."

"Yes sir."

The other bearded man picked up a piece of paper in front of him and flicked it with his finger. "It says here, lad, that you've been a sailing instructor for six years. Is that correct?"

Sam wondered where on earth that information had come from. "Yes."

"Where did you learn to sail?"

"In Germany, sir."

Stains resumed control of the conversation. "Being a lighthouse keeper is not for everyone. You will be isolated for long periods of time, yet you will have to live in close quarters with at least one colleague. In your case, it will be the Principal Keeper. Do you get on well with people, Mr. Hastings?"

"I believe so sir. What you describe is not so different from the shipboard life I've lived for the last eighteen months."

"That's good. Now here's a key question: We have lighthouses all around the nation. Do you have a particular preference for any location, or are you flexible?"

"I am flexible, sir." Sam allowed the searing wave of shame wash over him. It was unwarranted, but he still felt it acutely. "If I was allowed to have a preference, it would be for a lighthouse that was particularly remote."

"Are you sure about that, because those are the lighthouses we find it hardest to staff."

"Yes, I'm quite sure." He wanted to be away from people; somewhere where he could nurse his grief.

Stains raised an eyebrow and glanced at his two colleagues. Both gave him a small nod. "Well, Mr. Hastings; in view of all your prior experience, your training can be reduced to four weeks. Fortuitously enough, this training can take place in Portsmouth. We have a number of retired Principal Keepers there. They will be in contact with you. Where are you staying?"

"At the YMCA on Penny Street."

Stains made a note on a piece of paper.

Sam felt emboldened to ask. "After the four weeks, where is it likely that I will be sent?"

Stains sucked his lips and took a while to reply. "We are in desperate need of someone else to look after Fastnet. We look for single men to go there. The lighthouse is remote, and the quarters are cramped. Fortunately, it is now a whole lot easier getting there. We've just initiated helicopter reliefs to and from offshore lighthouses."

One of the bearded men broke in. "It's a damn sight easier than sending boat reliefs, I can tell you. We sometimes had to delay those for months due to inclement weather."

Stains nodded, "That's right." He hurried on. "You'll do your apprenticeship under the Principal Keeper there. We'll talk about where you will be sent after that."

"Does that mean I've been accepted?"

Stains rose to his feet. "You certainly have, young man. Welcome aboard."

Sophie giggled and said, "You can't do that. You're being completely irresponsible."

Isaac paid her no attention. He laid himself down beside her on the punt and put an arm around her.

The punt, with no one in command of the punt pole, swung sideways as the current took them gently downstream. Isaac needed to straighten the punt when they came to Clare Bridge, a feat he accomplished simply by sticking a leg out and pushing against one of the bridge's buttresses.

Feeling Isaac's arms around her was delicious. She let a finger play over his face as if drawing its contours. He took hold of the finger and kissed it. Then he heaved himself up onto one elbow and looked at her.

She smiled, seeing the softness of love in his eyes.

Then he brought his head down and teased her lips with his own, lightly touching them, until she could bear it no long and she hooked him round the neck and kissed him fully and fiercely.

A young couple standing on Garret Hostel Bridge clapped, but Sophie only half noticed them. Everything inside her was giddy with the heady feeling of love.

All too soon, they got to their destination, Trinity College and its Library. The two of them had come to view the library as 'their space.' It was where they chose to meet in order to talk. And they very much needed to talk. As giddy and wonderful as their love was, the dreadful things that Sam had so recently endured, ensured that he was always in the back of her mind. Isaac and Sophie had decided to meet in the library to continue doing what Oliver

Tremain had asked them of them – to examine the text they felt very sure had been inserted into Sam's notes.

Once they found their table, they put their heads together.

"What have we got so far?"

Isaac smoothed out a copy of the text in front of him. "I've been looking at the language of this text carefully. But first, let me read it to you out loud. You tell me if you think anything is odd and stilted. I don't just want to fill your mind with my convictions."

Sophie nodded, and Isaac began to read in a low voice:

The encryption equipment used by NATO is made by Crypto AG. The word is that this Swiss company – located in Steinhausen – is part owned by the CIA, and they have engineered their cipher devices so they can listen in to conversations through the back door. There is a strong suspicion that the CIA has done this in partnership with BND (the West German Federal Intelligence Service). Certainly, the Russians and the Chinese don't trust it, and neither, I suspect, should we.

When he'd finished, he said, "First impressions?"

Sophie took a while to answer. She furrowed her brow. Something was odd. Eventually, she said: The text is full of information. It's as if the person writing it wanted to get all the information down – all i's dotted and t's crossed. It's quite formal.

Isaac nodded. "Exactly. I know how Sam's mind works. All he needs is a few notes to remind him of the general theme, and his mind fills in the details." Isaac stabbed at the piece of paper with his finger. "Sam wouldn't have written all these facts. He wouldn't have written 'located in Steinhausen,' and I doubt he would have written 'the West German Federal Intelligence Service' in brackets. That's not his style. Sam is laid back. He uses the minimum of words, just enough to remind him of the issue – because he relies on his prodigious memory."

"Hang on," said Sophie. "I'm making notes so we can give this to Oliver Tremain." When she finished writing, she said, "What else have we got?"

For a long while, the two of them pored over the text.

Then an idea came to Sophie. She frowned, and then said, "We are very sure that the person who typed this was wearing gloves, aren't we?"

Isaac nodded. "Yes. Only Sam's fingerprints were found on the keys. Evidently, that was the killer blow that resulted in him being found guilty."

Sophie shook Isaac's arm. "But don't you see. If the person used gloves, some of the fingerprints will have been slightly smudged."

"What are you suggesting?"

Sophie found it hard to contain her excitement. "It would be reasonable to expect that those keys used more often by the gloved hand would be more smudged, wouldn't it?"

Isaac got the idea straight away. "So, if we count the number of times different letters appear, we should have a 'smudgeness' graduation."

"Precisely." She looked back down at the text. "I'll take the first half of the alphabet, and you take the second."

Isaac nodded, and the two of them set to work.

After twenty minutes, Sophie leaned back. "My eyeballs are beginning to wobble. What have we got so far?"

Isaac consulted the piece of paper he'd been writing on. "The text has no X, or Z, and there are no numbers or symbols. We would therefore expect Sam's prints to be clear on those keys. What have you got?"

"There's no letter J, but the letter E is used 50 times. I've compiled a list of the next most common letters. We would expect those letters to be particularly smudged."

Sophie leaned back. "You realize that this could break the case right open, or it could confirm Sam's guilt. How do you feel giving this information to Tremain?"

Isaac answered straight away. "I feel good. I've every confidence in Sam."

Sophie nodded. "So do I." She smiled at Isaac coyly. "You know he tried to chat me up, don't you? And I was tempted."

Isaac leaned across and kissed her on the nose. "He is a man of excellent taste."

Oliver Tremain drove down through Guildford and Petersfield to Portsmouth in his Austin 1300. It was a car that no one would notice, and he liked that. It was painted gray, the color of anonymity. As he drove, he reflected on the case he was currently engaged in – that of Sam Hastings. One of the reasons it troubled him was because he felt partly responsible for Sam's court-martial. He knew very well that he could have kicked up a fuss about the lack of clear evidence, and had the trial postponed or even canceled, but he hadn't. And the reason he hadn't was because he had bigger fish to fry. Whilst he knew some of the fish, there were others he had yet to identify. Oliver sought to salve his conscience somewhat by recalling that he had done all he could to help launch Sam in his new career with Trinity House. Nonetheless, he still felt guilty. Sometimes doing the right thing meant stepping into gray areas.

Oliver found his way to the naval dockyards. The guards at the gate told him where the Naval Police building was located.

It wasn't long before he was presenting a document to a Chief Petty Officer. "This is a court order sanctioning the release of the typewriter used in the recent Sam Hastings court-martial into my care."

The Chief Petty Officer examined the document, then reached for a ledger and began filling in the details. He then turned the ledger around and asked Oliver to sign it.

Ten minutes later, Oliver was in the car again, making his way out of Portsmouth. He drove up to the town of Liss, where he stopped for lunch. Then he turned off to Basingstoke. Forty minutes later, he pulled up in front of the Forensic Science Service there.

When he arrived, he presented a letter from the Home Office. "This letter sanctions the re-examination of a typewriter that featured in a recent case." Oliver looked at the chief scientist. "Have you, or any of your team seen this typewriter before?"

The scientist examined the letter and then went to a filing cabinet. After five minutes of investigation, he said. "No. This typewriter must have been examined in another of our facilities. We have a number of them around the nation." He looked quizzically at Oliver. "What is it that you particularly want us to look for?"

"Please examine the keys to tell me what fingerprints you find other than the one belonging to this man." Oliver pulled a manila envelope from his briefcase and handed it to the scientist. "You'll find the man's fingerprint details in there.

The scientist nodded. "That's pretty straight forward. Anything else?"

"Yes. I particularly want to know if the fingerprints on some keys appear smudged, or only partial. Can you do that?"

"Yes."

"Could you grade the level of smudge or partial clarity on a 1 to 5 scale?"

The scientist frowned. "I suppose so. We've never had to do it before. All we can give you is a subjective measurement."

"Could three of your staff grade them... and then give me the ratings from all three people? That should enable us to get at least some sort of statistical significance."

"Yes, we can do that." He paused. "What should I do with the results?

"Keep a copy safe with you, and courier me a copy – as fast as you can."

Oliver then made his way back to London.

Next day, Oliver exchanged his Austin 1300 for a large black Daimler. He didn't want to drive his own car to Scotland. It was a long trip, and he wanted to get there in comfort. He also wanted his presence to be as intimidating as possible.

He had with him the name of just one of the three people he wished to interview. He'd learned that at the court-martial. However, he was in no doubt that he would have the names of the other two very soon.

Oliver's name was checked off against a list, and he was issued with a pass by the guardhouse. Oliver took the opportunity to ask, "Do all visitors to Clyde have to pre-register in order to come?"

"It's usually only required for the one-offs sir, so we know who's about. The regulars pretty much just come and go."

"So, if someone was impersonating a naval officer, the chances are, he wouldn't be stopped."

"They would need a pass, sir."

Oliver didn't bother to say that passes could be easily forged. He grimaced and resolved to address the issue of security at a later stage. For the moment, he settled for getting directions to the officer's land-based wardroom.

A bored looking Lieutenant was sitting at the check-in desk of the wardroom. When Oliver showed him his credentials, the man sat up straight. "How can I help you sir?"

"Can you tell me who was the Officer-of-the-Day on these two weeks." Oliver handed him a piece of paper.

"That's not so long ago, sir. It should be easy to find." He reached for the register. After he'd leafed back a few pages, he found what he was looking for. "A midshipman stood the first week and a Lieutenant, the second."

"Where can I find them?"

"Both are billeted here. They are engineers on site and therefore non sea-going personnel. That's why they live here."

"Lieutenant, I will give you an hour to find both men and have them brought to me." Oliver looked at him without smiling. "Is there a room I can use to interview them?"

The Lieutenant stuttered. "The anteroom is free sir." He pointed across the hall. "Shall I book it for you?"

"Yes. And one more thing."

The Lieutenant visibly wilted two inches.

Oliver continued. "Please have leading hand, Daniel Richards, brought here as well. He's with the Royal Naval Police."

"Certainly sir. Anything else sir?"

"Yes. Where's the bar?"

Oliver learned nothing from the midshipman. However, he did

learn more from the Lieutenant who had been Officer-of-the-Day in the second week Sam Hastings had been at sea.

He'd made it clear to the Lieutenant that he was investigating an issue of national security. The man was instantly defensive. "I assure you Sir, I've not been involved with anything untoward."

Oliver knew that the man was not yet suitably cowed. "The penalty for withholding information in an investigation of this sort is ten years minimum in prison."

The man gulped.

"In the week in question, did you see anyone you didn't recognize going into the wardroom?"

The man looked at him helplessly. "Different people come and go all the time, Sir."

"Did any of them ask for a key, that you would have suspected should already have had one?"

"No sir." The Lieutenant raised a finger. "Wait. There was a Commander who said he'd locked his key in his room."

"Which room?"

"I can't remember. I didn't take much notice to be honest. He was a Commander. I just wanted to do what I was told."

"Did you see him again?"

"Only to return the key."

"Not afterward?"

"No."

"Didn't you think that odd?"

"No Sir. As I said: people are coming and going, and joining ships all the time."

"Is there a record of any Commander leaving the wardroom's accommodation during the week?"

The Lieutenant spun the register round and consulted it. "No Sir."

Oliver looked at the Lieutenant levelly. "May I suggest you become more rigorous in your duties, Lieutenant. Thoroughness does not mean disrespect."

The man's face became flushed. "Yes Sir."

Oliver waved a hand. "Send Daniel Richards in. He's waiting outside. You are dismissed."

The Lieutenant stood smartly to attention, saluted, and walked out the door.

Oliver learned just one important piece of information from leading hand, Daniel Richards.

"Were there any distinguishing features of this 'local' who drew your attention to Sam Hastings' dossier?" Oliver paused. "Take your time. Think carefully."

Richards shook his head slowly. "No sir. The only thing I noticed was that the man had a limp."

Oliver nodded. He'd learned enough.

Chapter 24

I t was now three weeks since the Westland Wessex helicopter had made its hair-raising descent onto the newly built helipad on Fastnet rock. Engineers had somehow managed to squeeze the helipad between the stub of the old lighthouse and the cliff face. The loadmaster on the Wessex had dropped Sam off, together with a plastic tank of fresh water and a large box of fresh food. The pilot had kept the rotor blades turning, anxious to be back up in the air.

A middle-aged man dressed in sea-boots, khaki trousers that looked to have been issued in World War II, and an Aran knit pullover, met Sam on the helipad. He was standing by a four-wheeled trolley. It was his first introduction to Joe Harris, the Principal Keeper.

If he wanted to be remote and away from people, he'd certainly picked the right place. The main coast of Ireland was eight miles away – a distant smudge on the horizon. Harris' opening remark was a memorable one. "Welcome to 'Ireland's Teardrop,' boy."

Once the victuals had been trolleyed to the store and packed away, he'd ask about 'Ireland's Teardrop.'

Harris put the kettle on to boil and grunted. "Fastnet is known as 'Ireland's Teardrop' because it was the last bit of Ireland the nineteenth-century Irish emigrants saw as they sailed to America."

Sam could have wished for a happier welcome, but in truth, the place suited his mood.

For the next two weeks, Sam nursed his grief and his loneliness. The work of maintaining the light was routine. But the lighthouse always threw up surprises that called on Sam's ingenuity. He'd had to fix both the generator and the bread toaster.

The Principal Keeper, Joe Harris, was easy-going but didn't say much. He had an encyclopedic knowledge of cricket and a passion for tying fly-fishing lures. He worked under a large magnifying glass with tiny pliers, thread, and bits of feather. Sam learned about dry flies, wet flies, bass bugs, poppers, and gurglers. To the best of Sam's knowledge, Joe had never used one of them to fish. He just enjoyed making them.

One night, a deep meteorological low over the Atlantic brought a storm down upon them. Sam could hear and feel the lighthouse shudder when the massive waves smashed against it. He was unable to keep the anxiety out of his voice when he said. "Gee, I hope this place can take all this battering."

Joe looked up from his fly tying. "The Lord bless you boy. Over 2,000 blocks of Cornish granite were used in buildin' this 'ere lighthouse. Each block were dovetailed into the next. They won't move. The bloke 'oo done it were James Kavanagh. 'Ee personally supervised the seating of every stone. And each of 'em weighed between two to three tons." Harris reached for his pipe. "Now the old lighthouse – that were a different matter. Gales shook it so much, that it threw the crockery off the table. One time, a seventy-gallon cask of water lashed to the gallery were washed away. And that were 133 feet above high water." He shook his head. "The boys did it hard, them days. The lighthouses were poor, and the lights weren't electric." He pointed with the stem of his pipe. "As you've seen, we use the stump of the old lighthouse as an oil tank now."

As he spoke, the MF marine radio stuttered into life. "Fastnet light, Fastnet light; are you reading me?"

Sam picked up the receiver. "Fastnet light. Sam Hastings. Go ahead."

"How are you reading me?"

Sam recognized the voice of their supervising officer, located in Plymouth. "Good evening, Mr. Harris. Reading you 'five.'"

"The weather map tells me you are experiencing a bit of a blow. How are you going?"

"Affirmative, sir. Force 9, but we are weathering it well."

"Good. I just wanted to check. And I have some news for you."

"Go ahead, sir."

"It has been requested that you be relocated to Skellig light. I say again: you will be relocated to Skellig light – one week. Please prepare."

Sam frowned. He had no idea where Skellig lighthouse was, or why he was going there. "Roger that, sir. Wilco."

"Good night. Stay safe. Over and out."

Sam replaced the handset into its pocket and turned to his colleague. "Joe, where on earth is Skellig lighthouse? I'm being transferred there next week."

Joe gave wheezy laugh. "Blast boy. But don't you get the pick of the crop. Skellig Lighthouse is one of the lights off the South West coast of Ireland. It sits on the Skellig rocks, eight miles from the mainland."

"It can't be more remote than this place."

"No it's not. And the lighthouse quarters are bigger. "But it's a wondrous strange place. I'm not sure what you'll make of it." Joe returned to his fly tying. "I'll be sorry to lose you, boy. You've fitted in well. You're reliable."

"It's all your good instruction, Joe."

"Boy, I'm not teaching you much. It seems as if you've done all this afore."

Sam grinned. "That's how good you are, Joe."

"No, I aint. Oi knows meself well. You're a natural; that's what it is." He paused. "I just hope that Skellig works out for you."

"Why do you say that, Joe?"

"At Skellig, you've got visitors – spirits and the like." He twirled the fly he was making between his fingers under the magnifying lens. "Tis a wondrous strange place."

"I have the results you asked for, sir."

Oliver Tremain pushed the phone closer to his ear. "Good. Tell me."

The department's statistician cleared his throat. "We've correlated the 'clarity score' of the fingerprints with the frequency of the letters that were typed."

"And?"

"There is an 80 percent correlation."

Oliver nodded to himself. "That sounds like a strong correlation."

"We statisticians like to work to 95 percent correlation before we claim statistical significance, but you can certainly say it is strong correlation."

"Thank you Claude. Send the results up to me when you can."

"Yes sir."

Oliver put the phone down, leaned back in his chair and tapped his fingers together. Sophie and Isaac had done well to suggest the possible correlation, and it had yielded fruit. He was now very sure he had enough evidence to overturn the results of the Sam Hastings' court-martial. But that wouldn't be happening any time soon. There were important things to do first. One of those was to put a close watch on Tony Chester-Smith. That meant organizing a surveillance team... and none of it had to go through the official channels of MI5.

Sophie was glad to finally be alone with Isaac at the end of what had been an emotional and testing day. The two of them had caught the train from Cambridge to Bury-St.-Edmunds in order to visit her parents. She'd been anxious that Isaac wouldn't be too shocked at her parent's humble status. Sophie smiled. She needn't have worried. Isaac had been very much at ease with her parents and had obviously been fascinated by all that went on at the estate farm.

As they'd walked down to the stables, Isaac had said, "I envy you Sophie. This place has an extraordinary sense of community. Everyone knows you, and you belong. That is very precious. My life has been very different. I've moved from place to place so often that it's been difficult to stay connected to anything, or make lasting friendships."

"You've been at Cambridge now for over four years."

"And that's a record." He'd looked at her. "And I've made good friends."

The only poignant thing that tugged at Sophie's heart was that Miss Chessington no longer lived in the cottage at the end of the spinney. She'd died a year ago of a heart attack. Sophie had attended her funeral at St. Peter's church in Thurston. The little church had been packed. Roslyn was there, of course. Seeing her was the only bright spot in what was otherwise a very sad day.

Sophie brought her mind back to the present. She was sitting at a table in the Angel Hotel in Bury-St.-Edmunds. Sophie's father had offered them the use of the estate's Morris Traveler in order to drive there.

They were sitting by the window, so they had a commanding view of the ancient city wall on the opposite side of the road. The wall had a Norman tower built into it, and an impressive looking gate, complete with portcullis. She turned her attention back to Isaac.

He smiled and took her hand.

Why are hands so wonderfully sensual? She allowed her fingers to play restlessly with his.

The lights of the dining room were dim and candlelight reflected off the silver dome-shaped carving trolley that the waiter was wheeling around the restaurant. It contained a massive haunch of beef, and it smelled delicious.

Isaac smiled. "Did you know that Charles Dickens stayed here?"

"Yes actually, I did."

"So this is a literary place." He slipped his hand away. "So I've got an early Christmas present for you."

She frowned with curiosity.

Isaac bent over, picked up a parcel, and handed it to her. From its shape, Sophie could see that the parcel contained a book.

She untied the string and unwrapped the plain brown wrapping.

Sure enough, the parcel contained a book. Sophie picked it up and read the gold-embossed title: 'Shakespeare's Love Sonnets.' She smiled. "You old romantic, you."

"Just to help you think of me when you read it."

She laughed, and opened the cover. Then she froze with surprise.

The center of the book had been cut out all the way through to the back cover, and there, nested in the small rectangular hole, was a diamond ring.

"Oh, and I forgot to say," said Isaac, smiling. "Will you marry me?"

Sam's replacement at Fastnet was a middle-aged man called Arnold who had a pronounced cleft lip. Sam hoped the man wasn't seeking the isolation of Fastnet in order to escape public embarrassment.

The loadmaster buckled Sam up in the Wessex and shouted into his ear above the noise of the rotors. "We're going to Karry Airport. You'll be transferred there into a Baron Beechcraft aircraft. It will take you to St. Davids. Someone wants to speak to you." He handed Sam some earphones.

Sam was bewildered as to who it might be, but nodded all the same.

St. Davids was the most western town in Wales and was therefore within relatively close reach of southwest Ireland.

It was a chilly winter's day, but the sun was out, which lent some color to the restless Atlantic Ocean below Sam. After one hour, the six-seater Baron made landfall, and the town of St. Davids came into view. Sam had a good view of the city from air. It was the smallest city in Britain with one of the smallest cathedrals. The cathedral looked to be a squat affair with very few adornments. The pilot, a cheerful Welshman, chatted to him through the intercom, telling him that St. David, the patron saint of Wales, was buried there.

The Baron flew over the city and landed at the airfield. Evidently, the airfield had been built and used by Coastal Command in World War II. Now, however, it served only as a relief landing area.

A black Daimler was parked fifty yards from where the aircraft taxied to a stop. The pilot turned off the engines and the propellers wound down to a shuddering stop. Sam clambered down the steps to the ground.

The single occupant of the car got out and stood beside it in his overcoat. Sam recognized him immediately. It was Oliver Tremain.

Tremain shivered. "Let's get in the car where it's warm."

Sam was dressed in his navy deck coat, but even so, he was grateful to get in the car. "What can I do for you, sir?"

"As you have probably surmised by now, it is no accident that you have been transferred to Skellig. I need you there to be my eyes and ears."

"And why is that?"

"Because I'm closing in on what I suspect is a Russian spy ring."

Sam's mouth dropped opened. "Good grief."

Tremain continued. "The difficulty I have, is that I don't yet know who I can trust. So I'm having to use a new team – one that includes you."

"I'm not sure how I can help, sir."

"I want you on Skellig, because I suspect that the Russians are aware that I'm closing in on them. We've managed to eavesdrop on some radio and telephone traffic, and it suggests a mass extraction of Russian agents is being planned." He pursed his lips. "The problem is, we don't know exactly where or when. But we know enough to think that one probable site is Skellig."

"Why Skellig, sir?"

Tremain smiled. "You've not been there yet, but when you do, you will know why. There's a manned lighthouse there, but it's right in the south. Here, let me show you." He reached behind him and took a folder from the back seat, from which he extracted an annotated aerial photograph of the island. "As you can see, the lighthouse is at the bottom of the island. The main landing point is in the northeast, at Blind Man's Cove. There's a small pier there with a derrick. The road, if you can call it that, runs from there to the lighthouse." He tapped a large cove on the other side of the island. "This is the place we need to keep an eye on – Blue Cove. It's on the other side of the peaks. There's a landing there but it's not used much because the path up from the cove is so treacherous. The good news is, you'll be able to keep an easy eye on it if you make for this place, Christ's Saddle. It's the dip between the two peaks, and it has a commanding view over Blue Cove." Tremain drew in a deep breath. The cove is shielded from the lighthouse by the peaks, and it is probably the remotest place you can expect to find anywhere."

Sam looked at the map. "Are those steps I can see going up from the road to Christ's Saddle?"

"Yes. There's a lot of them, so you will need to be fit."

Sam rubbed his chin. "I'm not sure I'll be very much use, sir, if I'm holed up in the lighthouse most of the time."

"I agree. I'm playing a long shot." He looked at Sam. "Do you think you can get to Christ's Saddle on a semi-regular basis. Any boat you see heading toward that cove has to be suspicious."

"Yes sir." He paused. "How do you think the agents will be extracted?"

"By submarine. If they run to form, they will send a couple of inflatables to a landing place when the weather is right."

"I take it, that the right weather means calm seas and preferably a sea mist."

Tremain smiled. "That's why I need a sailor – someone who understands when the time is right to cast an eye over Blue Cove. It's not quite as hard as it sounds as it's only possible to land at the cove on exceptionally calm days."

"It will still be incredibly lucky if I do spot anything."

Tremain nodded. "And if you do, it will probably be too late to intercept them. I can but try. I've got a team standing by at Portmagee. They have one of the new rigid inflatables. It's very fast." He handed Sam a slip of paper. "Use that frequency to contact me on the marine radio. Your call will be patched through to me."

Sam looked at the details and handed the piece of paper back.

Tremain gave him a quizzical look. "You'll remember that?"

"Yes." He paused. "May I make a suggestion, sir?"

"What's that?"

"Drop a passive sonar in the cove."

"A passive sonar?"

"You can put it ten feet underwater on a lobster-pot line, marked with a buoy. Passive sonars hardly use any power because all they are doing is listening rather than sending out sonar pulses. I could replace the batteries every fortnight – if the lighthouse has a boat."

"How would you know the sonar has heard a submarine?"

"I can rig it so that it trips an alarm onshore. But, for that to happen, I'll need some equipment."

"Tell me what you need."

Sam scratched his head. "Well, first I'd need…"

Chapter 25

Skellig shocked Sam. The island erupted from the sea like shark's teeth, its two peaks rising to a height of 750 feet. As the Wessex made its way down the eastern side of the island to the helipad, Sam could not conceive how the place could ever have been the site of a monastery. It must have been one of the hardest places on earth to live. He'd managed to catch a glimpse of the monastery complex out the window. It had been carved into the side of the northern peak, just south of its summit.

The island was certainly bigger than Fastnet. Fastnet was just a rock with a lighthouse stuck alongside it. Skellig looked to be a little over half a mile long, and a quarter of a mile wide. It would at least afford him some outdoor exercise.

As the helicopter shuddered down onto the helipad, Sam could see some Atlantic gray seals slip off the rocks into the sea. There seemed to be plenty of wildlife around.

A bearded Irishman met him at the helipad. He was driving a motorized buggy. "So it is yourself, Samuel. Welcome to Skellig." He held out his hand. "I'm Seamus McBride. My wife is Cara, and she's looking forward to having someone else at the dinner table."

He cocked a thumb at the truck bed of the buggy. "Throw your dunnage in the back, and let's get out of the wind."

Sam had to force himself not to grip the doorframe of the buggy in terror. The path only just clung to the edge of the cliff. For much of the way, they were separated from an almost vertical drop only by a low stone wall. An angry sea boiled amongst the rocks below.

It didn't take long for them to reach the lighthouse complex. It was a boxy white affair. A double story building was separated from the lighthouse by a single-story building. Sam guessed it was the machinery shed. The lighthouse itself was a modest fifty feet high – very different from Fastnet.

Sam heaved both rucksack and duffle bag over his shoulders and entered the accommodation block. Seamus pointed to the stairs. "You're upstairs. Cara and I are downstairs. It's easier for her legs."

The accommodation was modern and well appointed, if a little soulless. It only took a moment for him to unpack. He saw that someone had made up his bed.

Sam made his way downstairs and headed toward the voices coming from the kitchen.

Cara was stick thin, with thick gray hair, and she had distant gray eyes. She ran those eyes over Sam and nodded, almost to herself. "'Tis good to see you, Samuel. It's a poor table with so few knees under it."

Seamus laid a beefy hand on his wife's shoulder. "Cara loves the cooking. Strictly speaking, the person on watch prepares the meals, but you'll find it hard to have the kitchen to yourself if Cara is awake. She cooks more than her fair share of the meals."

Sam forced a smile. "I'm very grateful, but I plan to pull my weight."

Seamus nodded. "That's good, Samuel. There's a fair weight to pull. We've been understaffed for a while. Are you happy standing eight-hour watches? I'll walk you through it after dinner, and you can start at midnight."

"That's fine."

"Now, will you go to the machine shed next door and get the help? It's tea-time."

Sam furrowed his brow. "The help?"

"Ach, you'll find out." Seamus waved him away.

Sam shrugged into his deck coat and headed outside. It had been dark for some while and was very cold. He paused to listen to the mewing of seabirds as they settled on their roosts, and the booming thunder of waves. Above him, the 1,800,000 candle power light flashed three quick flashes every ten seconds. Fortunately, the light was shining above him, so he was not blinded by it. It was enough, however, to prevent him developing his night vision. So, he had to grope his way next door, until he was able to pull on the handle of the steel door into the machine shed.

As he opened the door, the thrum of the generator became much louder. Only two bulbs lighted the whole machine shed, so there were plenty of shadows. It therefore took a moment for Sam to see the figure crouched down at the base of the generator. He yelled to make himself heard above the generator noise. "Hello."

The figure was so startled by the voice that the head jerked up and bumped against the exhaust guard. Luckily, the figure was wearing a beanie.

"Ow!" The figure turned round with a scowl.

With a shock, Sam realized he was looking at a girl.

She rubbed her head. "You shouldn't go creeping up on people."

It took a while for Sam to find his voice. "Um, sorry. What are you doing?"

The girl stood up and put her hands on her hips. "I'm doing your job."

Sam blinked. "My job." He noticed that she had a smudge of oil on her cheek.

"The last assistant lightkeeper we had was a bit of a eejit. He didn't do half the maintenance jobs he was responsible for. And sometimes when he did, he rigged things up arseways." She looked him over. "How much experience have you had?"

"Two months on Fastnet."

The girl rolled her eyes. "Two months. The Lord help us."

"What have you been doing in here?"

"I've just changed the oil filter on the generator."

He nodded. "Cara asked me to say that dinner is ready. She said it was colcannon – whatever that is."

"It's mashed potatoes with cabbage. She will probably put some fish with it." The girl looked him over. "Who did you say you were?"

"I'm Sam, the new assistant. Who are you?"

"I'm Lily McBride. I'm Seamus and Cara's daughter."

"I didn't know you were also with Trinity House."

"I'm not. But I did much of my growing up here, so I know the ropes. Dad asked for my help because he was on his own for two days. He's fair knackered, I can tell you."

"So you don't live here."

"No. I live in on the mainland at Portmagee. I'm the local National Parks and Wildlife Officer."

Sam was intrigued. She was someone who shared a love of animals. "Where did you train to do that?"

"I did a bachelor's in Marine Science at NUI."

Sam guessed that NUI was the National University of Ireland. He would have dearly liked to talk more, but he remembered the reason he'd come. "I suppose we'd better be joining your parents."

She nodded and stripped herself of her overalls. Sam had the guilty feeling that he shouldn't be watching. It was absurd, of course; she was dressed in jeans and a pullover, but she had a figure that definitely disturbed his sensibilities. He did, however, venture to make one suggestion. He picked up a hand of cotton waste from a box on the bench. "May I wipe the oil streak from your cheek?"

"Certainly not."

She grabbed the cotton waste from his hand and rubbed her cheek. "Has it gone?"

"No," Sam lied. He took the cotton from her and wiped her cheek – feeling the contours of her cheekbone as he did. "There," he said huskily. "Perfect."

Lily felt slightly bereft after dinner when her father took Sam over to the lighthouse to familiarize him with its workings. She wanted to interrogate Sam further about his past. Her vague feeling of disappointment continued when Seamus came back alone.

"Where's himself, then?" she asked.

"In the lighthouse. He told me he'd take the rest of my watch, as well as stand his own at midnight." Seamus yawned. "I'm right grateful, that I am."

Lily was now regretting the harsh words she'd said to Sam when she'd first met him. "I'll take him over a mug of coffee."

Seamus shook his head. "You needn't bother lass. He has the makings over there. Samuel will look after himself."

She felt slightly thwarted, and mooched around helping her mother tidy up the kitchen and do a stock-take of the larder.

In the end, she could bear her restlessness no more. "Mum, can you remember how Sam took his coffee at tea-time?"

Cara's voice came from the larder. "Standard: milk and two sugars, I think."

Lily made the coffee, poured it into a thermally insulated mug, and pushed her way through the rising wind to the machinery shed that gave access to the lighthouse.

She found Sam in the communications room and plonked down his mug of coffee almost as an act of defiance, daring him not to accept it.

To her intense relief, he did. He smiled his thanks, something that caused his handsome face to come alive. Unusually for a young man in these modern times, his hair and sideburns were not long. She decided to open the conversation. "I'm after thinking: you're a navy fellah. Is that right?"

She thought she caught a flash of defensiveness in his eyes. "That's right. But just for four years."

He'd looked down, but as Lily made no attempt to leave, he looked back up at her. His eyes seemed to question her, but then he turned away.

Lily decided to answer his question by taking off her beanie and shaking her hair loose. It was an old feminine ploy, and she wanted it to work for her now.

Her strawberry blond hair fell down on her shoulders.

For a while, nothing was heard other than the sighing of the wind and the distant thunder of the waves. Sam nodded slowly. "So you are the local National Parks and Wildlife Officer. What can I expect to see on this island?"

This was one of her favorite subjects, so she allowed herself a long leash. "Skellig is an awful good place for birds and sea mammals. You'd be after seeing the petrel, gannet, fulmar, shearwater, kittiwake, guillemot, razorbill, and the Atlantic puffin. If you're lucky, you'll also see a peregrine falcon."

Sam nodded appreciatively. "The peregrine has the fastest dive of any bird. It has a modified beak so that its insides are not damaged by the air flow."

She frowned. "How do you know that? Are you an ornithologist?"

"Sort of. Before my brief stint in the navy, I contemplated studying biology." He smiled. "As a kid, I wanted to be a zookeeper."

Really?

He shrugged. "I've been a bit of a naturalist, ever since I was a child growing up in Malaya."

"So we have that in common."

He nodded slowly. "We do."

"How old are you?" She'd asked the question before she realized it might be rude.

"I'm 22."

She was four years older than him. But, she told herself, he looked older.

There was another silence.

When Lily could bear it no more she said, "You can also expect to see the gray seal, basking shark, minke whale, and the leatherback sea turtle."

Sam leaned back in his chair and crossed his arms. A small smile played on his lips. For a moment, she feared she might have overdone her enthusiasm. "I amn't boring you, am I?"

He laughed. "Certainly not. You obviously love your work."

"I keep telling my Dad that someday, Skellig will be a tourist attraction. They'll come for the wildlife and the history. But Dad disagrees and says that it is too rugged and remote for them."

"I saw the ruins of the old monastery as we flew in. It looks… fascinating."

"It is."

Sam picked up a pencil and started playing with it. "Do you suppose you could show me around the island in the next few days? I'd really like to try and understand it."

Lily laughed. "Try and understand why twelve mad monks would defy both nature and pillaging Vikings to live on this rock – good luck to ye."

"Would you show me around?"

She looked at his eyes. They were soft and invitational. But was he safe? Lily decided to take things to the next level. "Are you trying to hit on me?"

"I am legitimately interested in the island." He paused. "But that thought is definitely not unattractive." He looked up at her. "Would you mind?"

Lily experienced a thrill of electricity through her, but she decided to play safe. "We'll see." It wasn't quite a rebuff, but it did suggest that a long game was required. She had planned to call through for a boat and leave the island tomorrow, but she decided to reschedule her week. Fortunately, she had brought all the folders she needed to compile her monthly report for the Maritime Development Office in Dublin. She'd be able to do the work on Skellig.

Besides, Sam had asked for her help.

After breakfast, Seamus took over the watch from Sam. Sam was dog-tired and looking forward to a sleep. However he needed to talk with Seamus first.

"Seamus, have you got a marine chart of the island and surrounding waters."

"Aye lad, I do. I'll fetch it for ye."

Moments later, the two of them were poring over the chart. Sam had been wrestling with the question of how much he should tell Seamus about the task Tremain had entrusted him with. He looked at the old man. Nothing about him suggested anything else other than stolid integrity.

He drew a deep breath and decided to take the risk. "Seamus, a chopper will be arriving in the next day or so with some equipment for me."

"And what's that, lad?"

"It's a sonar and some electrical equipment."

Seamus leaned back in his chair. "Perhaps you'd better tell me what's afoot, because none of that sounds like standard Trinity House equipment."

"I've been given a project by the security service because of my naval experience. They want me to drop a sonar in Blue Cove to listen for submarines. As I said, the equipment will arrive by chopper in a few days, unless you tell me it's impossible."

Seamus' bushy eyebrows rose in surprise. "Is there likely to be a submarine nosing about in these waters?"

"A Russian one – yes. It's a real possibility."

"Then why isn't the navy sorting it out?"

"There have been some security leaks. So they've cobbled together a bunch of amateurs. And I, for one, am far from sure what I'm doing."

The old man nodded. "And where would you expect this submarine to be hiding?"

"If you had to wait for a break in the weather to pick people off from the landing in Blue Cove, where would you sit?"

Seamus lifted his shaggy head. "And what fellahs would these be?"

"It's a long shot. But they might be spies that Russia wants to extract."

Seamus started to laugh. "Ach, lad. When you invited me to stay for a wee craic, I didn't expect to be chasing Russian spies." His face then became serious. "I won't be doing anything that endangers Cara. So will it be safe?"

Sam nodded. "Yes. All we are doing is listening and reporting. If there is any action, it will happen at Blue Cove, well away from here."

Seamus nodded and scratched his beard. "If you planned to drop people off at Blue Cove, you'd have to pick your moment. It's only accessible about twenty days in a year."

"But if you were waiting to pick them up, where would you park your submarine?"

Seamus stabbed the chart with his stubby finger. "There's foul ground to the west and the north, which cuts down your options. The only place left is just off Blue Cove, here. I'd sit it down here in 160 feet. That's safe and gives room to maneuver. Blue Cove shelves a bit, but not a lot. The depth of water in the cove is about 65 feet."

"Could I drop the sonar on a mooring buoy in the bay?"

"I suppose so, lad. I've got an anchor line you could use in the storeroom."

"What about a boat?"

Seamus frowned. "This is no place to be arsing about in a wee boat, lad. It's treacherous."

"I'll be careful. Is there a boat?"

"Aye. There's one tied upside town at the head of the pier at Blind Man's Cove. Its outboard engine is in the store. But you'd better check it out. It hasn't been used for a while."

Chapter 26

L ily looked at Sam. "Lose the coat and put on an anorak."
They were getting up from the breakfast table, having just finished a meal of carrageen pudding. Lily looked out the window. "We'll only have about five hours of daylight, so we'll have to get moving."

Cara waved them away. "Seamus will take the daylight watch, won't you Seamus."

Seamus nodded obediently.

"I've put bread, cheese, and sausage in the knapsack." Cara gave Lily a push. "You've been wanting to check out the bird colonies somethin' fierce for days, but the weather has been against you. Go and make the most of the calm."

Once they were outside, Lily asked, "Where do you want to go first?"

Sam replied straight away. "I'd like to get up to Christ's Saddle and see the view over Blue Cove. After that, I'm in your hands."

"Ach, you'll be half way to the monastery there, so we might as well continue up to it."

Sam smiled. "Lead the way."

They clomped down the coastal path toward the helicopter

landing pad, but then they branched off on a narrow stone slab path that headed inland. Almost immediately, they came across a section of stone steps. The steps seemed to go on forever. At first, Sam struggled to keep up with Lily. "How many steps up to the monastery?" he asked.

"About six-hundred."

"Good grief."

She looked back at him and grinned. "You're sounding an awful lot like a soft Britisher."

He waved her on. "You're holding me up. Keep moving, girl."

Lily was content to allow the easy banter to continue through much of the morning. However, once they got to the ruins of the monastery, the stones that had been erected so many centuries ago seemed to call for more thought and respect. She pointed out the collection of beehive dwellings built of dry-stone. "These beehives are where the monks slept. They're quite small so I'm guessing only one person lived in them."

She was pleased to see Sam looking around in amazement at the ruins of the oratories and the stone crosses. "When did the monks get here? These look ancient. They haven't even used any mortar in their buildings."

"The only building where mortar is used is the chapel. That was built relatively late, in the tenth century. No one's very sure when the monks first arrived. The monastery is attributed to Saint Finian in the sixth century, but the first definite reference to monks is a record of the death of 'Suibhini of Skelig,' dating from the eighth century."

Lily was interested to see that the feature that most took Sam's attention was the tiny cemetery. It was a raised bed, edged with a low stone wall. The cemetery was just nine paces long and three paces wide. Yet, somehow, twenty-two gravestones had been squeezed into it. Sam shook his head. "What stories could this graveyard tell?"

It was not a question anyone could answer, so she kept quiet, content to leave the conversation to the ghosts of the past.

When they had finished exploring the monastery, they sat down against one of the fortification walls and ate their lunch.

Sam seemed very content. He caught her looking at him and asked, "Do you have any brothers or sisters?"

"I have a brother, Conor. He was born eight years after me and was a bit of surprise package. He's currently doing an arts degree at Hull."

"I thought Seamus and Cara were Irish."

"They are. Dad is from county Antrim in Northern Ireland, and Mum is from the south. She's a Kerry girl. Conor can go to Hull because Dad's from Northern Ireland."

Lily dusted her hands of crumbs and got to her feet. "We'd best keep going if we want to make the most of the weather."

"Where are you taking me next?"

"While the weather is this good, we'll go back down to Christ's Saddle, and then work our way to the other ruins."

"What are they?"

"'Tis the Hermitage. They're ruins built on terraces clinging to the southern peak, just 45 feet from the summit. You can't often get there because the winds get awful powerful – hurricane force, sometimes."

"Let's get cracking, then."

"Listen to him, would you. He's suddenly quite the mountain goat."

Neither of them said anything for the next forty minutes, as the path was so steep and treacherous. At one point, the track led through a dramatic natural rock chimney. Lily found enough breath to say, "They call this the Needle's Eye."

Sam seemed to be beyond words. Certainly, no words could do justice to the terrifying and dramatic views all about. Lily hoped it was also because Sam was out of breath, and that she'd managed to outlast him.

Alas, it was not to be. "Where next?" he said.

She looked at him in defiance. "You can either go back the way we came, or we can work our way down to the ruins of the old northern lighthouse. It's awful spectacular because it just hangs onto the cliff. There're also lots of birds. If it were summer, you'd be seeing puffins."

By the time they got to the ruins of the lighthouse, the light was beginning to dim. Sam looked around in evident disbelief. "The tenacity of people never ceases to amaze me."

Lily was well pleased with the day. It had gone well. The island was working its magic on Sam, and he obviously loved the place. It was a test she'd deliberately put him through, and he'd passed.

They wound their way via a twisting coastal path until they came back to the new lighthouse.

Sam turned to her after he hung up his anorak. "Lily, today has been the most memorable day of my life. Thank you very much." It was a curiously formal thing for him to say, but he didn't seem able to say anything more.

Lily smiled.

Sam made his way through the machine shed, and found Seamus wiping various pipes with an oily rag. The old man turned around on hearing Sam. "How was the day, young fellah?"

"Spectacular."

Seamus chuckled. "Aye. Skellig doesn't disappoint, if you pick the weather."

"I'll take over the watch, Seamus. Thanks for standing in for me."

"Ach, it's a pleasure. You did the same for me."

Sam held up a hand. "Just one question before you go. There was a small steel door built into the cliff by the old lighthouse. What's that about?"

Seamus smiled. "Best not go too close to that. That's the old explosive store."

"What?"

"Aye. In them days, we used explosives as fog signals – three quick reports every ten minutes, I'm told. The explosive charges were attached to retractable booms above the lantern, and detonated electrically. Sometimes the charges contained magnesium in order to provide a bright flare." He shook his head. "We haven't used explosive for sixty years, and there's been no call for us to give fog warnings since 1960."

"Why are the explosives still there?"

"The Lord bless you, laddie. No one's got the courage to take them off the island." He chuckled. "I hear tell of a time when the earth closet outside the old lighthouse became choked. The PK in charge in those days was a bloke called Brendan. He had the bright idea of clearing it by detonating some fog signals in the drain." Seamus chuckled again. "He blew the roof off the toilet and covered the place in shit."

Sam shook his head in disbelief.

Seamus yawned and made for the door. "I'm wrecked, so I'm off to bed. Just keep the light shining, boyo. Call me if there are any difficulties."

Sam waved him away.

When he was alone, Sam made his way to the communications room and put through a call on the marine radio. There was one more item he wanted Tremain to put on the chopper that was due to arrive next morning.

The man wore a shapeless gabardine raincoat. He liked things to be shapeless. You could hide a lot of things behind anything 'shapeless.' On this occasion, he was carrying a Makarov nine-millimeter pistol, machined to accept a suppressor. The length of the suppressor made the pistol unwieldy and difficult to balance – or it would have, if the man had not been well practiced at using it. It was just as well he was, given that most of his assignments required the use of a suppressor, or silencer, as it was more commonly called.

He had contemplated dressing as a postal officer who was delivering a parcel, but decided against it. The raincoat gave him more options.

The man pulled his hat down on his head, and pushed the doorbell.

There was no reply.

He pushed it again.

There was still no reply.

You never did anything a third time without drawing attention to yourself, so he walked through the foyer of the block of flats and out of the front door. Once outside, he paused beside the iron railings, ostensibly to light a cigarette. In reality, he was looking through the ground floor window.

He looked at the mantelpiece and noticed that the little display stand for Tony Chester-Smith's medal was empty.

The man nodded in satisfaction. He knew exactly where Chester-Smith would be.

It was a good day for death. The English countryside was still and bare under the frosting hand of winter. Nothing showed signs of life. The Russian handler had regretted recruiting Tony Chester-Smith for some time. Chester Smith had become a liability – a conduit through whom MI5 could reach him. The handler was not convinced that a connection had yet been made, but he had a feeling in his bones that things were getting critical. That's why he'd organized to shut down his operation. He and his team needed to disappear, and disappearing required loose ends to be tidied up. Chester-Smith was one such loose end. As an agent, he'd not turned up anything particularly significant, and nothing at all in the last year or so. It was this, as much as anything, that gave the Russian handler an uneasy feeling.

He made his way south out of London through Caterham and East Grinstead, until finally, he turned off to Hartfield.

Hartfield was such an English name. Although he hated to admit it, he liked England. Everything was so domesticated. England seemed to sit comfortably with its history – far too comfortably to his mind. Whilst the unions did their best to stir up dissent, the Russian handler had the dispiriting thought that the British were far too content to allow any revolution. However, they, and their NATO allies, were in a position to frustrate Russia's expansionist policies… and that was not to be countenanced.

He turned into Church Street and nosed his way down the narrow road toward St. Mary's Church. He noted with satisfaction that Tony's car was parked to the side in one of the rare places it was possible to park. There was a convenient car parking space just behind it, so he did a three-point turn in a driveway, and parked behind it – facing away so that his exit would be quick and unobtrusive.

With hat and Makarov in place, he walked down the laneway, alongside the iron railings that bordered the graveyard. There was no obvious sign of Chester-Smith.

The gate squeaked as he entered the churchyard. And then he saw his quarry. The man was slumped down beside a grave.

When he got closer, he could see that Chester-Smith had fallen over backward. Two neat holes pierced his coat, and a dark red patch had spread across his chest. Chester-Smith's arm lay across the grave. In his hand, was the medal he so prized.

The Russian handler walked away quickly, scanning the hedgerows as he did. This killing was not carried out by MI5. The people who had done this were infinitely more dangerous. This execution had all the characteristics of Russian intelligence cleaning house, ensuring that the work that had been assigned to him was carried out.

Isaac had the hand-piece pressed to his ear. "Hello," he said tentatively.

Almost instantly, a gravelly voice with an Irish brogue answered him. "Skellig Light. Seamus McBride speaking. Go ahead."

Isaac swallowed. "Good morning, sir. My name is Isaac Hastings. I was wondering if I could speak with my brother, Sam."

"Ach, you're the brother, is it? That's grand. He speaks of you."

"Is it possible to talk with him?"

"I'm afraid not, laddie. He's making the best of some good weather, and is away in a wee boat doing some fool thing."

Isaac was instantly concerned. "What's the fool thing he's doing?"

He heard a rich laugh. "Anyone getting into a small boat on this island takes their life in their hands. Let's hope St. Michael is riding on his shoulder."

There was a pause. Isaac wondered how much he should say.

"Have you got a message for him, laddie?"

"Umm…"

"Spit it out, man. I won't bite, although I'm curious about how you managed to get hold of a marine radio."

"An acquaintance made it possible for me to use the one at Trinity House in Ipswich. I'm speaking from there."

"And what's your message?"

Isaac wanted to tell Sam about the murder of Tony Chester-Smith. Oliver Tremain had told him about it the previous evening. It had come as a shock. Part of him was intensely relieved that there would be no more threats from Chester-Smith, but he couldn't fathom who would murder him. MI5 wouldn't simply kill someone who was a spy. They would want to capture and interrogate him. The only people he could think of who might want him dead were the Russian secret service. Perhaps Chester-Smith had double-crossed them. When he'd asked Tremain about it, he could give him no answer except to warn that things may be coming to a head, and that he needed to be on his toes.

Isaac had rung to inform Sam of everything that had happened. He drew a deep breath. "Sam is not in any particular danger, is he – other than the danger from the sea?"

"How much do you know about what he's up to here?"

"Just a bit." Isaac had the impression that he and Mr. McBride were like two cats circling, trying to find out about each other. Both were being careful not to give away information. McBride's very reticence encouraged Isaac to make a request. "Sir, many years ago, Sam and I swore an oath that we'd protect each other if ever there was need. I know that Sam is helping with some surveillance work. He's probably very safe and away from any action in Skellig, but I just wanted to warn him to be alert."

"Aye lad. I think I'm aware of some little bitty things. All I can say is that he's fishing for some big fish."

"I'm afraid I don't understand you, sir."

"Ach, but I've said enough."

Isaac frowned, trying to make sense of what he'd heard. It was obvious that Seamus McBride was aware of something clandestine that Sam was involved in. He was equally sure that the Irishman wouldn't tell him anything about it. "Sir, may I ask a favor?"

"And what's that?"

"Could you watch Sam's back? I can't be there to do it myself."

"What would you be wanting me to do, laddie?"

Chapter 27

S am was mildly surprised he was still alive. He hadn't given himself good odds for being so. It was curious; two weeks ago, he couldn't have cared whether he lived or died. But since he had come to Skellig and felt its spirituality, he had changed. He'd seen the faith of those who acknowledged the reality of something bigger than themselves – and who held to this with a conviction that rose above suffering. He'd also changed because of Lily. Sam shook his head at the memory of her. She was feisty, plain speaking, passionate about her work, and in every way beguiling. He had to admit that he'd regret dying before having a chance to pursue a romance with her. She was spending the day at the cliffs near the old lighthouse doing a bird count.

He forced himself to concentrate on the matter in hand, for he'd not yet found safety. He was actually in a small wooden boat rounding the northern tip of Skellig, with a rising westerly wind beginning to make life uncomfortable. To the northeast, he could see the jagged outcrop of 'Little Skellig,' a rock inhabited only by seabirds. Seabirds were also flying out from their roosts on the cliffs above him, disturbed by the noise of the Evinrude outboard motor.

Sam piloted his little boat down the east side of Skellig to Blind

Man's Cove, grateful for the promontory that led out to the pier as it was now protecting him from the worst of the wind. He breasted the boat against the stone pier and made the vessel fast. Sam then maneuvered straps under the boat and hitched them up to the derrick on the pier. After a lot of fussing about, the boat was lifted onto its trailer, and Sam was tugging it along the pier to where it was stowed below the cliffs.

The cliffs above him were daunting. They hung over him, as if wanting to devour him. The lower part of the rocky face had been blasted away to make the end of the track that ran all the way down the east coast to the lighthouse. Lily had told him that there had once been a northern path from Blind Man's Cove to the monastery, but the blasting had blown its lower reaches into the sea. Sam couldn't help but grieve at the history that had been lost – or think of the feet of those who had once trod the path up to their eyrie on the northern peak.

Sam slid the boat off the trolley and tipped it upside down. Then he pulled the trolley on top of the dinghy and tied them both down onto iron cringles that had been fixed into the cement. Finally, he lifted the outboard engine into the back of the motorized buggy.

It had been a testing day, but finally, everything was in place. A yellow diamond-shaped navy sonar was suspended ten feet below the surface of Blue Cove. It was hanging underneath a buoy Sam had made from a stout five-gallon plastic drum. He'd anchored the buoy to the seafloor with an old kedge anchor.

Accomplishing the task had been hard enough on a relatively calm day. It would have been impossible on a rough day. He knew he'd been lucky. Winter was the season for storms.

Sam climbed wearily into the motorized buggy, and wondered how long he would have to wait for the next calm day, a day when he would need to monitor the alarm and watch for boats at Christ's Saddle. Hopefully it would be a long while.

The alarm rang at 3 next morning when Sam was off watch. It took a moment for him to realise what it was, because he was still stupid with sleep. When he discovered where the sound was coming from, he reached for the headphones and slipped them over his ears. Straight away, he heard the unmistakable sound of a sonar making contact.

Sam listened to the sinister sound for the next thirty minutes, scarcely believing what he was hearing. The contact sound was now steady, signifying that whatever the sonar had picked up was now stationary. At 3:30 in the morning, there was not much he could do. He could, however, relieve Seamus on watch so the man could get some sleep – because Sam suspected that he would spend a long day tomorrow up on Christ's Saddle, looking for a boat coming from the mainland. Unusually, the day was again forecast to be calm – with the possibility of snow later in the day. Snow did not fall often on Skellig. The peaks were not high enough to attract it, and the warm North Atlantic Drift current discouraged it.

When Sam opened the door through the machine shed into the lighthouse, Seamus was staring moodily at the marine chart. "What are you after being here for?" he demanded. "Get some sleep."

"The sonar has picked up a vessel. We have to assume it's a submarine."

"Bajeebers. Is that right, then?"

"Yes. I heard the first signal 45 minutes ago. The signal is steady, so I'm assuming the vessel isn't moving."

"Well, it's 3:45am laddie, and you can't do much about it."

"I could report it."

Seamus gave a cough of derision. "No one will thank you for calling them at this time, particularly if all you've picked up is a fisherman doing some drift fishing. Go back to bed. You'll need your energy and your wits for tomorrow."

"Are you sure?" Sam asked.

"Away with you."

Sam wasn't sure how many of the 600 steps to the monastery he climbed to reach Christ's Saddle, but it was more than he could wish. He was dressed as warmly as he could and was now hunched down with his back against a rock looking at the spectacular drop into Blue Cove. No boats could be seen on the horizon, but it was early, and he hadn't expected to see any.

In the middle of the morning, Sam had an unexpected visitor. It was Lily. She came toiling up the slope to join him. When she finally breasted the top, she sank down gratefully behind the rock with Sam.

Sam handed her his hot vacuum flask. "Have a drink. You've earned it."

She waved it away. "You'd better have a good explanation for sitting here catching pneumonia. Dad is grumpy and won't tell me anything."

Sam did a lightning-fast mental review of what he could say. In the end, he decided that Lily deserved to know almost everything.

"Um… I dropped a sonar buoy in Blue Cove and rigged it up to an alarm." He pointed to the cove. "I suspect there is Russian submarine out there waiting to pick up people who will be dropped off at Blue Cove."

"You're kidding me, right?"

"No."

"Are you really a lighthouse keeper, or a spy?"

He laughed. "No. I'm a humble lighthouse keeper. But because of my naval background, I've been asked to observe and report. Nothing more."

"So, you being here is no accident?"

"No. I was transferred here to do what I'm doing now."

Lily looked at him. Sam could see the reserve and hurt in her eyes. "Just who are you, Sam Hastings? I want to know who I'm… getting to know."

Sam lifted a hand and sought to reassure her. "No, really Lily. I'm just an ordinary apprentice keeper. This is just a small job that draws on some of my naval experience."

"I'm thinking that anything to do with Russian submarines picking people up from remote islands, is anything but small."

"Perhaps so." He tried a smile. "But I don't think this sort of thing is going to happen very often."

Lily hugged her knees. Sam suspected it was a subconscious move of self-protection as much as a desire to keep warm. No one said anything for a while.

Lily broke the silence. "I watched you climb up here from the lighthouse."

Sam waited for her to say more.

She sighed. "You can't stay up here all day, so why don't we take it in turns and do two hours at a time. If the person off duty watches from the lighthouse, we can signal to each other if we see anything."

Sam nodded. "I'd want to check you were okay periodically, say… every fifteen minutes."

"That's easy enough. I'll stand up and hold my arms out in a T shape every 15 minutes, to signal all is well. And if I see anything, I'll stand with my arms straight up above my head."

"Are you sure you want to get involved with this?"

"You're involved with this."

"Yes."

"So I want to be involved." The tone of her voice left little room for protest, so Sam nodded.

Seamus McBride made his way slowly up the stairs and pushed though the entrance into the lantern at the top of the lighthouse. For a moment, he gazed out the window. However, he saw nothing of the view in front of him. All he could hear were the dreadful words he'd listened to through the marine radio whilst he had been on watch last night. *You will temporarily disable your marine radio for 12 hours from midday tomorrow, or your son, Conor, will be shot. Similarly, if you call the police, your son will be shot. Twelves hours, Mr. McBride… or your son will die.*

Seamus, jerked himself back into reality, and opened the door onto the lantern's balcony. Then, reaching for the antenna cable, he gave it a pull.

It was mid afternoon, and the watery sun was heading for the horizon. Sam was climbing up the steps to relieve Lily when he saw her suddenly stand to her feet and lift her hands above her head. She had seen something.

The muscles in Sam's legs were burning when he finally reached her. Lily bounced up and down with excitement and pointed to the north. "That's Finn O'Sullivan's boat. He's from Portmagee, and he takes people on boat tours. It looks as if he's heading to Skellig."

Sam took her by the arm to steady her. "It could just be a boat of bird watchers, but if they are, they're leaving things a bit late." He came to a decision. "I think it's time I reported this in."

Lily nodded, and the two of them trudged down the hill toward the lighthouse.

When they arrived, they went straight to the communications room. Sam pushed through the door and found Seamus sitting at the desk with his head in his hands. "What's the matter?" he asked.

Seamus lifted his shaggy head. "The antenna has got itself banjaxed. It's broken somewhere. We can't receive or send any radio messages."

Lily kept out of the way as the two men fiddled with this and that, trying to get the marine radio to work. Alas, it was all to no avail.

Sam sighed in exasperation and said that he'd head back to Christ's Saddle. But that first, he had to get something from his room.

When the door closed, Lily rounded on her father. He again had his head in his hands and was in obvious torment. She put an arm around his shoulder. "What's going on, Dad?"

"Nuttin' girl. Oim fine."

"Dad. Don't mess with me. I know something's not right."

"What d'ya mean?" He shook himself free. "Leave me alone, girl."

Lily persisted. "All I know is that the radio was working fine last night, and there hasn't been a storm to break anything. What's amiss?"

Her father shouted. "Leave me alone lass."

Lily watched the uncharacteristic behavior of her father with bewilderment. The man was now slumped over the desk. She thought she could hear a sob.

"Dad, I'm not going until I know the truth."

"Blast you, girl, Seamus sobbed. "I'm caught, don't you see."

"How are you caught, Dad?"

"I've been told to shut down the marine radio for twelve hours, or our Conor will be killed." Her father's shoulders heaved with sobs as he covered his face with his hands.

Suddenly, the awful reality of what they were all engaged in hit her. She was no longer just an observer reporting, she was involved… and her brother's life was in peril.

Lily left the communication room and made her way to her bedroom. She rummaged in her knapsack for a moment, and then went outside to join Sam at Christ's Saddle.

This was the third time that day she'd climbed up to the Saddle, and she was dog tired by the time she got to the top.

Sam was watching Finn O'Sullivan's boat as it chugged its way around the coastline.

She stood with her hands on her knees, fighting for breath. "Dad's sabotaged the marine radio."

Sam looked at her in shock. "What?"

"It's true. He received a message last night saying that if he didn't disable the radio, my brother, Conor, would be killed."

Sam groaned. "It can't be true."

"It is. Dad's a mess."

"Well. We know for sure now that something is going to happen today – probably fairly soon, when it's twilight." Sam closed his eyes in anguish.

Lily took the binoculars from Sam and studied the boat. There looked to be a small group of people standing in the cockpit. One of them was looking toward the shore with his pair of binoculars. She handed the binoculars back to Sam and fished in her haversack for her high-frequency hand-held radio. Being high-frequency, it was completely useless at calling over long distances. She'd only ever used it to co-ordinate field studies with colleagues in a boat or on a cliff somewhere.

Sam looked at it and shook his head. "I can't reach British Security with that."

Lily looked at him defiantly. "No. But maybe I can reach Portmagee with it. We're up high and if I walk a bit higher, I'll be in clear sight of the mainland. Perhaps we can relay calls to your fellah."

She could see the light of hope appear in Sam's eyes. Lily saw him rub his temples as if willing himself to think. "Yes," he said. "If we could get someone to call Isaac... who could contact Sophie, we might be able to do something. Sophie has a contact number for Tremain."

"I take it, Tremain is your security fellah."

"Yes." He gave Lily a gentle shove. "Let's get up to higher ground and see what's possible."

Chapter 28

Sophie was looking forward to Christmas. It would be the first Christmas Isaac would spend with her at the farm. From what she could gather, Isaac's Christmases with his parents as a child had never amounted to much. They were so often overseas that it had usually only involved the four of them. She smiled. Isaac had no idea what a Hunter Christmas would be like. There would be cousins, aunts and...

Her musings were interrupted by a knock on her door. It was Wendy from the room next door. "Hi," she said. "I'm sent to tell you that your boyfriend is at the front gate. He says he needs to see you urgently."

Sophie rushed downstairs and across the courtyard to the main gate. She could see Isaac pacing up and down, still with his motorbike helmet on. "What's wrong?" she said as he rushed up to her.

The college porter called after him. "Sir. You can't go in there."

Isaac ignored him. He grabbed Sophie by the arms. "Sophie. I need to get a message to Oliver Tremain... and it's urgent."

"Why?"

"It concerns Sam. He could be in trouble."

Sophie's mouth dropped open in surprise, but she quickly took herself in hand. Sophie turned to the porter. "George. We have an emergency situation here. May I use your phone?"

George was an amiable sixty-year-old who knew the wisdom of turning a blind eye and stretching the rules occasionally. "If it is an emergency, of course."

George led them into the porter's lodge. Posters of Liverpool football club were pinned above his desk. He pointed to the phone.

Sophie took a slip of paper from her purse and dialed a number.

A few minutes later, Oliver Tremain's voice could be heard. Sophie wasted no time on pleasantries. "Mr. Tremain. We have a situation concerning Sam Hastings. I'll let his brother tell you the details." She handed the phone to Isaac."

It was the longest hour Isaac had spent in his life. Tremain had ordered Isaac to stay at the porter's lodge with Sophie until he rang back. The two of them had explained this to George, who accepted it easily enough. The porter made them both a mug of tea, then sat himself down and began a fairly one-sided conversation about the fortunes and failures of Liverpool City's soccer season.

When the phone rang, Isaac grabbed at the handset, almost dropping it in his haste.

Tremain said, without preamble. "Conor is safe. Our people in Hull have him in their charge. It was a bluff. I will call your friend in Portmagee and try to get a message to your brother."

The phone cut dead before Isaac could ask any questions.

Sam had walked back from the high ground to the Saddle and was watching the boat nose its way into the landing at Blue Cove. He couldn't see the actual landing because it was below the lip of the cliff.

His attention was distracted by a yell. He looked up to see Lily running downhill toward him, waving her arms. "Conor is free," she yelled. "He's free."

He caught her in his arms.

Lily danced up and down in his arms. "Conor is free. Your Tremain fellah has him safe. Imagine that." In sheer exuberance, she grabbed Sam by the back of the neck and kissed him on the lips. The kiss was brief, but it was a definite kiss.

Sam didn't have time to dwell on it. He tried to settle Lily down. "Go tell your Dad. I've got to go now and get closer to the beach."

She looked at him in alarm. "Why? What are you going to do?"

Sam didn't have time to explain, but Lily grabbed him by the arm. "What are you doing?"

"I've got to get closer. To see." He broke away.

She yelled after him. "Well don't get too close. The path goes down in a giant zigzag. The top part has flagstones. It's steep and slippery. The bottom part of the path has been carved into the rock. It's treacherous."

Her voice faded as Sam bounded down the path.

Every now and again, he paused to look out to sea. The second time he paused, he saw it. A black fin had emerged from the water just outside the cove. It looked surreal. Sam grabbed the binoculars from his haversack. The light was now fading, so he didn't have much time to see the details. When the fin came into focus, he could see that it was the black conning tower of a submarine. Even as he watched, the upper deck of the submarine broke the surface. He could see the water sluicing off its deck. Almost immediately, he saw some men emerge onto the deck busying themselves around something at their feet.

Sam put the binoculars away and fished out a handheld garage remote control. Its power had been significantly boosted, but was it enough? He stabbed at the button.

Nothing.

He would have to get closer. Sam bounded down the slippery flagstones for another fifty yards. Then he stopped and pushed the button again.

Still nothing.

He skipped and slithered for another fifty yards, hampered now by another complication. Fluffy white flakes were floating down around him. It was snowing. He came to a halt, and then, with a silent prayer, he pushed the button again.

A searing light flashed from the middle of Blue Cove. It was followed an instant later by a thunderous explosion as two-dozen magnesium amended sticks of explosive blew themselves apart. Sam had hidden them in his makeshift buoy.

After the echoes of the explosion died away, Sam massaged his ears, trying to coax his hearing back to normal. After twenty seconds or so, he became dimly aware of gulls and guillemots swirling and calling as they flew in fright from the cliff face. His hearing was returning.

He was elated. His plan had succeeded, but was the explosion enough to frighten the submarine away? Sam pulled out his binoculars and focused them on the submarine. Its deck was only just free of the water, but he was still able to see what was going on clearly. The men on the deck scrambled for the hatchway in the conning tower, abandoning the object they had been working on. Sam adjusted the focus and realized that the object was an inflatable dinghy. He had the satisfaction of seeing it break free as the hatchway closed and the submarine moved forward, sinking lower and lower as it pushed into the Atlantic.

Sam punched the air and danced in triumph. It was a mistake. Sam slipped on the snow that was half melted on the flagstone. For a moment, he clawed at the air, then landed on his back… and lost consciousness.

The Russian handler cowered on the rock platform as the shock wave of the explosion punched through him. What on earth had happened? He shook his head and looked out to sea, fearful of what he might see. Had a British warship arrived? It took a moment for his eyes to focus. Then he remembered the binoculars around his neck. He snatched them and put them to his eyes.

He was just in time to see his worst fears confirmed. The submarine that was to take him and his three colleagues to safety was moving away. The handler wanted to scream and call for it to return, but he didn't. Instead, he looked up at the cliff above him to the path that had been chiseled into it. As he did, he caught sight of a man. It was only for an instant because the man fell backward with a yelp of surprise. There was no sign of him standing up again.

His colleagues were arguing and pointing. The man called Stan was one of them. He had his hands on his head in despair. Even as the handler took stock of the situation, a plan was formulating in his mind. He would capture the man who had fallen, walk him to the lighthouse and force him to make the marine radio serviceable again. They would be able to call the submarine back… and then he would kill all the occupants of the lighthouse.

Sam woke to find someone slapping his face. The sight of a pistol muzzle hovering twelve inches from his temple instantly dispelled any thought that someone might be attempting to help him.

Sam felt himself being hauled to his feet. A voice spoke in perfect English. "Take us to the lighthouse. If you do anything stupid, you will be shot in the back. Do you understand?"

The notion that Sam knew the full import of what was happening was debatable, but he understood enough to nod.

Moments later he was being pushed in the back up the steep rocky track. As Sam's sensibilities began to fully return, his mind was faced with the awful reality that four Russian spies were marching him to the lighthouse at gunpoint. Lily, Cara, and Seamus would be there, and they would have no idea of the danger they were in. He couldn't bring himself to lead these desperate men to the lighthouse. But a mocking voice inside him told him that they would get to the lighthouse easily enough with or without him. He was wracked with indecision, and he slowed his walking pace. His reward for doing this was a savage push in the back. Sam staggered forward.

As he did, he heard a BANG. It was so loud that Sam ducked down and cowered with his arms over his head. When he stood up and looked around, the man behind him was on his back writhing in agony. His upper arm and shoulder was a bloody mess. The man's pistol was clattering down the cliff.

A voice called from above him. Sam recognized it immediately. It was Seamus. The old lighthouse keeper called out: "Put your hands on your head and kneel on the ground. This is a pump action shotgun, and I've plenty more cartridges. At less than sixty meters, it's deadly."

The men behind Sam hesitated.

Seamus let off another shot. It hit the stone paving just behind them.

The three men hurriedly got to their knees.

It took a moment for Sam to locate exactly where Seamus was. He was above them on the path that zigzagged in the other direction. It gave him a commanding view of the path below where Sam was standing.

"Well, don't just stand there, Samuel. Frisk the bastards for weapons."

Sam did as he was told… and it was just as well he did. Two of the men were each carrying a pistol in a shoulder holster. Sam stuck one pistol behind his belt and kept the other in his hand. He cocked it and flicked off the safety catch. "Right, you three. On your feet. Move!"

One of the men pointed to his wounded colleague on the ground. "What about him?"

Sam was not in a charitable mood. "Take your coat off and put it on top of him." He pointed the pistol at the other men. "You too. I want two coats on top of him and one underneath. We'll come back for him later with first aid."

Moments later, Sam was walking behind three shivering Russian spies. Seamus walked ten yards ahead of them holding his shotgun over one shoulder.

In the distance, Sam began to hear the sound of beating rotors.

He couldn't conceive how any sane pilot would fly in snow, even in the light snow that was currently falling.

As the path leveled out at Christ's Saddle, the sky began to shudder as a big military helicopter came to a hover twenty feet above them. Seconds later, six men rappelled down ropes onto the tussocky grass.

Seamus had the good sense to raise his arms and surrender his shotgun. "Who are you?" he demanded.

The man who seemed to be leading the soldiers simply said, "SAS."

Sam surrendered both of his pistols and said, "There's a badly wounded Russian spy half way down that track." He pointed to the three men he'd been shepherding. "These three are also Russian spies. They're dangerous."

The soldier collecting his pistols said in a low voice. "So are we, matey."

The next thing to happen was Lily. She came flying down from the high ground and ran full tilt into Sam's arms. He held her close as she sobbed her emotions and allowed her adrenaline to dissipate. Sam wiped the tears from her face with his thumb and smiled. "All's well, Lily."

She shook him by the arms. "Don't you do that to me again, Sam Hastings."

Sam was unsure what 'that' was, but said nothing. Instead he drew her back into his arms and gave her a long lingering kiss.

Chapter 29

Seamus and Cara's tiny parlor was crowded. The three SAS soldiers with them had combed through the lighthouse complex and rejoined them. The other three were retrieving the wounded man and taking him and the other spies to the helipad where the helicopter had landed.

Cara stood in the kitchen door, in her safe place. "Would anyone be wanting tea?" she asked.

The SAS soldiers declined her offer. "We don't have time for tea, Ma'am."

Lily didn't say anything. She was still close to tears and was holding Sam by the hand.

"One tea for Lily," said Sam. "With extra sugar." Sugar was good for those suffering shock. It was comforting.

Cara nodded. "I'll be pleased, so I will, when this place gets back to normal." She bustled off into the kitchen.

Seamus was sitting in his armchair. His craggy face looked grim and haggard. Sam extricated himself from Lily and squatted down beside him. "You found us pretty quickly up there with your shotgun."

"Aye. I was half-way there already, when our Lily came flying down the steps from the Saddle and tells me about Conor."

Sam paused. "What made you change your mind?"

Seamus looked at him. "I decided to honor a promise I made to your brother that I would watch your back."

"My brother?"

"Yes."

Sam closed his eyes. The Scorpion Stone had again proved to have a long reach. A wave of emotion washed through him. Once he had himself back under control, he asked quietly, "How's the marine radio?"

"Ach, the thing is working fine. I'd only pulled a lead out the socket up the mast. I've gone up and plugged it back in."

"I don't think there is any need to mention the temporary radio failure, do you?"

Seamus nodded and laid a beefy hand briefly on Sam's shoulder. No words were needed.

The soldiers told Sam that he was required to fly back with them for a debrief. Sam dearly wished he didn't have to. He'd been climbing up and down dizzying peaks all day and was exhausted. He was far from sure he even had the energy to walk the quarter mile to the helipad.

Lily must have seen his weariness, for she said, "If you have to leave us for a few days, Sam Hastings, the least I can do is drive you to the helipad." She nodded to the soldiers. "You can ride in the back, if you want."

Sam raised a cautionary hand. "Who's going to look after the light?"

Seamus reached in his pocket for his pipe. "I'm Principal Keeper. It's my responsibility to keep the light. So I'll be staying." He said it as a matter of fact rather than a subject for debate. Fortunately, the officer in charge of the soldiers nodded and said, "Time to go."

Sam protested. "But who will share the watch with you Seamus?"

Lily pushed him toward the door. "That would be me, Sam Hastings. I will be covering your arse, as usual."

Oliver Tremain had never seen the Admiral in charge of MI5 look uncomfortable. However, he was giving a passable impression of it today. The reason for his discomfiture was plain to see. Oliver had walked into the Admiral's office in the company of the Lord Chief Justice, Head of the Judiciary of England and Wales.

The Admiral's secretary had called out to him as he swept past her. "Sir, you can't go in without an appointment."

Oliver had simply said. "Cancel his appointments this morning," and kept walking.

He was now facing the Admiral, who was sitting behind his desk.

The Lord Chief Justice slipped into a chair at the back of the Admiral's office, making it plain that he was there only to observe.

Oliver did not mince words. "I have incontrovertible evidence that you have knowingly conspired to have an innocent man accused of a crime."

The Admiral picked up a letter opener with both hands and said carefully, "And who would that man be?"

"Midshipman Sam Hastings. You used your influence to blunt the defense and ensure Hastings was found guilty. I am assuming you wanted to convince Russia that such a clumsy trial would make them suspicious that Crypto AG's encryption was not something we wanted the Russians to use."

The Admiral turned the letter-opener between his fingers. He stretched his neck and said, "Our world is full of gray areas. Sometimes we have to sacrifice things for the greater good. If the Russians really knew that Crypto AG was part owned by the CIA, it would be disastrous. And if we could get them to use it, it would be a coup."

"What is it, Admiral, that you are fighting for?"

The Admiral did not reply.

Oliver continued. "If we do not aspire to justice and truth as the highest ideals, then we are no better than any tin-pot totalitarian regime that tramples on those values."

The Admiral leaned back. "Do we actually know what is good and true, Oliver?"

"No. Not without the Judeo-Christian ethic."

"And do we still have that ethic? Is it still foundational for today's society?"

"It has been the only thing that has rescued us from the 'might is right' mantra of despots." Oliver threw up his hand. "Dammit, Admiral! Do you want to turn your back on civility and return us to the Dark Ages?"

An awkward silence hung in the room.

"What's going to happen now?" said the Admiral.

Oliver pulled himself fully upright. "These are the things you will do, Admiral."

When he had finished speaking, Oliver did not wait to hear the Admiral's assent. He turned, and made for the door.

The Lord Chief Justice levered himself out of his chair to follow him. He paused for a moment and faced the Admiral. "Admiral, you were going to ask for a two-year extension to your tenure here." He turned back toward the door. "Don't."

When Oliver and the Lord Chief Justice were on the pavement outside Leconfield House, Oliver shrugged himself into his coat and said, "Give my best to your daughter, Roslyn, sir. And, if you would be so kind, ask her to pass on my kind regards to Sophie Hunter. She is a remarkable woman."

His companion smiled. "I will."

Chapter 30

I t was madness, as Lily well knew. But she had to see if a life with Sam was even remotely possible. If she didn't, she knew she would regret it. Their romance, such as it was, had been wild, brief, and unconventional. For much of that time, their love had not even been declared. She'd been content to sit in his company in the long watches of the night tending the light at Skellig. He'd told her of his life as a child, living in exotic corners of the world. There was no doubt that he was someone who thrived on adventure. But he also had a gentle side. He was passionate about nature and had an innate kindness. Sam had taken a double watch so that her father, Seamus, could catch up on much needed rest. These qualities were too rare to pass over. And if that were not enough, the very first sight of him with his lean, angular face and muscular body had disorientated her from the very first time she'd seen him.

But it was the hours they'd spent huddled together behind a rock on the tussocky grass at Christ's Saddle that had allowed her to see something of his heart. He'd talked of his first love, a puppy love, for a girl from the Tiwi Islands of Australia… and his nascent love for Sophie, a girl now engaged to his brother, Isaac. Sam had told her he'd never been lucky in love. Even as he said it, her heart ached for him. And, oh, the sweet release when they'd finally kissed.

But where was it going now? Sam had joined the navy. What could she hope for? It was a question she had pondered for days, ever since an audacious idea had begun teasing her sensibilities. It was an idea that had been fueled in part by a growing conviction that it was time she left home. Her community of family and friends in southwest Ireland had protected her from the wider world for her entire life, but now she was beginning to feel the need to spread her wings.

Where should she fly?

Even as she pondered it, she tapped her finger on the job advert she'd cut out of the 'New Scientist.' It was for the position of Marine Conservation Officer for Langstone and Chichester Harbors in the south of England. The new position would require collaboration with Portsmouth Polytechnic's marine biology station on Hayling Island. It was a dream job, and one that she was now eminently qualified to apply for. She'd written a healthy number of peer reviewed scientific publications over recent years.

However, she was in a storm of indecision.

The phone rang. Her heart leaped with delight as she recognized Sam's voice. "Hi Lily. How are you bearing up with all that's gone on? Gee, I wish I was there with you." He paused. "There are things we need to talk about."

"And what things would they be?" she asked coyly.

"Us. I've only just found you, and I don't want to let you go."

"Surely your first priority needs to be the navy, Sam." Even as she said the words, she felt a knife twist in her gut. She was giving voice to a brutal, unpalatable reality she'd been trying to hide from for the last two weeks.

There was silence on the other end of the phone for some time. Then his voice came back to her. "Lily, I would be a shadow of a man if I made the navy my ultimate priority. I may have entertained the idea at one time – particularly as I'd not done well in relationships before. But you've changed that. I don't want to lose you. Surely you know that."

"Are you asking a girl to commit her life to a sailor; one who has lost his heart to other women in the past?" She was unable to keep a touch of bitterness from her voice.

"No. I'm saying that I want to commit my life to you. And if that means leaving the navy, then so be it."

"Are you serious?"

"Deadly."

Lily was conscious of a wave of relief flooding through her. In truth, the very last thing she wanted to do was to force Sam to leave the navy. But knowing that he would, if it meant keeping them together, was wonderful. She smiled. "Then you and I have a great deal to talk about, Sam Hastings."

She heard him chuckle. "Did you get your invitation to attend the ceremony at Portsmouth in three weeks time? It's just a small ceremony. Only close family members are invited."

"Close family members? Then how come I got an invitation?"

"I said that you were my fiancée."

Lily's mouth dropped open. "But, but that was a lie." She didn't trust herself to say more.

"Lily, you are the only one able to call it a lie, because I cannot."

"You are crazy, Sam Hastings."

"Have I lied?"

The joy of being loved, of Sam making her the highest priority in life, overwhelmed her. It took a moment before she found her voice. "No Sam, you did not lie."

Lily was very aware that things were moving fast in her life, but whether or not they would advance to become anything significant depended on her next two phone calls. The first was to the number on the job advertisement that potential applicants were invited to call if they wanted more information. She wanted to make sure that her application would be given serious attention if she applied. Lily didn't want to be one of six-hundred people applying for a job that had already been promised to an internal candidate. As a result of her phone call, she found herself speaking with the professor in charge of the Hayling Island Marine Biology Center. He interrogated her on her qualifications and encouraged her to apply, saying that he would give her application his personal consideration. She would need to be quick, however, because the cut-off date for applying was in two day's time. They would be interviewing next week.

Lily's second phone call was the one that represented the greatest risk to her heart. She rang Sophie Hunter at Girton College, in Cambridge. It took some time for Sophie to be located and brought to the phone. She heard her say, "Hello. Sophie Hunter speaking."

Lily swallowed. "Hello, Sophie. My name is Lily McBride." Before she could say anything more, Sophie interrupted.

"Lily. It's lovely to talk to you. You're Sam's girlfriend, I understand. Sam's brother, Isaac, has told me about you."

Lily was relieved to hear Sophie's friendliness. It didn't, however, make what she wanted to say next any easier. "Well that's just it, Sophie. I've lost my heart to Sam, but I've hardly had time to get to know him. I understand that he has fallen in love with women before, and I wanted to know if he still carried a torch for them in his heart."

"Wow, this sounds serious. But I can't see where I come into it."

Lily drew a deep breath. "Because you were the last woman he fell in love with."

"What? Did he tell you that?"

"He admitted that was the case for him." Lily rushed on. "He didn't say that you returned that love. Sam said it was only idle fancy on his part, but I think he felt it to be real enough." She paused. "He said that Isaac always seemed to get the girls he loved. Sam didn't blame Isaac. He just mentioned it as a reality."

"So why are you ringing me, Lily?"

"I just needed to know if there was any chemistry between you and Sam – and whether or not I was stepping into anything that was, er, complicated."

Sophie laughed. "Sam is handsome, guileless, and a natural

leader. Of course I noticed him. Between you and me, I even toyed briefly with the idea of him being my boyfriend. But the real deep spark was never there, and I doubt it ever could be."

"And why's that?"

"Two reasons. The first is: I need someone who can be my emotional and spiritual soul mate. The second is: I found that soul mate in Sam's brother, Isaac." She paused. "We are, as you probably know, engaged to be married – and marriage is something I won't allow to be threatened – at least, as far as it depends on me."

Lily could hear Sophie's sincerity and caught a whiff of something that smelled of goodness. "I think I could learn a bit from you," she said.

"I'm sure we could teach each other." Sophie changed the subject. "Will you be coming to the ceremony at Portsmouth?"

"Yes. But I'm hoping to get down there a week earlier for a job interview."

"Really. That's fabulous." She paused. "I wonder…"

"You wonder what?"

"I wonder if we could spend some time together." Sophie rushed on, "but only if you'd like to."

Lily frowned. "How's that possible?"

"I've an uncle who has a holiday cottage in Emsworth. I'll ask him if we can borrow it. In truth, I'd welcome a quiet spot to write up my thesis. I could do that in the week before the ceremony? So, why don't you join me? We can keep out of each other's way when we need to work, and have fun together when we don't."

"Wow!" said Lily. "I think I'd like that very much."

Lily was seated in an easy chair in front of a coffee table. Professor Peter Malik and Professor Ann Souter occupied the two other chairs. All three of them had a mug of coffee in front of them, bearing witness to the informal nature of the interview. The interview was being conducted in Professor Ann's office at the Hayling Island Marine Biology Station. Whilst the setting may have been informal, the interview was rigorous. Lily had learned that she was the last person being interviewed, as her application had been the last to arrive.

Professor Malik moved his glasses down his nose and peered over them at Lily. "You did what, Miss McBride?"

"I visited here yesterday – to get a feel for the place and bring a few samples from Langstone Harbor. Your lab technician kindly showed me around, and we ended up looking at some of my samples through a binocular microscope."

The professor shook his head in apparent disbelief. "And what samples did you bring?"

"Some seaweed. I suspected it was *Sargassum muticum*, the Japanese seaweed that is threatening the inter-tidal areas of the south coast. I'm sad to say, I was correct."

The professor swore under his breath. "Dammit, Ann. It's now in Langstone Harbor as well as at Bembridge."

His colleague nodded. "What other samples did you bring?" she asked.

"I brought some hermit crabs, *Pagurus burnhardus*, that were inhabiting whelk shells."

"And why did you do that?"

"Because hermit crab shells are colonized by a host of invertebrates. They therefore give a good indication of what's around."

Professor Souter dropped her pen on the coffee table and leaned back in her chair. "What did you find?"

Without a word, Lily handed across a piece of paper listing the species she had found.

The Professor scanned the list. It included protozoans, annelid worms, arthropods, and sponges. Forty species were listed. She handed the list to her colleague. "Did anything surprise you?"

"Yes. I found tiny strands of non-organic filaments, some of which were blue in color. I very much suspect they are microplastics." Lily shrugged. "They are now beginning to show up in samples around the British Isles."

"Good grief." Professor Malik frowned. "Have you still got the samples?"

"Yes. Judy, your lab tech, has them under seawater in the lab. I asked her to keep the microscope out in case you wanted to view them."

"Good girl." Both professors got to their feet and made their way through to the laboratory. It took Lily ten minutes to find one of the tiny strands on the shell. When she did, she invited the professors to inspect it.

They both did, and the two scientists spent a good deal of time murmuring to each other and speculating about what they were seeing.

Finally, Professor Ann Souter turned round on the lab stool. "My colleague and I have both agreed. You have the job, Miss McBride." She held out her hand. "You will be notified officially in due course, but I want to congratulate you on what has been a most interesting and unusual interview. Well done."

"Have you made up your mind whether or not to accept?" ask Sophie.

Lily wasn't quite sure how to answer. The job was ideal – just the thing she was hoping for. She was still giddy with disbelief that she'd won the position. Lily also desperately wanted to be as close as she could to Sam – and therein lay the hesitation. Could he commit himself to her for life after such a brief period of knowing him? Was it even fair to expect him to at this stage in their relationship? And yet, Sam had called her his fiancée. Fiancée! She couldn't believe it.

The two girls had decided to make use of the daylight hours and explore the area around Emsworth. They were currently in the grounds of the old Saxon church of St. Thomas à Becket at Warblington, a mile or two to the west.

Sophie pointed to two small huts built of flintstones. "Do you see those huts?"

"Yes. What are they?"

"Believe it or not, they are grave watchers huts. As you can see, this is a lonely churchyard, and body snatching was rife years ago."

"Goodness. Really?"

"Yes. And have a look at this." Sophie pointed to an old headstone. "It says that the bloke buried here was a pirate!" She laughed. "Fancy having 'pirate' listed as your profession on your gravestone."

Lily looked at Sophie speculatively. "And why did you bring me here, Sophie?"

"Just as a reminder."

"A reminder of what?"

"That some things in the past should remain buried. You and Sam are standing on the threshold of something new and very beautiful."

An hour later, the girls were back at Emsworth. The tide was out, and the two of them were sploshing around in the mud and rock pools looking for anything that might be of interest. The unpretentious village of Emsworth charmed Lily. It huddled at the top of Langstone Harbor and made no concessions at all to the modern, high-tech world of expensive yachts. The village, however, was really a town, as it was becoming a dormitory suburb for Portsmouth. She'd discovered this when she visited a local real-estate office. Lily fervently hoped that the old part of the foreshore would retain its character and not be spoiled by hard-edged commercialism.

The girls had now drifted fifty yards apart, each absorbed in their own world of exploration.

Suddenly, Lily heard a yell. "Hey, you two!"

She looked up with delight. It was Sam. He'd obviously managed to get some time off to visit them. The navy had kept him busy for the last week.

Sam stood on the foreshore, equidistant from Sophie and Lily. He removed his socks and shoes, rolled up his trousers and headed out through the mud... straight to Lily.

Lily sobbed as she clung to him. The last vestiges of doubt had been removed. She kissed him and said, "I've got something to tell you."

Chapter 31

A sword lay on the table. On its hilt, was a lion's head... and the hilt was pointing toward him.

The Commodore in charge of Portsmouth Royal Naval Base got to his feet and walked out from behind the baize-covered table. He stood directly in front of Sam. "Midshipman Hastings. Pick up your sword."

With a sense of unreality, Sam did so and sheathed it into the scabbard he was wearing. Sam was dressed in his new 'full dress' uniform. Evidently, the navy had paid for it as Sam had sold his old uniform two months ago. In fact, everything that now comprised his naval kit was new.

Isaac, Sophie, Lily, and Oliver Tremain had been invited as guests to the Admiral's cabin of the *Victory*. Two marines stood to one side of them. No marine guarded the door. There was no prisoner to guard.

The Commodore continued to speak. "Midshipman Hastings: you will suffer no loss of time before being made up to Lieutenant."

Sam was standing stiffly to attention. "Thank you, sir."

"And I have one more duty to perform." The Commodore nodded to one of the marines. The marine stepped forward. He was holding a cushion in both hands. A medal that Sam did not recognize sat on top of it. The Commodore picked it up and pinned it to Sam's chest.

"It is my very great pleasure to award you the British Empire Medal. The Crown awards it for meritorious civil or military service worthy of recognition. You, Midshipman, have demonstrated that service." He stepped back and saluted.

Sam's head was spinning, but he retained enough sense to return the salute.

The Commodore nodded to the other marine who barked. "This court is now out of session."

Everyone came forward to congratulate Sam. Lily claimed his arm and gave it a shake. "I've found a place to rent in Emsworth."

He looked at her speculatively. "But that's not all, I'm guessing."

Lily grinned. "There's an old stone barn on Tower Street, just thirty yards from the foreshore, and it's ripe for conversion."

Sam laughed and gave her a kiss. "You're sounding like the perfect sailor's wife – innovative and self-sufficient."

"I'm not all that self-sufficient, *macushla* (my darling). I'll be needing you right enough."

Isaac came forward and slapped Sam on the shoulder. "Well done, mate. It is richly deserved."

Sam held his gaze for a moment, then put his hand in his pocket and pulled out the Scorpion Stone. He let the dim winter light coming in from the stern windows play on it, and then he handed it to his brother. "I have a feeling I won't be needing this for a while."

Isaac laughed. "I sincerely hope so."

Just then, a marine interrupted them. "Sorry to interrupt sir. You have a telegram from Commander Holman on the *Cleopatra*."

Sam took the slip of paper and read it. 'YOU ARE LATE ON WATCH - STOP - JOIN SHIP ASAP.'

Note from the author

Thank you for reading *The Scorpion Stone*. I hope you enjoyed it. If you did, please consider leaving a review on Amazon to encourage other readers.

Much of what you read was based on my personal experience of growing up in Malaya with my twin brother. There was a brothel at the end of our street. Indonesian infiltrators did explode bombs, and my best friend was Rohit, the son of a Ghurkha. Similarly, all the adventures in Germany (except for the fictional Tony Chester-Smith who broke his knee) happened in real life.

It would be fair to say that the events of the 60s and early 70s were troubled and exciting times.

I'm pleased to report that the "Stone Collection" now includes:

The Atlantis Stone
The Pharaoh's Stone
The Peacock Stone
The Dragon Stone
The Fire Stone
The Celtic Stone
The Syrian Stone

The Viking Stone
The Martyr's Stone

I invite you to keep up to date on new releases, by signing up to my mailing list at www.author-nick.com. New subscribers will receive a free novelette, *The Mystic Stone*.

About the Author

Nick Hawkes has lived in several countries of the world, and collected many an adventure. Along the way, he has earned degrees in both science and theology—and has written books on both. Since then, he has turned his hand to novels, writing romantic thrillers that feed the heart, mind, and soul.

His ten full-length novels are known as, 'The Stone Collection.'

Nick Hawkes' first novel, *The Celtic Stone*, won the Australian Caleb Award in 2014.

Also by Nick Hawkes

The Atlantis Stone

Benjamin is part Aborigine, but nightmares from the past cause him to disown his heritage. Unfortunately, he feels no more at home in the Western world and so struggles to know his identity. Benjamin seeks to hide from both worlds in his workshop where he ekes out a living as a wood-turner. However, an attempt on his life propels him into a mysterious affair surrounding the fabled "mahogany ship" sighted by early white settlers near Warrnambool in Australia.

Felicity, a historian, is seeking to rebuild her life in the nearby town of Port Fairy after a messy divorce. The discovery of the "Atlantis stone" whilst scuba diving results in her joining Benjamin in an adventure that takes them overseas to the ancient city of Cagliari in Sardinia.

An anthropologist dying of cancer and an ex-SAS soldier with post-traumatic stress, join Benjamin and Felicity in an adventure that centres on a medieval treaty, a hunger for gold… and, of course, the Atlantis stone.

More details at www.author-nick.com

(See next page for more)

The Fire Stone

Sebastian, a young farm hand living in the Australian mallee, is being watched by Val, a fugitive hiding in the forests on the banks of the River Murray. Val has an official document that confirms his death fourteen years ago. There is no official document that confirms his particular skill: assassin.

Pip divides her life between her musical studies at the Adelaide Conservatorium and her work as a barista. Her ordered life is shattered when bullets fired through the window of her home reduce her cello to matchwood. The violence appears all the more bewildering given that she lives with her father David an Anglican cleric and retired missionary.

A web of violence draws all four of them together.

Everything in Sebastian's life begins to change when he is given the gift of a Koroit opal—*The Fire Stone*. It begins a journey in which he is challenged by David's wisdom and confronted by Pip's love.

The four of them seek to escape the violence that pursues them by sailing across the Pacific to the islands of Vanuatu. There, in the village community of Lamap, the final drama is played out…

…before *The Fire Stone* makes an unexpected return.

More details at www.author-nick.com

13329542R00178